53 SLEEPLESS NIGHTS

SHORT HORROR STORIES

TOBIAS WADE

HAUNTED HOUSE
PUBLISHING

First Edition: March 2021
53 Sleepless Nights

HAUNTED HOUSE
PUBLISHING

CONTENTS

GRAB YOUR FREE BOOK!

Read more from Tobias Wade
download a **FREE BOOK!**
TobiasWade.Com

READ THE FULL COLLECTION

Click the image or get it on
TobiasWade.Com

AN OLD MAN'S LAST SECRET

MY GRANDFATHER IS 95 YEARS OLD AND NOT LONG FOR THIS WORLD. There's nothing but a mess of tubes and wires to tether him here with us. It's difficult for him to speak, but each rasping whisper carries a severe weight that cannot be interrupted. My family doesn't talk about things like death though, so whenever I visit with my dad we tend to spend most of the time sitting in near-silence.

"What a news week, huh?" my dad might say.

"Mmmm," Grandfather will grunt. "Crazy world."

Then silence again. Small talk seems almost disrespectful to the gravity of the situation, but no-one wants to be the first to broach the irrevocable goodbye. When the silence gets too loud my dad will start to fidget with his phone or pull out a book until one of us makes an excuse to leave. That's how it went yesterday, with my father mumbling something about a dentist appointment and hurrying out the door almost as soon as we arrived.

"You'll stay though, won't you?" my grandfather said when we were alone in the room together. "You'll listen to an old man's last secret."

This was it then. The end of the road was in sight. "Would you like me to call dad back?" I asked.

Grandfather shook his head as far as the oxygen tubes would allow it to turn. "I'd rather he didn't know."

I already knew some of the story he told me. It began when my grandfather was 20 years old living in Nazi Germany. He'd been working forced labor on a farm, but managed to smuggle my grandmother and infant father out of the country hidden in a grain shipment. He'd been caught almost immediately and sent to the concentration camp at Buchenwald where he endured the next two years until he was liberated by allied forces.

"You don't have to tell me what happened there if you don't want to," I told him. I wasn't sure I wanted to hear the gruesome details. He was unusually animated and persistent though, promising it was something that needed to be said.

He wouldn't have survived the ordeal if it hadn't been for a friend he'd met there. One of the Nazi officers, a Rottenführer squad leader, had taken a special interest in him because of their striking similarity in age and appearance. The two would sit on either side of a barbed wire fence and swap stories about their childhoods. My grandfather would talk about my grandmother, how beautiful she was, and how he wouldn't give up until he found her again.

The SS officer had gone straight from the Hitlerjugend (Hitler youth group) to the army, and had never been intimate with a woman. He became enraptured in my grandfather's tales of romance, and the two became close friends despite the circumstances. The officer twice spared my grandfather's name from work assignments that meant certain death, and he'd often slip extra rations through the fence which my grandfather would then distribute to other prisoners.

"It wasn't a good life, but it was life, and that was good," Grandfather said.

Things changed as the war began drawing to a close. The Nazi officers became increasingly paranoid and desperate as the allied forces moved in. It became common practice for lower-ranking officers to be held as scapegoats when impossible work orders were not met. Besides that, the rumor that the Rottenführer was protecting my grandfather put him in a dire position with his own officers.

Faced between protecting my grandfather and his own hide, the Rottenführer signed the order for my grandfather to be sent to a nearby armaments factory. Eighteen hour work days, starvation rations, no medical attention—the factory might as well have been a death sentence. The three month survival rate was less than 50%.

In the name of love, my grandfather pleaded, let him survive to find his sweetheart again. She was waiting for him in America. The Rottenführer was moved, but his decision was final. His only compromise was to record the address of where she went, promising to send her a letter to let her know what happened to him.

"So how did you survive?" I asked. "Did he change his mind? Were you rescued from the factory?"

"Shielded from the worst of the camp by the Rottenführer, the transition to the factory proved too difficult for the young farmer. He didn't last the first week."

"What do you mean, 'didn't last'? How d'you get out?"

The exertion of the long story was taking its toll on my grandfather. He coughed and wheezed, struggling to draw breath for several seconds before clearing his throat a final time.

"On April 11th, 1945, the Buchenwald camp was liberated. Many of the Nazis had already abandoned their position and fled into the country. Others decided to lock themselves inside, pretending to be prisoners themselves so the allied forces would have mercy on them. This was especially convincing for those who had taken the time to get to know the prisoners and could assume their identities. When an SS officer gave the information and address of his lost love, he was allowed to board the next transport ship returning to America to be reunited with her."

The gears in my head were turning. Turning. And then stopped.

"Your grandmother was suspicious at first when I met her, but she accepted that the war had changed me. Besides, I knew so many stories about her that she couldn't deny our shared history. I raised his boy as my own, and lived the life he dreamed of every night until his death. Do you think your real grandfather would forgive me if he knew?"

I didn't have an answer for him then, and I didn't get another chance. He died in his sleep that night after a long and happy life that wasn't his.

MY DAUGHTER IS AN ONLY CHILD WITH A TWIN

DON'T YOU DARE TELL ME THAT THERE ARE LOTS OF KIDS WHO LOOK THE same. Don't pretend this is some sort of funny coincidence either, like the kindergarten teacher does. I'd know my baby girl anywhere. I know the way her hair smells, and how her soft little hands feel in mine. I know her giggling laugh, the way she puffs out her cheeks when she's angry, and the light in her eyes when she sees me across the room. I know all the things that only a mother can know, but for the life of me I still can't tell them apart.

"Elizabeth, go put your crayons away. It's time to go home now."

"I'm not done yet."

"Don't talk back to your mom. You can finish tomorrow."

"You're not my mom. You're just a lady."

That was the first shock, when the girl I thought was my daughter shied away from me at the kindergarten. I grabbed her arm and started dragging her, thinking she was just misbehaving. She started to struggle and howl in protest, but I wasn't in the mood so I picked her up and slung her over my shoulder. I would have walked away with her and never known if the real Elizabeth hadn't come skipping around the corner.

"Hi mom! Hi Taylor!"

"Put me down! I don't wanna!" shouted the child I was carrying. I'd always thought double-takes were just something people did in movies. I must have done a quadruple. Everything was identical, from their blonde pigtails tied exactly the same way all the way down to their matching floral overalls.

"Whicha cowa," my daughter said.

"Zookiah gromwich," Taylor replied as I put them down.

"Isn't it adorable?" Mrs. Hallowitz, the kindergarten teacher, was just returning from the bathroom leading another toddler by the hand. "They even talk in their own language. None of the other kids can understand them."

My daughter leaned over to Taylor and whispered something that sounded like: "Priva priva mae."

Both girls looked at me pointedly and began a hysterical giggle in perfect synchronization. Even the intakes of breath and the sudden high-pitched squeals lined up.

Honestly? I didn't think it was adorable at all. I thought it was beyond creepy. I wasted no time scooping my real daughter up and getting her out of there. I might have been able to find it cute under different circumstances, but the truth is that Elizabeth did have a twin. At least in the womb. Her sister was stillborn though, and seeing Taylor just brought back a rush of memories that I hadn't allowed myself to touch for five years.

By the next day, I'd convinced myself I was overreacting. I should be glad that my daughter made a friend. This was only going to be weird if I let it be weird. I don't know if I was just trying to prove something to myself, but I even made an effort by reaching out to Taylor's parents and inviting them over for a play date. They were really sweet people, and we laughed about the 'weird coincidence' while the kids played with LEGOs on the floor.

In theory, this was supposed to make me feel better about the situation. It didn't. The more we talked, the weirder it got. Both girls would sit exactly the same way with their knees drawn up to their chins. They both liked to peel apples and eat the skin—both liked the same obscure cartoon about a digital world—both liked cats more than dogs. Their favorite color was blue.

Even worse, the whole time they were playing together they only spoke in their secret language, laughing in unison. Taylor's mother looked a little uncomfortable when they both asked to use the bathroom at the same time, but she just laughed it off and commented on how impressionable five-year-olds are.

"Did you have fun today with your new friend?" I asked Elizabeth when I was tucking her into bed that night.

"She's not my friend. She's my sister," Elizabeth declared in that pompously imperative way children have.

"You don't have a sister. Taylor has her own parents, remember?"

"It's okay, mom. I know she died." Elizabeth's eyes were already closed when she said it. She spoke as casually as though saying goodnight, nestling further under the covers as she did. "Don't worry. She's all better now."

I'd never spoken aloud about Elizabeth's twin since the day she died. Never even dared to think it too loudly.

"Did your father tell you that?" I asked, trying to keep my voice calm.

"No. Taylor told me. Goodnight mom."

"Sweet dreams, little one."

I'd just turned off the lights and was about to leave the room when Elizabeth said: "Baree fanta lan, Taylor."

"What did you just say?"

Elizabeth started giggling. Then she was silent. Then giggling again, rambling away in her unknown language.

I can't explain exactly why I decided to call Taylor's parents right then. I guess I was just feeling overwhelmed and needed a little reality check.

"Has Taylor gone to bed already?" I asked.

"No, she's in the kitchen drinking a warm milk," Taylor's mom replied. "Is something the matter?"

"Is she... talking to herself?"

A shuffling. Then a pause. I heard Elizabeth mumble something, then start to giggle again. On the other end of the line, I heard Taylor giggling at the same exact instant.

"She's not saying anything," Taylor's mom said. I breathed a sigh of relief, but it was cut short. "Not real words anyway. Just pretend words."

I thanked her, wished her goodnight, and hung up the phone. Not before I heard Taylor replying in the background to whatever Elizabeth was saying to herself. They were communicating somehow. I don't know why that terrified me so much, but it did. I sat outside her room and wrote down as much of the gibberish as I could make sense of. In the morning, I tried asking Elizabeth what it meant. She only laughed and said it was a secret.

I felt like I was running in circles. I couldn't stop thinking about it, but the more I thought, the more confusing it got. Had my other girl survived after-all? Could she have been adopted by another family somehow? But that still didn't explain how they were talking to each other.

As a last resort, I tried hanging around the kindergarten until after Taylor's parents dropped her off and left. Then I went in and signed Taylor out, pretending that she was my daughter. She trusted me this time since we've played together at my house, and I promised her some treats if she went along with it.

Once we were alone in my car, I showed her all the gibberish words I wrote down from the night before. I told her she had to help me figure out what they meant for her to get her treat. Taylor was happy to oblige.

"Lizzy (her word for Elizabeth) and I were talking last night."

"What were you talking about?"

"We were trying to decide which of us was dead. What kind of treat did you bring?"

"Soon, honey. Can you tell me what that means?"

"Ughhh." Taylor rolled her eyes in exasperation, just the way Elizabeth always does when I make her wait. "One of us died when we were little. I think it was Lizzy, but she thinks it was me."

"You both look pretty alive to me."

"I knowwwwwwwww," she whined. "That's why we can't agree. But I can't live unless she's dead, so that's going to happen. Can I have my treat now?"

"What's going to happen?" I understood her, but I still couldn't believe a five-year-old would say such a thing.

"Lizzy has to die," Taylor said emphatically. "There's only supposed to be one of us."

"That doesn't make sense. It's insane. I never want to hear you say that again."

Taylor shrugged. "If we get ice-cream, can it be—"

"Chocolate," I cut her off. "I know."

Taylor giggled.

"Are you going to hurt my daughter?"

Taylor's eyes widened, fearful. She shook her head rapidly. I let out a breath I didn't even know I was holding.

"You can't hurt someone who is already dead," Taylor said matter-of-factly.

This part is hard to type, but I need you to know why I did it. I need you to know that Taylor didn't suffer when I wrapped my hands around her little neck. She barely even struggled, and it snapped so easily that I know she barely even knew what was happening. She said so herself. You can't hurt someone who is already dead, and I had my own daughter to worry about.

I'm sorry Mr. Sallos. I'm sorry Mrs. Sallos. I know this letter will be hard for you to understand, but your daughter didn't die yesterday. She was my daughter, and she died five years ago before she ever left the hospital. I know what it must have seemed like, but you never had a daughter of your own. You had a dream about a life that could have been, and this pain you feel is just the surprise of waking up.

I just wish Elizabeth would stop talking to herself. I wish she wouldn't look at me the way she does, or laugh when she's alone.

MY SELF-HELP TAPE TOLD ME TO KILL MYSELF

I HATE MY JOB.

I hate selling days of my life while barely earning enough to sustain it. I hate my boss who tells me I'm lucky to find stable work in such an uncertain world. I hate my friends who treat dreams like an unfortunate symptom of youth that need to be outgrown.

And most of all, I hate myself for not doing anything to change. I keep waking up at the same time every day to sit in traffic. I read the same lines on the same billboard with the same happy models leering down at me. I don't think I could go on if I thought this was all there was, but if I'm waiting, then I don't know what I'm waiting for.

That's why I started listening to self-help tapes in the car. Motivational speakers would tell me about how I had the power to change my life, and for a few minutes at a time, I'd believe them. That obstacles, no matter how great, were only in my mind, and that anyone could be happy if they just willed it hard enough. And if I wasn't happy yet, then I just had to buy another book and keep trying.

My favorite speaker was a guy named John Fallow who claims he used to be a day laborer making less than minimum wage. When there weren't any jobs available, his fellow workers would play cards or chat, but he kept going door-to-door, knocking on businesses until he found one that needed work done.

Pretty soon John had enough clients and extra money that he started hiring the other laborers to work for him instead. The more jobs he got, the more workers he hired, until lo-and-behold he was running a business of his own. Then they had a second location, and a third, and before you know it, he was a millionaire with five hundred stores across the country.

But it was never about the money, says the guy selling $30 audiobooks. He gave it all up so he could give motivational speeches and help others achieve their dreams. And sure it was a lot of hard work and took many many years, but he was the man he wanted to be doing the things he loved to do, and that's all that mattered in the world.

"Of course, hard work isn't the only way to solve your problems," John said on one of his tapes. "In fact, there's a lot of you who are probably getting discouraged right now because you were hoping for a shortcut. Well I've got good news for you, because there's a solution as easy as apple pie. You go on now and kill yourself tonight."

I couldn't believe I heard that right. I had to rewind, but there it was.

"Are you too fat? Well diet and exercise is a lot of work, but you could put a gun in your mouth and never eat again.

"Or maybe you're feeling down because your relationship didn't work the way you wanted? No problemo. Just slip on that noose, and suddenly your ex will be the one who hates herself, not you."

John's warm, bubbling voice didn't miss a beat as he proceeded to list a number of foolproof ways to die, 100% satisfaction guaranteed.

"Now some of you are probably skeptical that this is the right choice for you, but don't you fret about it. I'll be hosting live demonstrations around the country, so check my website for details and come see if suicide is right for you."

Part incredulous, part morbid curiosity, I visited his website and found he was hosting an event in my city next week. Sure enough, his website had a video of him standing on stage with a man who hung from the rafters by his neck. The crowd was cheering like wild as the dying man's body was wracked with its final spasms. John Fallow lifted the dying man's hand to reveal a thumbs up, and the crowd cheered even harder as though their team had just scored the final goal.

I bought a ticket and printed out the confirmation code. I don't know why I did it, but for the first time in a long time I really felt like I had something to look forward to.

John was a man's man, rugged and handsome as they come. He wore a cowboy hat pulled low over one eye, faded Levi's, and a button-up shirt the day of the event. He greeted everyone at the front door with a firm handshake and a beaming smile, laughing and carrying on with people he'd just met like they were his oldest friends.

I expected there to be at least a little outrage, but everyone who showed up seemed legitimately happy to be there. The feeling was contagious, and by the time I sat down with the rest of the audience, I already knew several people by name.

"Silly old me, I forgot what speech you all came to hear," John Fallow announced from the stage. "Was it the one about working hard from morning till night, day in and day out?"

"No!" chorused a hundred voices around me. I was half surprised to recognize my own as one of them.

"How about the speech about it being your fault if you aren't happy, because you ain't trying hard enough?"

"No!"

"So you telling me all you fine folks showed up just to hear how to fix all your problems at once in less than five minutes? That what you want to hear?"

The enthusiasm was deafening.

John Fallow mimed whipping out a pair of pistols from an imaginary belt and rattled off shots into the audience. Everyone remotely close to the line of fire made a dramatic show of taking the bullet and collapsing into their chairs with great big grins on their faces. Then cheers again, an ocean of sound beating against my eardrums.

"Well let's get started then," John roared. "How about a volunteer?

Come on now don't be shy. There ain't nobody going to look down on you where you're going."

A sea of hands like a flock of birds all taking flight at once. John stepped down from the stage and took the open hand of a middle-aged woman to help her into the spotlight. He led her to a stool on stage where she sat down.

"What's your name, gorgeous?" he asked. The woman swooned and mumbled something I couldn't hear.

"Katylin, is that right?" John said in his booming voice. "Tell me Katylin, what's wrong with your life? Loud and clear, come on now."

"I was supposed to get promoted this year," she said, her voice trembling but audible. "They gave the job to some young slut instead."

"Well you aren't getting any younger, sweetheart. It's only going to get worse from here."

She nodded and smiled as though that's exactly what she wanted to hear.

"I got just the thing for you though," John said. "A little medicine for what ails ya."

He produced a pill from a small leather bag in his pocket and offered it to her. She snatched it gratefully and clutched it in both hands.

"That's gonna take the sting right out. Go on now. One quick swallow. Cyanide tastes just awful if you let it dissolve in your mouth."

I watched with horrified fascination as Katylin tossed the pill back and washed it down with a water bottle that John offered her. She gave a feeble smile as her face flushed bright red. The room watched in anxious silence as she started panting for breath, each labored heave more desperate than the last.

"Almost there, 'hun," John whispered, his microphone washing the sound over the audience "Let's see those bastards at work take this one away from you."

Katylin fell off her stool and began rolling on the ground. The audience began to woop and whistle. Within seconds Katylin lay still. Two men wearing 'Staff' shirts hustled out to drag her off stage.

There was a brief silence when she stopped moving. I had the sense that everyone was trying to read the room, unsure of whether or to scream or cheer. Then the applause began to ripple, tentative at first, but growing by the second until the whole auditorium vibrated with its intensity.

I felt sick. An anxious feeling flooded my body, but the cheering confused me and made me think that it was alright. If we were doing something wrong, then surely someone would have said something by now. Unable to shake the uncertainty, I staggered from my chair and headed for the bathroom to clear my head.

Outside the auditorium I saw the two men wearing 'Staff' shirts exit a side door. The woman wasn't with them anymore. Was she still back there? Was she alive, or dead? Maybe she needed help.

One of the staff noticed me, his face screwing up with suspicion. I snatched a nearby trash bag and made to enter the door they'd just exited from.

"Hey, where you think you're going?" one asked.

"Bringing some rope for John," I said, hefting the trash bag. "Back stage is that way, right?"

The staff nodded, and I slipped inside. I could hear the audience cheering again through the wall and felt the urge to cheer with them, but I thought better of it and stayed quiet.

The hallway skirted the perimeter of the auditorium, and I was able to track my progress toward the back of the stage by the sounds coming through the wall. Another uproar—perhaps a second demonstration concluding. Another body to be dragged off stage.

Not just a body. A human being. A father or a mother, a son or a daughter. That thought should have horrified me, but it didn't. They didn't ask to be alive. They didn't make the world the way it was. So why shouldn't they leave when they're ready?

"Looks like we've got a bleeder here," John's voice carried. "That's it, boy. Let it all out. You're the lucky one—the rest of us have to clean up that mess."

I must have been directly behind the stage at that point. The place was dark and cluttered with electrical and sound equipment. I saw no sign of the woman's body. The thought of stumbling across her splayed out on the ground nauseated me. I shouldn't be here.

A shaft of light tore through the room as the stage curtain was pulled aside. The staff were dragging a college aged boy by the hands. His throat was cleanly slit, and a sheet of blood soaked through his shirt and drained onto the floor. I hid behind an upright speaker and watched the staff prop the boy against the wall before they turned to exit.

"Let's all take a break while they get this cleaned up," John said from the stage. "Fifteen minutes, then you'll all get your chance."

The boy was still alive. Spitting and gurgling blood, he panted with feeble wet gasps. His red-smeared teeth were locked in a vicious grin. I started to creep toward him, but another blast of light made me scramble back to concealment.

John Fallow moved through the shadows to stand over the dying boy. The boy's grin twisted into one of agony. He struggled to stand, but John put a boot on his chest and forced him back down.

"Shh shh," he held a finger to his lips. "Don't fuss. Lot of folks are dying to be you." He laughed at his private joke.

The boy tried to answer, but the wet sucking sound which escaped his lips carried no words.

"You did this to yourself. You wanted to fit in so damn bad that you didn't care what you had to do. Now look at you."

It was too late to save him. The boy was barely breathing now, and the pool of blood encompassing him was still growing by the second. John dropped to his knees to bring their faces level.

"It don't matter what other people expect from you," John said softly. "The government wants you to make a lot of money to pay taxes. A holy man might tell you not to make any because it corrupts you. The people who sell burgers want you to be fat, and the people who sell diet pills want you to hate yourself for it. They all want something different from you, but you don't belong to them. You belong to you."

The boy had stopped moving. I couldn't make out the faintest sign that he still drew breath.

"So what if you flunked out of school? Does that make the stars any less bright, or the taste of strawberries more sour? Will you no longer feel your lover's caress, or the ocean lapping your bare feet? Fear, pain, doubt—they're just passing clouds, and floating in front of the sun don't mean the sun ain't still there.

"So I'm going to give you another chance," John continued. "You get back up and go outside and tell me what you see. And if it's nothing but clouds, then pick one and call it beautiful and love it forever, because it's all part of the same sky."

With that John Fallow pulled out a syringe and stuck it in the boy's chest. He began to buckle and squirm, but John held him down while wiping the blood from his neck with a handkerchief. It came off like makeup, leaving clean fresh skin below.

"Get out of here," John said, "and don't let me catch you back either."

The boy scrambled to the door and disappeared.

"You too," John said, looking into the shadows where I hid. "Or it won't just be blood capsules and a temporary paralytic for you."

I ran for it.

Outside I saw the boy with his head thrown back, looking straight up. Beside him was the woman who'd taken the fake cyanide pill, head back and staring at the sky with wild eyes. I don't know whether they thought they'd really died and came back, or whether they knew it was a trick, but one thing I'm pretty sure is that neither of them had ever looked at the sky like that before.

I know I hadn't.

WHERE THE PEOPLE WHO DISAPPEAR GO

WE DON'T TALK ABOUT THE ONES WHO NEVER COME BACK. NOT IN MY house, not at school, not anywhere in my town. But not talking about them doesn't bring them back, and it doesn't stop more people from disappearing, so I'm going to tell you everything I know.

The first disappearance I remember is Julie Wilkins in the 3rd grade. She had blonde pigtails and always wore a bright red sweater even in the summer. I didn't think anything of it the first day she was gone, but I asked my teacher about her by the second day.

"Julie? She's sitting right over there in her usual spot," Mrs. Peterson replied.

The girl sitting in Julie's spot wore the same bright red sweater, but she had black hair and a mean face and didn't look anything like Julie. I tried to explain that to the teacher, but Mrs. Peterson wouldn't listen.

I kept insisting, louder and louder, growing red in the face and screaming when the teacher wouldn't listen. I ran over to the imposter and pulled her hair, demanding with the single-minded fury of a 9-year-old girl to know what happened to Julie's pigtails. She cried and started pulling my hair back, and soon both of us were sent home early.

I watched the mean-faced girl get picked up by Mrs. Wilkins, Julie's mom. The woman hugged the girl and helped her into the backseat, and they drove away together. And every day after that the girl with the black hair would sit in Julie's chair and chat with Julie's friends, until after about a month I finally let it go and started calling her Julie too.

Kate Bennet in the sixth grade. Steve Oshaki in the eighth. Lisa Wellington, junior year. There was never a fuss about it, so there were probably more that I didn't notice. I actually liked the new Lisa considerably more than the old one who used to stick gum everywhere, but that didn't make it okay.

Because every time it happened, I couldn't stop thinking about what it would be like if I was next. I didn't like the idea of someone else sleeping in my bed or hugging my mother. I liked the idea of what might have happened to the original people even less.

As I got older, I started thinking there was something wrong with me. If their closest friends and family didn't notice the change, then maybe there was no change at all. Maybe I misremembered or hallucinated. Maybe there was something wrong with my eyes, or my brain —some unseen tumor quietly swelling until the day I won't know anyone and no one will know me.

I still lived in the same small town during college though, and I didn't forget the lesson I learned in the 3rd grade: I kept my mouth shut and pretended not to notice. But it was a lot harder to pretend when I woke one morning to find a stranger sleeping next to me where my fiancé used to be.

I didn't wake him. I just watched him sleep, trying to imagine what would come of us. The new Robert wasn't unhandsome. He was in better shape than my fiancé had been. If the other replacements were any indication, then he'd still know who I was and what I meant to him.

I tried to go along with it, but couldn't even make it through the first morning. I flinched when he kissed me, and just watching him getting dressed in Robert's clothes was enough to make me miss my real fiancé.

I lay in bed pretending I was sick until he left for work, then I jumped up and started packing my things. I was gone before he got back. No message, no letter, no explanation—why should I try to mend a stranger's broken heart when I had no one to mend mine?

The new Robert didn't let me go that easy. I blocked his number, but messages kept slipping through. Social media—email—he even renamed our shared Netflix account to say he misses me. I finally confronted him when he found out which friend I was staying with and knocked on the door.

It's not you, it's me. Weeks of suffering from an invisible wound, and that's the best I could come up with. I tried to convince him that I was sick and needed to be alone, and he tried to convince me that he would help me get better. I'd almost gotten rid of him when my stupid friend started crying and thanking the stranger for not giving up on me.

I guess that's when I gave up on myself. I let the man take me back to the place that used to be my home. I stood stiff as a board when he hugged me, and the hair on the back of my neck stood on end when he stroked my head and told me we would get through this together. Then I lay beside him in the bed we shared and wondered how the warmth of his body felt so much colder than what love was supposed to be.

I didn't sleep that night. I guess that's why I was the only one to hear the knock on the door after midnight. A burst of tentative taps, almost like someone wanted to be heard and was afraid to be noticed at the same time. I thought about waking the stranger in my bed, but I decided that I felt safer when he was asleep.

I lay in bed for several long seconds before I heard the knocking again. It was faster this time—more urgent. I slipped out of bed and crept down stairs, not turning on any of the lights. Checking that the door was still locked—then up to the peephole—

"It's cold out here, and I can't find my key," Robert said through the door. I stared at my real fiancé through the peephole. "Are you in there? Hello?" Then rapid knocking once more.

How could I open the door? How could I invite him into our home with another man upstairs in the bed? But how could I not, and risk losing him again? I stood frozen at the peephole, watching him huddling under his jacket for warmth.

"Let me in," he pleaded, louder this time. The other Robert would wake soon, if he hadn't already. "Let me in, let me in!" Suddenly he leapt at the door and started hammering on it with his fist.

I jumped away from the shuddering wood in surprise, tripping over myself and collapsing onto my ass. The original Robert fell instantly quiet, no doubt hearing me.

"I know you're there. Don't do this to me. Let me in—let me in!" And the hammering returned, stronger than ever. The whole door was trembling in its frame. The first light turned on upstairs, and then the creak of wood from the steps.

I unlocked the door and flung it open.

I clenched my eyes and braced for impact, expecting the real Robert to come flying into the room from his momentum.

"Honey? What's going on down there?" the stranger's voice.

"I don't know. I thought I heard something," I said, my voice ringing hollow in my own ears as I stared at the empty darkness. I took a step outside and welcomed the freezing air enveloping my skin.

"You're already sick—don't make it worse."

I moved farther into the cold in defiance. "I'm not sick," I told him, my voice more level than it had ever been. "I just don't love you, that's all."

His snarl lasted less than a second, but it left enough impact that I couldn't see his face again without remembering it.

"Don't you dare follow him," the stranger said.

"Follow who?" I asked innocently, taking another step into the freezing night.

The snarl returned, and this time it took several seconds to fade. He half-turned away from me, then apparently changing his mind, he lunged through the door after me. I was already running as fast as I could, the icy concrete driveway stinging my feet as though some skin was left behind with every step.

"Don't go out there!" he shouted behind me. "You'll disappear too!"

I wouldn't have minded disappearing though. I could disappear with Robert. The other ones can have the house. They can get dressed in our clothes and laugh with our friends and eat Christmas dinner with my family, but they won't have us. So I just kept running, calling for Robert and hoping that he'd find me before my lungs froze stiff. Before the stranger caught me and dragged me back and fussed over me until I believed that I was sick too.

I ran for as long and hard as I could, screaming until my throat was raw, but I didn't find Robert. The stranger had given up hours ago, but I kept going until morning when my fingers and toes were black and blue and my blood felt like ice in my veins. And by the first touch of light I found myself back at the house that had been my home, back to wondering whether I really was sick, and whether it would be the death of me.

Only it wasn't my home anymore. The stranger who had replaced Robert was kissing his new fiancé who had replaced me. And there was our neighbor, greeting them good morning as though he'd known them both for years. And life goes on for the rest of the world who don't talk about the ones who never come back.

As for me? Without friends, or family, or a home to call my own? I finally know where the ones who disappear go. They can go anywhere they want, because there's nothing left to hold them back.

MY REFLECTION SMILES MORE THAN I DO

IT'S NO SECRET THAT I DRINK. MY FRIENDS WILL MAKE JOKES LIKE 'YOUR idea of a balanced diet is a beer in both hands'. I'll laugh with them, but I don't miss their pitying smirks. When I'm out, I'm out to have a good time, and when I'm in... well either way, it feels like I'm only smiling once I've knocked back a few.

I have this weird habit when I'm drinking alone where I like to watch myself get drunk in the mirror. I start off by seeing this drab, aging, overweight slob, and I'll make a game out of drinking until he looks happy. I'll grin and make faces and watch myself laugh and wonder why I can't be like this all the time. I can steal a few hours from reality until my girlfriend gets home from work and we start to bicker, and then everything that didn't exist a moment before is suddenly there again.

The second she walks in the door and sees that I've been drinking, the smile disappears from the mirror. Usually we'll have a "discussion", although she's the only one talking so I tend to think of it more as a "lecture". Sometimes she'll give up and let it go, but then there are cases like the other night where she works herself into some kind of frenzy. I guess I'd forgotten to pick her up—I knew it was my fault and I apologized—but it didn't matter. Nothing I said got through to her anymore. It was like she couldn't even hear me. And she just kept getting louder and louder until all the words morphed into one long angry blast, not ceasing until the door slammed behind her.

It was just me and the mirror after that, so I took another drink and watched it smile. A big sloppy smile too, as wide as I'd ever seen, stretching my face into a caricature of itself. It would have been heart-warming to see if I really had been smiling. I turned my head slowly from side-to-side, watching the mirror from my peripheral vision. The man in the mirror turned too, matching my movements exactly, giving me full-view to all its leering teeth. Meanwhile I felt my own closed mouth with my hand just to be sure. The mirror was smiling, but I wasn't.

That unnerved the hell out of me. It was a wake-up call. I emptied the rest of my bottle down the sink and went to lie down for a while. The weird thing was that I didn't feel that drunk though. I was walking straight—thinking clearly. I was barely even buzzed.

Lying there in the dark and thinking about what happened wasn't any better. I felt like I was going to start sobbing. After about an hour of tossing and turning and hating myself, I got up to use the bathroom and looked in the mirror again. I wanted to see myself smile, even if it wasn't real, just to know that it was still possible.

I was even more sober now than last time. I could feel the miserable weight of it. My reflection though? A coy dimple at first, but before my eyes it was stretching into a beaming grin. I felt my slack, loose face again with both hands. Then reaching out to touch the smile in the mirror, my hand tensed into a rigid claw. I didn't feel the glass. I felt the warm, moist, tightly pulled lip. The stubble of its face, the curve of its chin, my hand slipping through the mirror as though it wasn't even there. I wasn't afraid exactly—more mesmerized by something so far beyond my understanding. Then when my reflection turned to walk away, it felt like a part of me was leaving with it.

I watched myself exit the bathroom on the other side of the glass. Now the mirror showed an empty bathroom, my reflection gone. I touched the glass again and felt the cold, smooth surface. I was about to try to sleep whatever this was off, but then I heard the door open.

She's back! She changed her mind! Suddenly the mirror didn't matter anymore. I raced through my apartment faster than a kid on Christmas morning, stumbling to a halt when I reached the living room. It was empty. The door was locked. No-one had entered, but then I heard her voice:

"Look, I know I said I wasn't coming back, but—"

Her voice was coming from behind me, sounding muffled almost as though she was speaking underwater. I raced back to the bathroom —the mirror still empty of my reflection. I was beginning to think it was another hallucination when I heard:

"I'm so sorry. I'm going to be a new man from now on, I promise."

My own voice. Coming from inside the mirror. It was muffled too, seemingly a long way off. But even if my reflection had left its bathroom and gone to its version of my living room, how could my girlfriend have entered that living room instead of my own?

"You do look different somehow," she said. "I can't quite put my finger on it."

Unless of course... I had changed places with my reflection somehow. If he was in my real living room, and I was behind the mirror.

"Did you do something with your hair? It's usually parted the other way," she added.

"I'm just happy to see you, that's all," my voice said. "I guess you're not used to seeing me smile."

"Maybe you're right. It's a good change..."

I'd climbed onto the bathroom counter at this point. My face an inch from the glass, but still no reflection. I mapped the entire surface with my hands. Then harder—pounding my fists against the mirror, watching the whole pane rattle against the wall.

"Hello! Can anyone hear me?" I shouted.

If they could, they made no sign. I heard them talking softly for a while, then she started to laugh. I don't remember the last time I heard her laugh. I was getting desperate by this point. I wanted to smash the mirror to pieces, but I was afraid the action would block my only route home. I sprinted back to my empty living room—threw open the door—searching for something—anything to make sense out of this madness. I didn't make it far before I heard her scream though, and I felt compelled to run back and see what was going on.

My heart leaped when I saw my reflection again in the bathroom mirror. He was still smiling, even humming to himself while he washed his hands in the sink. Washing the blood from his hands. I couldn't hold myself back anymore. I threw my whole body against the mirror. It exploded on collision, splintering shards of shrapnel showering me in a thousand bloody hands. I didn't stop, hurling myself again and again into the empty frame, smashing and driving each fragment of glass into my hands until there was nothing left but diamond dust.

I was heaving for breath when I walked back into the living room —my real living room. I know it was real because I saw her on the couch, her throat and mouth cleanly slit from end to end, smiling wider than she ever had when she was with me. I took my keys and my wallet and I ran, leaving everything else behind for good.

The police caught up to me about a week later. They interviewed me and took prints, but apparently the one's on the knife didn't match me. They were completely backward, in fact. I haven't had a drink since that day, but God knows I've wanted to. I guess I'm just too afraid to look in the mirror one day and see myself smile.

MOM I'M 14, I CAN HAVE MY OWN DEMON

My family has a secret. It isn't the mundane type of secret either: Dad isn't hiding any affairs, Mom doesn't drink herself to sleep, and my sister doesn't sneak boys or drugs up to her room. They do, however, all have their own demons, and they keep them hidden from the rest of the world.

Dad's demon has swollen eyeballs which protrude at least six inches from its floppy, boneless face. He said it's because he reads so much, but it's probably because he's always snooping on other people's business. Mom's demon is something between an eel and a slug, although every once in a while it'll turn itself inside-out and leave bloody, oily stains on the carpet. My sister Sandra only got her demon a few months ago. It's always eating things: clothes, pencils, books—anything it can fit into its distendable jaw. I can only imagine how much trouble they'd get up to if they weren't kept in cages all the time.

"Sandra had to wait until she was 18 for her own demon, and so do you," my father would say.

When you're a freshman, a four year wait might as well be a life sentence. It wouldn't have been so bad if I hadn't seen how much Sandra had changed after she got her demon either. Mom says that when we summon a demon, we take all the worst parts of ourselves and bind it to the creature.

Sandra used to stress eat. She could clear a family sized pizza in under 10 minutes. I don't think she even tasted it. When she was a junior in high school, she weighed 240 pounds (although she'd kill me if she knew that I knew).

When she went to prom her senior year, she weighed 110. I wasn't allowed to watch the actual summoning ceremony, but I can only imagine the demon crawling (or eating) its way out of her and taking all her bad habits with it. It's not like she magically transformed overnight though. Not physically, anyway. She went on an all liquid diet the next day, running an hour every morning, yoga in the afternoon, and another two hours of gym at night.

At first I was supportive. That lasted about a week. Then the jealousy set in. Don't get me wrong, I'm not a fat cow like she was, but it was hard to even stand next to that goddess without feeling insecure. Just being alive is enough to make me anxious and uncomfortable though. I have this magic power where I can walk through a crowd of strangers and telepathically infer that everyone is laughing at me, even though logically I know they don't give two shits. And forget actually trying to make friends. I'd rather kill myself than talk to a cute boy (not really, although I'd be lying if I said the thought never crossed my mind).

So why torture myself through high school like my sister did? If she hadn't wasted 3 years sitting in the corner and feeling sorry for herself, she could have had the best time of her life. I must have begged my parents a thousand times to let me summon my demon early, but the point was non-negotiable. I wasn't "mature" enough. I was just going through a "phase". They thought I was still "developing", and that it was still too early for me to know who I really was. But I did know who I was. I was a sad, lonely girl who was sick of feeling like this, and I knew the longer I waited, the worse it would get.

I got my chance last Friday when Mom and Dad went out for a date. Sandra was at the gym, so I had the house to myself. I was a sock-footed commando slipping into my parents room to search for their summoning book.

Dad's demon perked up right away from its cage on top of the dresser. It pressed its bulging eyes against the bars so hard that they squished straight through. Mom's demon was in an empty aquarium, squelched up against the glass. I ignored them and started to search: under the bed, in the closets, in the bathroom drawers—all the obvious places. Nothing. My search widened: inside pillow cases, hidden between clothes, rifling through their other books to see if one had a fake cover. Nothing. I was growing frustrated and was about to give up when Dad's demon started squeaking.

It was pointing a long, thin finger at the AC vent. I followed its advice, and sure enough the grate cover was loose. The book was inside, a heavy leather affair entitled "The Demonicum". I replaced the vent cover, thanked the bulging eyed creature (even though Dad said never to talk to them), and hurried back to my room to study the book.

The spell was way simpler than I imagined. No ingredients, no sacrifices, just a short verse and a silly dance. It seemed weird because I remember them being gone for hours for Sandra's ceremony, but they probably just had to drive a long way to get to a sacred spot or something. Even better, there was an unsummoning spell which bound the demon back to me just in case things got out of hand. Nothing to lose and everything to gain, I started to read.

As soon as I pronounced the final syllable, I felt a heavy burden lift from my heart. It felt a bit like dreading an impossible test all week, only to arrive at class to find out its been replaced with a field trip. I hadn't just been carrying that dread for a week though—it was a whole lifetime of doubt, and resentment, and insecurity that separated itself from me.

Then came the scratching from the inside my chest. An insatiable, internal itch. I watched in morbid fascination as a small claw pushed out of my skin. It retreated, and a moment later a long, thin tongue slipped out to taste the air. It didn't hurt, so I ran to the bathroom mirror to watch it slowly widen the hole and begin to work its way out. My demon was small and round, covered with bristling black fur like a hamster that had been plugged into an electrical outlet. It had just gotten the hole wide enough to stick its head out when I realized that I didn't have a cage ready for it.

The old me would have gone into a panic attack on the spot. Not anymore. I was cool and collected as I glided to my closet to look for a container, the demon wriggling its way out of me the whole time. The best I could do was a backpack, but the creature was so small and feeble looking that even that seemed more than sufficient. I waited until it pulled its full torso free before snatching the demon and dragging it the rest of the way out. It squeaked and whined in protest as I stuffed it into the backpack and zipped it up. The hole in my chest was already closing, and a few seconds later I was as good as new.

No, I was better than new. For the first time I could remember, I was happy with myself. The only damper was the pathetic, terrified squeaking coming from inside the backpack. I stuffed it under my bed and tried to forget about it, but my demon was loud enough that I was sure it would be discovered. I yelled at it to shut up, but it only responded with pitiful whimpering.

I pulled the backpack out and unzipped it about an inch. My demon was cowering in the corner, trembling all over and clutching itself with its little paws. Like it or not, there was a part of me inside it. I couldn't help but relate to it, knowing that all its anxious fear was exactly what I had been feeling every day of my life. Then it looked up at me with those quivering eyes and my heart broke completely.

"Okay, you can come out. But only if you don't make a sound, okay? And you can't let anyone see you," I told it.

The demon nodded vigorously, so I unzipped the backpack and let it crawl free. It stayed silent and didn't try to get away. I patted down its bristling fur, which was surprisingly soft, until gradually the trembling stopped and it started to relax. Sandra came home shortly after, but the demon was true to its word and stayed hidden.

The next few days were heaven. It's amazing how different the world can be with a simple shift in perception. I wasn't afraid of making mistakes or being laughed at anymore. I started speaking up in class, joined new people at lunch, and felt myself becoming accepted and admired almost immediately. I even caught a few glances from boys which lingered on me longer than I've ever noticed before.

I was so happy that I barely paid any attention to my demon which continued to cower in my room. It was growing every day, but any attempt to trap it again elicited such a woeful sound that I quickly gave up. I was sure my parents would take it away or unsummon it if they found out, and that wasn't a risk I was willing to take. I told it to stay under my bed until it got too big for that, then I made it stay in the closet. By this point it was about the size of a large dog, already far bigger than the other demons and showing no signs of stopping.

I wasn't anxious anymore, so the heavy breathing didn't bother me. I didn't worry about the half-eaten squirrels I sometimes found in the corner of my room. I didn't dread what would happen if it kept getting bigger. All I cared about was how good it felt to not be dragged down by those negative feelings all the time. I didn't realize how bad it had gotten until I heard the screaming in the middle of the night.

Glass shattering.

"Let go of her, you brute!"

Savage snarling.

"Dad, get the book!"

It was coming from Sandra's room. I leapt out of bed and raced across the hall. The door was open, and my demon was cowering in the corner. It was almost as tall as my sister now, its black fur rising like so many blades. Broken glass glinted in the carpet, and Sandra's demon was nowhere to be seen. Dad shoved past me and rushed back toward his room. My demon launched off the wall in hot pursuit. I tried to hold on to it as it sped by, but the spikes of fur were sharp enough to cut my hand and I immediately let go.

"It ate her!" Sandra was wailing. "It ate my demon!"

I heard another smash before I got to my parents room. The wire cage was empty, twisted wide open. More glass sprayed the ground where the aquarium once was. My demon was chewing like a starved animal, a path of oily blood running down its chin.

My parents' demons were barely a mouthful for it, but they distracted it for long enough. Dad was reading something from the summoning book, but I could barely hear him over the sound of Sandra's screaming. My demon had finished swallowing, and it was crouched again, ready to leap on Dad...

But not before he finished the spell. The demon rippled once, twice, and then just as it flew into the air it dissolved into a wave of black mist. The mist reared to a halt in the air before turning to crash down on me in a freezing wave. It poured into my nose, and my mouth, and my eyes—flooding me with an overwhelming fear and hatred. It was a second skin over my skin, and a third skin under it, encompassing and filling me to the brim. The demon was being bound to me once more, only it was bigger than ever, with it all the weight of my family's demons inside of it.

I can't get rid of it again. It's become too powerful to contain. I guess I just have to get used to the new me.

HAUNTED HOUSE PUBLISHING

"Great men do not lie still in death. Our words echo across time, a light for others to follow when their own fire burns low. Thus shall my torch be taken up again; thus shall I dwell once more among the living."

THOSE WERE THE LAST LINES ALEXANDER NOTOVITCH'S EVER WROTE. I know they belonged to him because I watched his frail hand tremble the tortuous route across the page. I know they were his last because I watched him die in that leather chair the same evening.

You may have never heard of him, but I guarantee you've seen the light of his torches. Alexander wrote in a hundred different styles under a hundred different names. His work has sold millions of copies and has been translated into 112 languages. But the most important thing he's ever written, his Magnum Opus, has never been read by anyone except me.

I think he would have died years ago if it wasn't for that book. Alexander was never married, and neither did he keep any friends. I don't think anyone could stand to be in the same room as him long enough for that. The dark scrutiny of his eyes pierce the most sacred part of you, leaving you naked in a way that you have never seen yourself. The only reason I endured the weight of his frightful presence was the promise of publishing his final volume.

I've always fancied myself as a writer as well, but reading that book humbled me to my core. I read the whole thing in a single 14 hour stretch after his death. The poetry of his words taught me what it was to be human, yet made mockery of my presumption to call myself the same species as him.

I wept many times through the silent vigil of that reading, but it wasn't for loss of the man. I wept that the highest peak of my life would never rise above the lowest shadow of his. I hated myself for how hollow my ideas were, knowing my intellect to be forever incapable of approaching his mastery.

It wasn't fair. If I had written that book instead of him, then I would never need to prove myself again. If I wrote it… but who is to say that I didn't? Only a dead man and these empty halls. What good was fame to him who hid behind pseudonyms as impenetrable as the veil of death?

I took a pen from Alexander's desk and wrote my own name at the head of his manuscript. Though only a single line had changed, I could feel the holy relic in my hands somehow turn into a thing of evil. No more was this a testament to the greatness in man, but rather a tribute to his most vile and jealous desires.

I couldn't bear to look at the thing anymore. I hurled it down upon the dead man's desk, half expecting it to burn a hole straight through. Yet there the crumpled sheets lay, a forgotten pile of rubbish but for me. I reverently sorted the papers once more, and opening the word processor on my laptop, began to type. I watched my fingers write my own name at the top, and I did nothing to stop them.

It took several days to type the entire manuscript, made longer by my constant need to re-read passages that I'd somehow skipped the first time. It wasn't a matter of two pages sticking together either—there were unfamiliar sentences within memorable paragraphs, unnoticed notes in the margin, and even a whole chapter that I had never seen before.

It was almost as though someone had edited the work during the night. I dutifully recorded everything regardless, telling myself that I had been too excited to register these details the first time around. I didn't allow myself to question the genius until I'd reached the very last sentence of the very last paragraph on the very last page.

"Thus is my torch taken up again; thus I dwell once more among the living."

The first time I'd read that line, it was written in the future tense. Now it was written in the present. I was sure of it. The lines had been seared into my mind as surely as my own name.

Alexander's house no longer felt as empty as it had a moment before. Those who have stood alone beneath a storm-ravaged sky would understand the brooding electricity I felt around me. The soft whir of the overhead fan seemed to grow louder, its motion stirring the papers on the desk for the first time. Before my eyes the metal beads beneath the fan slid downward until a clear click resonated.

The fan increased in speed again. I fumbled my way out of the chair and reached to turn it off, but before I could, the chain had already pulled once more. The blades were slowing on their own accord.

In the sudden silence of the dead air I heard footsteps downstairs. They were soft and deliberate, a panther stalking an unsuspecting prey. I raced to the top of the staircase to settle my rebellious imagination, but stopped short as I reached the first step.

The outdoor porch light had just turned off. A second later, the kitchen light extinguished. Then the living room directly below the wooden stairs, dissolving the whole first floor into shadows.

The creak as someone stepped on the bottom stair. Footsteps again—faster now, something sprinting directly up the flight of steps in an avalanche of buckling wood.

I yelped and scrambled backward into Alexander's study. I couldn't hear the footsteps over the thunder of my own blood. I slammed the door behind me. There wasn't a lock, so I thrust my back against the door and braced my legs against the floorboards to pin it shut.

Straining with static tension, I forced slow breaths and willed the drumroll of my heart to slow enough for me to listen. Nothing. Nothing. So quiet that there was no marker to separate the fleeting seconds, the frozen moment colorless and eternal. So quiet that I could almost hear the self-deprecating laughter of my own thoughts.

I was being absurd. All I'd really seen was an electrical abnormality —more the rule than the exception in an old house like this. The sound—the soft tread that I'd mistaken for footprints—nothing but the thrumming of a blown fuse or transformer outside.

Alright wise-guy, my thoughts seemed to retort. Then why don't you explain those snuffling sounds running up and down the door frame? Those dry, dusty snorts, like methodical sandpaper grating against rough wood?

The study lights cut with such vicious swiftness that I jolted and grunted in sudden alarm. The sniffing doubled in urgency in response, something butting against the door on the other side with an assault which grew more frenzied by the second.

Soon I was heaving with exertion, each blow making my skeleton dance to a tune that the rest of me didn't hear. Three inches or more I'd be pushed back by the impact, and before my full weight had even slammed the door into its frame another numbing cascade ricocheted through my body and I'd be flying again.

And then the howl, the chilling echo of a sound buried deep within the dormant animal instinct of my psyche. A sound more beast than man, yet more man than any beast for the tortured guttural syllables which rolled across its alien tongue.

More terrible than the splintering door, more terrible than the bestial anthem or the shrill symphony of my nerves, came the pitter-patter of gentle keys and the soft shadow blocking the light. As horrifying as the creature sounded beyond the door, at least it was on the other side.

Illuminated by the halo of my computer's light, I saw a strange creature hunched over the keyboard. Its shoulders extended so far past its head and stretched the skin of its back so transparently thin that it appeared like a deformed bat. A dozen long crooked fingers on each hand deftly picked out the keys one by one, each bending subtly with several too many joints.

I couldn't leave my post at the door without letting the other monster in, so I was helpless but to stare as the thing completed its work. Once satisfied, it leaned back in the chair and stretched its arms luxuriously behind its body, the elbows bending 90 degrees in the opposite direction to wrap around itself.

At once the pressure on the other side of the door vanished. The dry sniffing left a moment later, growing fainter until I could hear the creak descending the stairs.

No longer needing to hold the door, I cautiously approached my computer and the thing in the chair. It watched me with beady fascination, tracking my slightest movement with a micro adjustment from its head. I got just close enough to read the title page and see that my name had been removed. The original pen-name Alexander had written under was in its place.

"You wrote this?" I asked the creature.

It shook its head and pointed a long finger out the door. The creature pulled itself out of the chair in a sudden lurch, causing me to backpedal. Dragging itself by the arms, useless vestigial legs sliding behind, the thing moved to the bookshelf in the corner and produced another volume.

It pointed at the book, then at itself.

"But there are hundreds of them—"

The creature swept its too-flexible arms in an encompassing gesture. The distant shuffle in the attic—the creaking on the stair—the rush of shadow behind the wastepaper basket—all absorbed in an instant.

To think I was jealous of the old man. All he's ever done is sell the books these mute monsters have produced. And if I'm careful, and if I'm kind to them, then through me they'll write a hundred more.

SOMEBODY BROKE HER

You know the kind of girl I'm talking about. She looks like life chewed her up and spit her back out.

You can see it in her eyes if you could even see her eyes. Her loose tangled hair covers most of her face, and she's always staring at her feet. You can see it in her hunched shoulders, hear it in her mumbling voice. She's both desperate and afraid to be heard, hating herself for everything she says and everything she doesn't say.

She doesn't live in my building, but I see her almost every day when she visits her boyfriend in the apartment next door. I've said hello to her a few times—she always flinches when I talk to her. The first thing out of her mouth is inevitably an apology—sorry for being in my way, or for being here too often, or for taking up one of the dozen empty parking spots. I asked her name once, but she said it didn't matter.

"Why not? What am I supposed to say when I see you?" I asked.

"Nothing. You don't need to. I'm nobody."

"Well my name is—" I began.

But she just kept walking. Head leaning against my neighbor's door, hands in her pockets, looking like an ostrich trying to disappear into the sand.

"Bye nobody!" I chimed as the door opened to let her in.

I couldn't be sure under the hair, but I think she almost smiled. "Bye somebody," she murmured, disappearing into the doorway. My neighbor Jeff poked his head out—scrawny fellow with a soul patch and a beanie which seemed permanently fixed to his head. He nodded sharply at me like a fighter paying insincere respect to his opponent, slamming the door.

I liked watching Nobody from my balcony when she was parking her car. I liked the fluid grace of her movements which transformed regular motions like opening doors and stepping over obstacles into a choreographed dance. I must not have been the only one to notice either, because there always seemed to be someone hitting on her whenever I saw her. Not the charming kind either—fat oafs jumping out of their car like they were waiting for her, or pushy street rats backing her up against the building. I thought she was a prostitute at first, but she always rebuffed them so vehemently that I figured that wasn't the case.

Often at night I'd see her leaning on the railing of my neighbor's balcony, smoking a joint and staring off into space. I got the feeling that she was staring into a world that only she could see, but looking at her face, I also got the feeling that it wasn't a very pretty world. I wish I could see it too. Sometimes I'd go out onto my own balcony and try to make an excuse for conversation, but she'd invariably duck back inside the moment she saw me. If I was lucky, and she seemed to be in good spirits, I'd hear a "Bye somebody" before she went. A stupid joke, but it always made me smile.

She couldn't have been happy, but I suppose it wasn't any of my business. I'd hear her boyfriend yelling at her through the walls sometimes, although I never heard her say anything back. I figured that she was her own person with her own choices to make, and if she was being really mistreated, then she wouldn't keep coming back. It's not like I had proof that she was being abused or anything—and what I did guess, I quickly dismissed as petty jealousy, resolving not to interfere with her life.

That resolution lasted for about two months, but it ended last night. It was after dark and I was getting home late when I spotted Nobody pressed up against my building. Two men in leather jackets were several inches too close for innocent conversation, practically pressing themselves on her while she squirmed to get away. I honked my car horn at them, and one looked over his shoulder. Fat stupid face, mouth hanging part way open, he stared at me for a few seconds before turning back to her.

"I got to go," I heard her say. "Somebody is waiting for me."

I honked again. Fat-face turned to walk over to my car. "Cool it, asshole," he shouted. "This target only has 11 points left, anyway. Get your own damn girl."

I rolled down my window. "What's that supposed to mean?"

"You new or something?" he asked, fishing out his phone. He showed me the screen which depicted a GPS map of my neighborhood. Scattered throughout were little targets, each with a name and a life-bar like a video game character has. The target against my building was named 'Cillia', with 11/100 life remaining.

"I don't know what the fuck that is, but I'm not playing," I told him.

He laughed. More like a guffaw really—deep and guttural without the slightest hint of mirth. "You're after that piece of shit and you're not even getting points? Hey Mark—he actually wants this bitch."

The other guy—presumably Mark—still had the girl against the wall. He made a half-lunge at her as she wriggled free, but it was just to scare her. She looked like she was about to run toward my car, but seeing the fat one over by me, she sprinted to her own vehicle instead. We all watched as she tore out of the parking lot, the biggest smile I'd ever seen plastered across her face.

"Don't waste your time. Somebody already broke her." Fat-face slammed my car with the palm of his hand as he turned to leave. "Let's go Mark. There's two more of them on this street."

I was so relieved to see them go that I didn't try to ask more questions. Nobody had a name. It was Cillia. And something was tracking her location and broadcasting it out to these creeps. It didn't feel like I was meddling in someone else's business anymore. I couldn't just play dumb and let her sort this out for herself.

A few minutes later and I was hammering on my neighbor's apartment. "Hey Jeff, you in there?"

"Bug off," came the muffled reply.

"It's about the game you're playing with Cillia." It seemed pretty vague to me, but if he was involved, then he'd know what I was talking about.

Loud shuffling like someone crossing the room in a hurry, and the door opened a moment later. He was wearing nothing but his boxers and his beanie, skinny body blocking the door.

"Yeah, what about the game?" he asked. I hesitated, unsure what to say next. He must have misread my silence because his face became animated and hopeful. "Hey did I win the prize or something?"

I nodded stiffly. Jeff threw the door open to welcome me in, practically dancing with excitement. "Holy shit, I knew it! I've been on the leader-board for weeks—it was only a matter of time. Seriously competitive shit, you know? I've got everything ready for you, come on in." He rushed to a cabinet under the sink and began hauling out cardboard boxes. I still didn't know what the hell was going on though, so I had to play along to get more answers.

"How many points are you at now?" I asked.

"723," without hesitation. "19 separate targets, although I've been getting most of the points from Cillia, as you know." He plopped two cardboard boxes on the coffee table beside me, flaying them open for inspection. The greasy smell of stale sex was nauseating. "This one's got all the condoms in it," he said. Hundreds of them—all used—neatly tied off into little balloons. "Then this one has all the recordings."

"723 is a lot," I said, pretending to be impressed. "Tell me how you were keeping score."

He looked suspicious for a moment, but it passed. If my question raised any red flags, then he was so pleased with himself that he didn't dwell on it. "It's legit, I swear. I used the 'Break Her' rule-book and everything. 10 points for humiliating her. 15 points for taking a personal item or making a big decision for her. 25 for unwanted sex or something physical. Then I've got a bunch of the small ones I've been building up—the daily criticisms, isolating her from friends and family, that sort of thing. What's the prize going to be?"

"Hold on a minute, I got to ask all the questions first. Standard procedure, you know."

"How come you never told me you worked for 'Break Her'? You must have known that I played," Jeff asked. Again the suspicion, this time lingering on his face.

I shrugged, making notes on my phone as though I was dutifully recording his answers. "What do you think the purpose of the game was? And how did you get into it?"

"Isn't it obvious? You just got to break her. I started playing when my buddy got dumped by his ex. He paid to have her registered in the system, and I thought it would be fun to join so I could start harassing her. At first it was just to support my buddy, but it was pretty helpful seeing where all the vulnerable chicks were. Turned out I was pretty good at it, so I decided to try to get enough points to win the prize."

"Uh huh." I typed as he talked. My fingers were literally shaking. "And Cillia? Did you ever love her?"

He laughed. It wasn't a pleasant sound. A pause, then: "Oh, are you serious? Come on, man. It's just a game. So what's the deal? Am I getting the prize today or not?"

I didn't look up from my phone. I was so disgusted that I couldn't even look at him. The silence was excruciating.

"Is this legal?" I breathed. Silence again, as both of us digested what I said. My cover was blown.

"You lying piece of shit," Jeff grunted, protectively ripping his boxes of prizes away from me. "You trying to steal my points or something?"

He was on me before I even realized what was happening. Bony arms wrapped around me, the momentum flinging me to the ground. He got in a good hit to my jaw before I flipped him on his back. I was bigger and stronger than him, but he twisted under me like a feral animal.

"She's mine! You don't know how much work I put into that bitch!" he roared. I punched him to shut him up. He spit blood at me, and I hit him again. I never thought it would feel so good to hurt someone, but now that I started, I couldn't stop myself. Next I knew my hands were so soaked in blood that it ran between my knuckles like rivers. Jeff wasn't moving. And I was okay with that.

Jeff's phone beeped where it lay on the ground. Somehow the weight of what I'd done didn't hit until I heard it. It beeped again, and I lifted the phone to see what was going on.

It was a notification from 'Break Her'. I opened the app and saw a short questionnaire. Humiliation, abuse, control—a daily checklist for him to go through to get his points. What the hell did I get myself involved in? And who was I to think I could make any difference when a whole world of terrible people were trying to destroy her?

At the bottom of the form it asked: 'Did you see her smile today?' Numb and overwhelmed, I clicked 'yes'. Immediately Cillia's life-bar jumped a point, up to 12/100.

Well that's some difference at least. Not much, but it's a start.

ANY SOUL WILL DO

MADNESS ISN'T USUALLY LOUD LIKE IT'S PORTRAYED ON THE SCREEN. IT'S not bright either—no supernova of unfettered emotion or physical deformity to hint at the rot inside. I didn't bellow until my throat was raw, or bloody my hands on my walls and mirrors. I didn't splatter my paints across my skin or shred the half-finished canvases which taunt my chosen identity.

My wife Joana even commented on how methodical I was when I gently placed each brush in its case, never to be opened again. If you count finger painting in pre-school, then it's taken me forty-one years to fully accept my failure. I should have realized it sooner, but I always managed to concoct one excuse after another.

I didn't try hard enough. That's a good one. It makes it sound like I could just flip a switch in my mind and force myself to become a master through sheer willpower.

I wasn't taught well enough. Even better: shifting the blame onto someone else. If only my teachers had been more qualified—if only they'd devoted themselves to nurture my potential like Domenico Ghirlandaio devoted himself to Michelangelo.

I'm not good enough—the hardest pill to swallow. I set out to capture the intrinsic beauty of the human spirit and display it for the world to see, but there is no beauty in me to share. I didn't scream and throw a fit. I didn't think much of anything at all. I just let my body move through the familiar motions of life and hoped no one would notice there was nothing below the surface.

Joana asked why my eyes were watering, but I blamed it on the movie we were watching. She punched my arm playfully, calling me a big softy.

"Aren't you working on something tonight?" she asked.

I blinked hard, not taking my eyes off the TV.

"I remember you talking about that comic book store commission. How's that coming?"

"It's coming," I lied. She tried to snuggle against me, but I slipped free and snuck off to the bathroom. It felt wrong to even let her touch me. She had this conception of who I was in her mind—just like I used to—but that person doesn't exist. I'm a failure, a hack, a fraud. And that's all I'd ever be. I stared at myself in the mirror, tracing the unfamiliar lines on my face. Poking at the bags under my eyes. Hating what I saw, and hating even more what I couldn't see.

I mimed a gun with my fingers and put it against my head. Cocked the thumb, grinned my best phony smile, and BLAMO.

"Honey, can you get me a soda on your way back?" I heard from the living room.

But I couldn't take my eyes away from the mirror. My reflection showed a crater in the side of my skull where the imaginary bullet entered. Blood, fragmented bone, and fleshy gray lumps splattered across the bathroom walls, with more gushing from the exit wound on the other side of my head.

"Ooh and one of those Nutella cups," Joana added. "Thanks honey!"

I traced my fingers over my temple, withdrawing them clean. My reflection still wore the phony smile, although it was barely visible now under the torrent of blood flooding down its face.

"Two years, maybe less," came a voice. I spun, startled, unable to find an orator in the empty bathroom. "First comes the depression. Then the withdrawal. Joana will pretend she's just going to visit her family for a while, but you'll know she really just can't stand being around you."

My bloody reflection was talking to me. That's normal. This is fine.

"She'll expect you to call and explain what's going on, but you won't. She'll extend her trip, thinking you just need time to yourself. And you do, but only because you're too much of a coward to pull the trigger while someone's watching. The silence will become too loud, and before you know it..."

The bloody figure mimed a finger to its head, the phony smile flashing through the red.

"You okay in there?" Joana called from the living room. "Mama wants her chocolate!"

"Okay," I mumbled, replying to both.

"Or..." the reflection said.

"Or what?"

"Or you become the best painter the world has ever known, your name spoken with reverence a thousand years after your death."

"Okay," I mumbled, numb to the whole show. "Yeah. Let's do that."

"This is where most people ask 'what's the catch?'" My reflection's voice was coy.

"Probably my soul or something, right? That's okay. I'm not using it for anything."

"You don't have to sell your soul. Any soul will do."

"Never mind I'll get it myself," Joana said. "Geez, I wish I'd married a butler instead."

"Think about it," the reflection bubbled rapidly, spraying blood between his teeth as he did. "You won't be able to enjoy your success without a soul. And your wife—she was going to leave you anyway. If anything, this would spare her a lifetime of regret and guilt over your death. You owe it to yourself—you owe it to both of you."

"I can't give something that isn't mine," I replied, immediately hating myself for even entertaining the thought.

"Anyone who loves without reservation exposes their soul. Paint her—not as she appears, but as she truly is. I'll take care of the rest."

"What are you doing, giving birth in there?" Joana asked from right outside the door. The handle rattled. The door wasn't locked. I leapt to stop her from entering—too slow. The door swung inward and there she stood: tank top over pajama bottoms, hair frizzy and wild, licking Nutella off her fingers. My heart was beating so fast, but as much as I loved her, I think my fear was even stronger.

Back to the mirror, I stared into my reflection. No blood. No bullet wound. Just a tired, aging face, equally terrifying in its own way.

"Come on," Joana wrapped her arms around me from behind. "The movie's no fun without you blubbering over the dialog."

"I can't," I said, still staring into the mirror. "I have a painting to finish."

A feverish intensity imbued my work all night and into the next morning. A drowning man struggling for air could not have done so with more urgency than the flight of my desperate brush. No thoughts endured more than a second before they were replaced by the endless cycle of anticipation and release each stroke demanded. When my canvas was filled, I didn't hesitate to slash the lines onto the walls on either side of my easel. Then the table—the dresser—my own body a vessel to carry the glory of her design.

My brush was unconfined by any shape, but in its erratic patterns I felt myself carving something out of nothing—something that had never been seen by mortal eyes before.

In the subtleties of the blending colors I captured Joana's wry humor and gentle grace. Her laughter exploded like shrapnel across the space, the light in her eyes reflected in my cascading colors. The way her heart broke when her aging dog nudged her goodbye—the anxious thrill of stepping off the plane in Paris—even her love for me and her unspoken dread of the great beyond, naked and frozen for all the world to see.

Paint beneath my fingernails, in my hair, blazoned across my body, a testament to the frenzied passion which had possessed me. Though working alone, I danced with Joana the whole night through. I have never seen her more plainly nor loved her more strongly than those forbidden hours, and not until morning's light did I stop to understand what I had done.

'Are you insane?' That's what I was expecting to hear. Any second the door to my studio would open and Joana would see the chaos I had the audacity to unfurl. She'd laugh at me, making a thousand playful guesses at the madness which leaked from my mind all night. We'd both laugh, then she'd say something like 'I'm just happy to see you enjoying your work again,' and offer to help me clean. That's how kind she was: when I did something stupid she'd be there to help me fix it without a trace of accusation or blame.

Maybe I really was insane. But either way, she couldn't fix this one for me.

She didn't enter the room though. Not in the kitchen making her coffee, not in the shower singing herself into lucidity. Joana never got up that morning. She said she wasn't feeling herself, and I was too much of a coward to tell her why. If I'd taken a break in the night to check on her, I might have noticed the rot that had already started to set in. She managed to prop herself up on her elbows, leaving several layers of flaking skin on the pillow. Ashen cracked skin, yellowed eyes, balding patches where clumps of hair had already started to fall —my wife was still in my studio where I'd captured her. The woman struggling for breath was nothing but a stranger to me, and I left her without a word.

I slept little and ate less. I sought only to paint, vainly trying to recapture the intimacy I'd felt with her the night before. There was a brief thrill as I marveled at the dexterity of my fingers, although they lacked the passion that haunted me before. I could trace every mental image I dared conjure and map them flawlessly onto the canvas, but they were dead things being carved into a dead world.

It didn't take long for me to sit back in exasperation. I had the technical skill to conquer any challenge, but it wasn't an infernal magic which had possessed me the night before. I knew in that moment that there was nothing I could ever create that was more beautiful than the pandemonium of Joana's soul. I heard that hollow thing call my name from the bedroom with a voice like wind through dry leaves, and Heaven and Hell as my witness, I wept for what I'd done.

"Give her soul back to her," I begged the aging face in the mirror. "Take mine instead—"

"What an ugly painting that would be," the demon with my face replied.

"Then another—it doesn't matter whose. I'll give you as many as you like!"

"Does another love you as she did? Have they exposed themselves to your capture as she has done?"

I had no reply to give. Coward that I was, I merely returned to my painting. Lifeless hollow forms came marching through my work, each accompanied by the soundtrack of my wife's body slowly deteriorating without its soul. Each time I looked at her there would be another piece missing: fingers decomposing and littering the mattress, cheeks worn so thin that I could see her blackened teeth and languid tongue even when her mouth was closed. I'd listen to her moan while I worked, always stealing longing glances at the portrait of her soul splashed across the room.

I couldn't take it anymore. I set fire to that place with her inside. And watching the smoke curl into the night sky, all that's left is to hope her soul escaped its prison and is now soaring somewhere with its dignity returned.

As for me, I returned to my work. Until the day I paint something so marvelous as to trick some poor innocent into loving me. Then I will paint what I see, and sell them until Joana is home again.

THE OTHER SIDE OF SKY

WHEN I WAS ABOUT TO DIE, MY LIFE DIDN'T FLASH BEFORE MY EYES. ALL I could think about was what my father once told me from a beige couch in an unlit study.

"Above all else, humans are survivors. When one has exhausted all possibility of survival, the mind will expand its idea of what is possible. Think of it this way: You're alone in the woods and hiding from wolves which are hunting you. Do you call for help?"

"Of course not", I had said. "Then the wolves would know where I was."

"Exactly. But if the wolves found you anyway, and you knew there was no hope of escape. You might as well shout then, right?"

"You might as well."

"The only difference, then, was your desperation. In the same way, your subconscious mind is prudent enough not to shout into the dark for fear of what might hear. When all hope is lost though, the mind begins to scream at random. It screams across time, across dimensions—and just sometimes, something will be listening."

"What kind of something?" I'd asked.

"There's only one way to find out, and I wouldn't recommend it."

I wouldn't recommend it either. Taking a bullet in the stomach isn't all that. The head would have been better. Nice and clean. Arm or leg? No problem, I can still get myself to the hospital. The stomach though—that bleed is slow, and there's too much time to scream at the emptiness between stars.

It doesn't matter how it happened. I made some bad decisions, and the man who shot me made a worse one. That's not what this story is about. This story is about an asphalt parking lot, my twelve-year-old daughter Lizzie, and the best pizza I ever had in my life.

Let's start at the parking lot where I died. You ever jump straight from a hot tub to a cold pool? It was a little like that, only I didn't feel it on my skin. I felt it deep inside, radiating out from where the bullet sat between my ribs. It seemed to move about an inch a minute, and I could hear it the whole while—kinda like the slow tear of fabric that kept getting louder and louder, until I was pretty sure every cell in my body was screaming itself apart. Like the worst static you ever heard. And the louder it got, the slower it spread, until each POP was a supernova and each plateau between was death itself.

And I knew—deep down I knew, like I knew fire burns and gravity drags me down—that soon one of those POPS will be the last one I ever hear. And that for the rest of time, I'll be suspended by the anticipation between. But that never happened, because something spoke to me before I went.

"Want to stick around?"

If that was the voice of God, then God is a lonely old man at a diner with nowhere else to be. I didn't know how to answer, but I really did want to stick around. Lizzie needed a dad, and I needed another chance to make up for fucking up the first time. I wanted it so hard that I think the voice must have felt it too.

"You won't get to leave again."

I'll never leave her again...

"Not now, not in a hundred years when your daughter is dead, not in ten-thousand when the last man has killed his brother, and you're left to watch the survivor grow old and blow to dust. Or you can get off now, and that will be that."

I don't know how long I sat there thinking, but I did know that I hadn't heard a POP in a long time. That silence sure can be heavy. I also knew that I'd rather spend the rest of time thinking about how I tried my hardest for my daughter than let my last thought be self-hatred and regret. And as soon as I knew that, the voice knew it too.

POP

To the other side of sky and back. But not back—not like I ought to be. I was less than the shadow of a shadow, a ghost of a light breeze wafting on a calm day. And nothing broke my heart like lingering in Lizzie's room and watching her watch the door for me to come home. And nothing hurt so much as not to be able to hold her and tell her I was here, or watching her push away her food until I could see her collarbone like it was a snake beneath her skin.

But hurt is a lot like desperation, because sometimes you don't know what's possible until it really sets your blood on fire and gets you screaming. Because one night it hurt so bad and I lashed out so hard that something quite miraculous happened.

A water bottle fell off the side of her nightstand and fell onto the carpet. Lizzie hadn't pushed it. She was lying on her back, staring at the ceiling like she did most of the time. It was me, and with some concentration and practice, I could do it again. Little things—sliding a pen on a desk, or popping a bubble, or kissing her on the forehead as light as a butterfly. Then once I caught her smile and touch her fingers to her skin, and I knew she felt it too.

I could learn how to be in her life, but it would take time. But I didn't have the luxury to wait forever.

It's not that I was afraid Lizzie would hurt herself. Not on purpose anyway. She had to move and live with my sister though, and like a flower in the sun, I could see her wilting day by day. She stopped seeing her old friends, and she didn't talk to anyone at her new school. My sister didn't have the first idea how to reach her, so she'd just give my daughter money whenever she felt guilty.

What's a 12-year-old going to do with nothing but time, money, and pain? Sneak cigarettes at first, but it didn't stay innocent for long. Apple doesn't fall far from the tree I guess; pretty soon she was buying a bag of pills from the school janitor every week like clockwork. What could I do about that? Breathe down the bastard's neck? Blow some sand in his eye?

The flower was wilting faster than ever, and Lizzie never kept money in her pocket for very long. To make matters worse, my sister's guilt didn't last into the third month. Lizzie's allowance was cut off, and suddenly the only thing she'd done to numb the pain was out of reach. All I could do was be the breeze on her knotted brow when she sweat herself to sleep or bit her nails until they bled.

Lizzie confronted the janitor the next day, and it wasn't pretty. She shoved him in the hallway in the middle of the day, practically shouting at him in front of a dozen kids. If she'd picked up one of my bad habits, she'd gotten them all. Watching her little face seethe, I knew that things were only going to get worse from here.

I had to try harder. My next breakthrough came in the form of a house fly. I was nudging it back and forth when I began falling into the rhythm of its motion. Pretty soon I was that rhythm, and before I knew what was happening, I was inside looking out, swerving wildly to avoid slamming into a wall. The shock knocked my mind straight back to where I was, but it wasn't hard to get back in again. Next a spider, crickets, even a squirrel for the fraction of a second—my spirit was breaking its way into simple-minded animals.

The animal mind was in there too, but I was getting better at keeping them down. Pretty soon I might be able to send her a message somehow, or even become her friend through a dog or cat. But pretty soon wasn't soon enough.

Lizzie was stubborn, and just like her father, she wouldn't take no for an answer. She slipped from her bedroom one night and snuck out the house while my sister was asleep. She didn't have a car, or money, but she did have a hammer, and that scared me even worse. She walked the whole 2 mile route to her school, her face as blank as if she were still lying in bed and staring at the ceiling. I tried to intervene by slipping into the minds of a few moths we passed, but even these were suddenly too difficult for me.

I couldn't get into their rhythm. I didn't feel like a moth. I felt like her father, the worst father in the world who was helpless to stop whatever happened next. She broke into the window of the computer lab and stole a dozen laptops from the school. She hid them in the bushes around the corner, then walked all the way home and slipped back into bed as if nothing happened. The next morning she ditched after the bus dropped her off, then straight to the hidden computers and a pawn shop nearby. An hour later and she was back in school, a giant wad of cash in her pocket and a fake doctor's note for the front desk.

I would have been almost proud if I hadn't been watching her face the whole time. I hadn't seen that much quiet, self-loathing since the last time I had a body to look in the mirror.

"How much did you bring?" was her first question for the janitor after school. They were under the bleachers of the soccer field.

"How much you got?" he asked.

Don't. Don't be that stupid.

She pulled out the entire wad of cash. I don't think she ever once counted it. She didn't care, as long as she got what she came for.

The janitor's face lit up like a kid on Christmas. He reached out to take it, and she let him. She stuffed her hands into her pockets and waited while he flipped through it, checking surreptitiously over his shoulder as he did.

Maybe this will be the last time. Maybe she'll take a bunch of pills and get sick and never want to touch the stuff again. Or maybe she'll be stoned for a month, and by the time she sobers up I'll be a little further from her mind. Maybe I'll be stronger by then, and I can hold her like I'm supposed to, and tell her that everything is going to be okay...

But the janitor didn't believe in 'one day'. He stuffed the cash in his pocket and, as cool as a cucumber, started to walk away.

"Where the fuck are you going?" Lizzie whispered as loud as she dared.

The janitor started walking faster. If she is anything like her father... right on cue, she charges at him, hurling herself onto his leg and wrapping herself around it. He kicks her, but she holds on fast.

"Just give it to me. I'll tell everyone."

"You wouldn't dare. I can guess where you got the money. The whole school is talking about it. Get off of me."

"Fuck do I care? I'm going to tell the principal. And the police. And your fat cow of a mother—"

I don't know if he intended to stomp on her. It all happened too fast. She was already wrapped around his leg, and the shaking wasn't getting her off, and—BAM, his foot planting right in her face. But she held on, and that seemed to make him even angrier. She didn't cry—she didn't even whimper. She just closed her eyes and clung on like a drowning man on the last stick of wood in the world.

"You never... talk to me... again," the man said between kicks. Each one was harder than the last, like he was trying to get out a whole lifetime of frustrations all at once. He kicked her like she was every woman who had ever failed to love him, and every man he'd ever looked up to and let him down. Like it was the only power he'd ever had in his miserable life, and he couldn't stop because he'd never get that power back again. He kicked her and he hated himself for doing it, and that made him kick her even harder.

That rage—that pain—that helpless despair—now that's a rhythm I could understand. I was inside his head all at once, and I wasn't going to let go. I felt his mind screaming inside me, but Lizzie wasn't getting kicked anymore, and that's all that mattered. Everything that he had poured into hurting my daughter, I poured into him, crushing his spirit until it was a shadow—less than a shadow—and then nothing but a distant thought in the back of my mind.

I was alive again. I had a body. I didn't get bounced out, I couldn't get out even if I tried. And I was standing over my barely conscious daughter who lay bleeding and crying into the dirt. I fell onto my knees right beside her and started crying too. There wasn't anything else to do.

I tried to reach out for her, but she recoiled as if I was a serpent. How could I blame her? She'd just seen this body beat her bloody. How could she ever speak to me after this? She started running, but I couldn't let that happen. If I let her out of my life, she'd never trust me enough to let me back in. This was my one chance, and I couldn't waste it.

She wasn't hard to catch in the state she was in. And the janitor had picked his spot well—there wasn't anyone else around the soccer field. I've been watching long enough to know which car belonged to him, and it didn't take long to force Lizzie inside and stomp the gas.

Doesn't hatred get tired eventually? I'm going to be there for her, and I'm going to protect her from here on out. She'll understand how hard I tried one day, and she'll forgive me. Who cares if the lines on my face are different, or if I sing her to sleep in an unfamiliar voice? I'm her father, and I'll love her until the end of time.

It took her almost a year to speak to me, and almost three before she said: "Can we get pizza tonight, dad?"

But you know what? It was the best pizza I ever had.

THEIR LAST WORDS

IT TAKES SOME BY SURPRISE DURING THE NIGHT—I THINK THEY'RE THE lucky ones. I think others are holding off for something—their daughter's marriage, their grandchildren—something powerful enough to give the last grains of the hourglass some weight. Others simply make up their mind that it's time. There's one man in particular I remember who hadn't moved a muscle for a day. Several of us at the hospice thought he was already gone a half-dozen times, but then all at once he stood up. He carefully put on his suit, tied his tie, fastened his shoes, and then laid back down. He was dead within the hour.

Its their last words that really stick with me though. Logically I know they're a random line of conversation slipping from a deteriorating mind, but somehow it also feels like their truest reflection. In that moment when I'm holding her frail hand, I know her better than her husband or her children ever did. People can hide their whole life long, but they can't keep hiding into death. That's how I feel anyway, and it's why I started keeping a journal of all the last words I hear.

"I don't know where to go next." That hit me hard. She was 94 years old, hardly bigger than Yoda, and she usually just watched me in silence while I cleaned her room. It was late and I was tired—I didn't know how to comfort her, and I just pretended that I didn't hear. She was gone when I checked in the next morning.

"Am I in the way?" Seems silly, doesn't it? Inconsequential. But the man was a world war 2 veteran. He told me once about how he and a dozen men broke over a thousand people out of the camps. He wanted to go home at the end, but I saw his two sons fighting over who would take him in the lobby. Neither took him and he died in the hospice, his last words being: "Am I in the way?"

"Not going without a fight." I liked that one. Barrel chested bearded man, looked as healthy as could be. The fight was a seizure though, and one of the worst I'd ever seen. It must have lasted half an hour, bucking and flailing and gasping for breath. He would have done better to go quietly.

"Dead... dead... dead... dead..." over and over. Ever since the woman's stroke, she was convinced that she'd already died. She never stopped muttering to herself, "dead...dead..." being one of her favorite mantras.

Sometimes I wonder if thoughts can linger in the air after their thinker has died. I can swear that the rooms are darker for at least a week after someone goes. If its a violent death, sometimes I'll feel a tension in the air—something like anger without a body attached to it. I decided to start keeping track, my hobby of journaling became a bit more of an obsession, if I'm being honest. I took a calendar and marked down how I felt about the rooms each day. I didn't fill in the deaths until the end of the month, and sure enough, each death marked the change in a room.

Now I know this isn't an exact science, but in the process I did notice something that I couldn't explain. For the last four deaths in my building, their last utterances began with the following words:

"I. Am. Not. Dead."

It's silly, right? Here were four unrelated people who never talked to each other. And their last words formed a sentence. It was a silly coincidence, it meant nothing, and it kept getting stranger.

"Can you get me a little water?" 11B, a few days later.

"You look like an angel." 23A, a heart attack during the night.

"Hear the birds outside? I do love the spring." Sitting by her window, the sun on her face. It should have been the most peaceful one for me, but the moment she closed her eyes I knew the word fit.

"I. Am. Not. Dead. Can. You. Hear."

Can I hear what? I found out this morning.

I wasn't there when he said it, but everybody at the hospice knew I was keeping track. My friend told me the moment I walked in the door.

"Me and my buddies are going to see each other real soon."

I am not dead. Can you hear me?

The rooms all seem dark today.

CHILDREN TASTE BETTER

A SINGLE ENGINE PRIVATE PLANE, SKIMMING LOW OVER THE ALASKAN wilderness. Glacial waters as clear as a polished mirror, reflecting the vast primordial forests and savage peaks which loom above us: a testament to the stoic grandeur of an Earth which existed long before humanity and will continue to endure long after the footnote of our existence has been forgotten. For one glorious moment it feels as though the world was created just for us, but that was before the engine stalled mid-flight. Before the violent plummet and the mercy of a deaf God, before the ground accelerating toward us, all happening much too fast to regain altitude before the crash.

An explosion so loud it was silent—light so bright I saw nothing. Bone-jarring impact, everything lurching so bad it felt like my soul must have been ripped clean from my body. I wish I'd died the second we hit the ground. I wish my husband had too, but he lingered in that broken body until nightfall. Our hands had never clasped so tightly as when sealed together with his blood, and no words were as precious as those escaping between his shallow breaths.

"Promise me that you'll survive," he'd said. "Whatever it takes."

I wasn't in much better condition than him. One of my legs was broken, several ribs had snapped, and three of my fingers were still clinging to the bottom of my seat where I'd braced for the crash, now a dozen feet away. I didn't expect to last the night, but I still made that promise. I'd like to think that hope gave him some small comfort before his eyes closed for the last time.

After that came the war between slow starvation and my desperate hope of being saved. A hungry animal could easily find me first, lured by the scent of charred flesh and fresh blood which teased my nostrils. But there was another war going on below the surface: my human dignity against my will to survive.

I lasted almost four days before I took the first bite. Just a mouthful, holding the strip of his skin in my mouth and wetting my parched throat with his blood. By the end of the week I'd become more methodical, stripping the flesh clean to roast, cracking the bones for their marrow, wasting nothing. By the end of two weeks, there was nothing left of my husband.

I'd given up on ever being rescued, and instead started the long walk back toward civilization. I was amazed at how quickly my leg had healed, and as I trekked, I felt myself filled with a restless vitality which I could only attribute to my will to live.

I barely slept at night, barely rested during the day. It's almost as if I'd spent my entire life being sick, but I'd gotten so used to the feeling that I thought that's how everyone is supposed to feel.

I can tell you right now that life is a lie. Your blood is not supposed to pass sluggish and unnoticed through your veins, its power dormant. You should feel the electricity of your flexing muscles, each explosive fiber primed to your will. Those pristine wildernesses were not where I had been banished to die. It's where I came alive.

I don't know how long I traveled in such a state, falling into a a trance from my single-minded determination. I think my husband's spirit must have been guiding me though, because I found sudden understanding in how to navigate the stars, just like he learned from the navy.

Eventually I found what I was looking for: a couple of campers fresh from the big city. I was so relieved at hearing another human voice through the trees that I surged forward like a wild thing. All my pain and sacrifice had been building to this moment. Elegant French words, a woman's laughter, a way home—this is what I'd kept myself alive for.

But when I saw them... him panting and sweating to move his grotesque belly, her screaming and carrying on as though I was less than human... well it just goes to show you that sometimes you need to take a step back in order to see things clearly. After everything I'd been through, I couldn't feel anything but pity and disgust for these torpid creatures, willing victims of what their artificial life had deformed them into.

The husband was bigger, but the wife tasted better. Cleaner. I lived more vibrantly in those next few nights—feasting and regaining my strength from their unused bodies—than all the years they'd wasted on being half-alive.

I wasn't only getting stronger either. I started catching my thoughts slipping in and out of French. I'd thought my husband had been guiding me through the woods, but now it seemed more appropriate to say that I had consumed some aspect of him, just as I had done with the French couple.

I was hungrier than ever. Gnawing, incessant hunger almost as soon as I'd finished, like my stomach threatened to digest itself if it didn't get more. I tried eating some of the trail mix and granola bars in their packs, but it tasted like so much sawdust and dirt. Even the beef jerky tasted like cardboard (although that's not unusual by itself).

Human meat. It was obvious that the more I ate, the more I needed it. The prospect of returning to my frail old self? Unbearable. But the idea of living in the woods, biding my time in agonizing solitude while waiting for my next chance meal? I don't think that's any better.

Unless of course, I go back to my old life without giving up what I need to survive. And such easy targets, there at the kindergarten where I used to teach.

I didn't even waste time stopping at a hospital. My wounds had mended on their own, all but the missing fingers. I only stopped off at home long enough for a shower and some new clothes before heading back to the school.

Surrounded by a sea of little shaggy heads, not even reaching my waist. I could almost taste them. The other teachers were shocked to hear what happened of course (their version was lighter on the details), but despite their generous offers to help, I insisted that I wanted to be back in the classroom as soon as possible.

"See guys? I told you she wasn't dead!" That was Roddick. He likes to finger-paint. I hope it doesn't have a bad flavor.

"What happened to your hand? Ewww gross! You're gross!" I'd be lying if I said this was the first time I'd contemplated Tiffany's horrible demise.

"You don't have to come back. We were having fun without you."

"Oh don't you worry." I squatted down to Sandy's level. "Having me around will be even more exciting. Now take these and hand one out to everyone in the class."

I may be hungry, but I'm not an idiot. I'd never be able to take more than one or two children before causing such a scene that it became impossible to continue.

"What's she handing out? What is it let me see!" Tiffany shouted.

"It's a permission slip," I told her. "We're going on a field trip. You, me, the whole class. We're going camping."

It's not just the taste that makes children special. It's their innocence. And if I ever want to start over and live a normal life, then I'm going to need to eat until I'm innocent again too.

THE SMALLEST COFFINS ARE THE HEAVIEST

IF SOMEONE POINTED A GUN AT ME AND FILLED ME WITH LEAD, THEN NO one would question my right to remove the bullet from my body. It was forced into me against my will, and I would be a fool not to fight tooth and nail to stop it from destroying my life.

The child growing inside me is the result of another wound: one much deeper than a bullet could reach. A wound that my mother says is a blessing in disguise, but I don't see it.

I don't mind telling you how it happened, but I won't because I don't want you to think it matters. Whether or not he loved me, whether one or the other was drunk or lonely or beaten into submission doesn't matter, just as it wouldn't matter whether the gun went off by accident or deliberate malice.

The only thing that matters is that I'm hurt and want to be well again, and an abortion is the only way to make that happen. At first it seemed like my mother was sympathetic to the idea, but as the weeks dragged on it became clear that she was only stalling for time.

I trusted her though, and I kept promising to wait. Just until I talk to one more person—just until I read one more pamphlet filled with comforting faces and sourceless facts.

I waited as if one morning I'd wake up and realize I was making a big deal about nothing. As if I'd just failed a test or bumped a car that would be forgiven and forgotten. Day by day the child grew inside me, and day by day the child I used to be died to make room for it.

"You don't have to decide anything yet," my mother kept saying. By the time I realized that 'not making a decision' was itself a decision to keep the baby, it was already too late.

12 weeks had come and passed without me noticing, and no clinic in my state would take me now. My mother didn't need to pretend to be patient or kind anymore. All the talk about my well being was replaced with accusations about my responsibility. I had to get a job—find daycare—find a man. I had to sacrifice myself to this wound, and offer it my dreams for a future that I had only just begun to plan for myself.

My mother said I was being selfish. Hadn't she sacrificed everything for me? No, I told her, she hadn't. She'd wanted a child, so anything she'd been willing to trade for that was an exchange, not a sacrifice.

I couldn't talk to her anymore, so I confided in a close friend. A few days later my friend slipped me two bottles of pills which I treasured more than a thousand sweet words. The first ones were supposed to detach the embryo from the uterine wall. The second set dispels it. I like that word—"dispel". Like magic, vanishing it away without a trace.

This was no disappearing act though. I'd never felt such excruciating pain in my life as when I took the first pills. I got through it because I knew it was a cleansing pain, like I was stitching myself back together to be whole again.

I had to wait at least 24 hours before taking the second set. Sometimes it hurt too bad for me to keep a straight face though, and my mother was quick to notice. She wanted to take me to the hospital, and the more I protested, the more suspicious she got.

There was no hiding it anymore after I took the second pills. I was rolling on the bathroom floor and couldn't stop her from reading the empty bottles. The wound was healing though, and it was too late for her to do anything about it.

"What have you done you evil girl?" she shouted at me while I clutched my stomach in pain. "Nasty, vile, wicked girl. God will not forgive you."

Her words couldn't reach me anymore though. There was nothing left to hide. If God was watching, then he was the only one who should feel ashamed.

The whole process was a lot bloodier than I expected. Whenever I thought it had all discharged, I'd clutch my stomach again and another wave would wrack my body.

To my mother's credit she stayed with me the whole time. After the initial outbursts she held my hand and prayed for me. I told her I was sorry that I wasn't ready to start my own family yet, but she said all the family she needed was already in this room.

I guess I was too relieved to understand what she meant until the next morning. After everything I'd been through, how could I expect to see my child waiting for me in the kitchen?

In a high chair pulled up to the counter. I thought it was nothing but an old doll until I got close enough for the smell to hit me. The stuffing had been replaced with the gore I'd left in the toilet. Congealed lumps that could have been premature organs or bones stuck haphazardly from the mess, and blood dribbled down the thing's legs and onto the otherwise spotless floor.

I threw up in the sink. I felt my mother's hand on my back, but it was cold and damp and brought no comfort.

"Still having morning sickness?" she cooed. "Don't worry, that won't last now that you've had the baby."

"I didn't have the baby. I don't have a baby," I told her as soon as I'd stopped gagging.

Her smile didn't falter. "How silly of you not to remember. You must have known you were pregnant."

"Yes but—"

"You didn't think you could really interfere with God's plan, did you?"

I didn't want to look at the gruesome doll, but I couldn't help it. I immediately began to hurl again.

"I've been thinking of names," my mother prattled on. She reached out to hold my hair back, but I recoiled from her touch. "She is a girl, isn't she? It's so hard to tell."

"Mom please. Don't do this. Get rid of it now."

"Sally is nice, isn't it? Silly Sally—you've got to think about what the other kids will think too."

My breathing came in ragged gasps. I couldn't answer.

"Or Lizzy, that's cute. Then when she grows up she can be Elizabeth, which is very—"

I was seeing red, and it wasn't just the blood. I rushed at the doll, meaning to throw it in the trash. My mother was more lucid than she appeared though, and she immediately blocked me behind the kitchen counter.

"Don't you dare!" she howled. "You have to let her sleep!"

"Which of us do you want, mom? You can't have us both."

"You're being selfish again. Can you imagine Lizzy saying that to you when she has a child of her own?"

I made another rush, this time ducking under her arms. I almost reached the horrid doll before mom grabbed me by the hair and yanked me back. She was pulling so hard I can't believe the hair didn't uproot.

"You aren't saving your grandchild!" I screamed. "You're killing your daughter."

She let go all at once. For a tense moment we stared at each other. There was still intelligence in her twinkling eyes. There was still love in her trembling lips.

"I don't have a…" she mumbled.

"Say it. Admit she's gone. Please mom, you have to."

She pressed her lips into a thin, hard line. Whatever came next wouldn't be a slip of the tongue. It would be deliberate and conscious and utterly irrevocable.

"I don't have a daughter," she said at last, turning away from me. "My daughter wouldn't do this to me."

I packed my things and left that night, never to return. She'll call from time to time, but I never answer anymore. She sends me cards, but I throw them away unopened. What else does she expect when she writes "your daughter misses you" on the front?

SELF-PORTRAIT FROM THE DEAD

MY MOM HATES HER FATHER. GRANDFATHER JACK'S NAME MIGHT AS well have been a swear word when I was growing up. Dad told me the story once, on the condition that I never tell mom I knew.

Jack was married to my Grandmother Kathy for 22 years before he cheated on her. It wasn't a midlife crisis or an intoxicated indiscretion either—he'd been going on fishing trips every other weekend for almost a year before Kathy figured out the fish was named Sally, and that she was half his age. Either dad doesn't know the specifics, or he wouldn't tell me, but I guess Kathy decided suicide was a less sinful way out than murder or divorce. That was before I was even born, but mom hasn't spoken a word to her father since.

I still got to know him though. It took 8 years of his begging and pleading after I was born, but mom finally gave in and arranged for us to meet. She used my father to deliver messages between them, as she 'was afraid of what she'd say if they spoke'. I was pretty scared when dad told me we were going to drive an hour into the desert to visit grandpa Jack's house, and mom only made it worse in the days leading up to the meeting.

"He might be an axe-murderer by now for all I know," Mom said.

Dad said he's a professor of art history.

"Or maybe he'll say nasty things about me. Whatever he tells you, I don't want you to listen to him."

Dad made a joke about how I've already had a lot of practice not listening to my parents. Mom didn't smile.

"In fact, it would be better if you didn't talk to him at all. Just let him see that you're a happy, healthy, well-adjusted boy, and then go play by yourself until Dad takes you home. Okay?"

"You're going to have a great time," Dad told me on the way. "He's got a whole art studio setup with everything you can imagine. Clay pots and sculptures, water and oil paints, brushes and tools of every size and shape—we can hang out all day if you want."

"Does Grandfather hate me?" I asked.

"Of course not. He wouldn't have kept sending letters all those years if he hated you. All he cares about is his seeing his grandson."

"Does he hate mom?"

"Your mom is a saint. No-one could hate her."

"Did he hate Grandma?"

Dad looked uncomfortable at that. "You'll have to ask him yourself."

So I did. That was the first thing out of my mouth in fact. Grandpa Jack was a pudgy old man, straight bald with discolored blotches on his scalp, and a huge mustache that wiggled when he talked. He came rushing at me, arms wide for a hug. Right away I asked him if he hated my Grandmother. Froze him in his tracks. Dad stepped in front of me as if trying to protect me from being hit, but Grandfather Jack just squatted down to my height and looked me solemnly in the eye.

"I never loved any woman half as much as I did Kathy. Except your mother, of course. Just because two people love each other doesn't mean they make each other happy though. I guess I just wasn't strong enough to spend any more of my life being unhappy, and not brave enough to hurt your grandmother by telling her the truth."

He smelled like old spice, and that seemed like a pretty satisfactory explanation to my eight year old self. I let him show me his studio and we painted a big landscape together. He did all the hard stuff and the details, and he helped me transform every messy blotch I made into something beautiful without painting over my contribution. He asked if I was going to visit again, and I said I wanted to—as long as mom allowed it, anyway. I've never seen a man go so red, so fast, his mustache bristling like a porcupine.

"Your mother got no right to tell you anything. She can throw fits and slam doors all she wants, but you're my family and the only thing left in this world I give a damn about. You tell her that, okay?"

I didn't get to visit as often as I liked, but at least every month or two dad would drive me out there. Mom was reluctant at first, but I convinced her that I wanted to be a painter and that she'd be crushing my budding dreams if Jack didn't teach me how. I loved the landscapes, but Jack's specialty was portraits and his passion for them soon rubbed off on me.

"A good portrait only depicts the subject," he told me once. "It'll get the scruff on his chin and the wrinkles under his eyes and everything else that makes him who he is. But a great portrait—" here he took a long drink from his iced tea, liking to draw my attention out as long as it would go. "A great portrait is always a portrait of the artist. Doesn't matter who he decided to paint, he put so much of himself into it that it's going to tell you more about him than the person he's painting."

Jack had a special gallery just for self-portraits. He did a new one every year, the passage of time immaculately mapped onto his many faces. Seeing all the paintings together like that, I couldn't help but notice that every year his brow seemed a little heavier. His smile was a little sadder, his eyes a little more weary. I didn't like seeing him change like that, and I told him so.

"Don't you worry, I still know how to paint a happy picture. I'm just saving it for the year when your mother finally forgives me."

I told mom that too. She told me that he'd be better off figuring out how to decorate Hell.

The self-portraits made me sad, but they didn't start to frighten me until Grandfather showed me his latest work when I was 19 years old.

"Where are your eyes?" I asked, staring at the blank pools of flesh dominating his latest portrait. The lines were more jagged than his previous work, making his sagging face seemed to be carved from marble.

"Right behind my glasses, silly," he said.

"Why didn't you paint them?"

He studied the picture, seeming to notice for the first time. "Would you look at that," he mumbled. "Doesn't matter. You can tell it's still me, can't you?"

More features were missing in the portrait next year. The whole face seemed to be sliding, almost as if the skin was a liquid that was dripping right off. He couldn't figure out why I was making such a fuss over it. "Looks like me to me," he grunted.

Shortly later Jack was diagnosed with Alzheimer's disease, and it was all down hill from there. He'd retired as a professor several years back, and painting wasn't a hobby anymore—it was an obsession. Now that I wasn't living on my own it was easier to visit him, but even in the span of a week he'd finish three or four more self-portraits, each more disconcerting than the last. I don't know why he even called them self-portraits—they weren't even recognizable as human anymore. Just tormented flesh, grotesquely and unevenly contoured as though the underlying skeleton was replaced with a haphazard pile of trash.

He'd get angry if I didn't recognize him in his pictures. He said he was painting who he was, and if I didn't see that, then I was the one who was blind. A few days later and he'd be excited to show me his next one, completely forgetting that the last one even existed at all.

"When is your mom going to come see? I've been calling her all week."

He even forgot that she hates him too. Every time he'd ask, and every time I'd make a vague excuse and promise she'd be there next time.

He was 86 when he had his stroke. He didn't paint again after that, and within the year he was gone. Dad and I went to the funeral, but mom just locked herself in her room. Grandfather still left everything to her anyhow, saying in the will that "I may not be able to give her a home, but at least I can give her my house." She didn't want to even set foot in the place though, so a week or so later I went to start boxing up the stuff for her.

That's when I saw his final painting. I was dreading going into his studio, and not just because I knew it was going to be the biggest job. I started stacking the abominable canvases face down so I wouldn't have to look at them, but I couldn't help but notice this one was different.

It was so perfect that it could have been a photograph. The self-portrait showed Jack lying peacefully in his casket, hands crossed over his chest, eyes closed. It was strange that he'd been able to paint it so precisely though, considering the rest of his recent work littering the room. I sat there for a while, thinking how heartbreaking it was for him to predict his own death like that.

I left the painting out while packing, thinking of hanging it in my apartment to honor him. There were plenty of less morbid pictures to choose from, but this one felt like it was really him who painted it, not the disease which had ravaged his mind. It made me think that his spirit was at rest somewhere, and that made me glad. I hung it in my bedroom that night, saying goodnight to him just as I'd done on the dozens of sleepovers where I'd lay my sleeping bag at the foot of his bed.

I fell asleep quickly, exhausted from the day of clearing stuff out. I slept straight through the night, not even dreaming as far as I can remember. Then sitting up in the morning, the first thing I saw was Jack staring back at me from his portrait. The one that had shown closed eyes last night. They weren't closed anymore. Maybe it was like that yesterday and I hadn't noticed, but that didn't sit right with me at all. I remembered how Jack always used to get angry when I didn't see the same thing as him in his pictures—maybe he was right and I really was just blind. I didn't think too much of it until the next night when I woke up and the painting was screaming.

No sound—I'm not that mad yet—but the mouth was open, twisted and frozen in unending agony. I just sat in bed, breathing hard, staring at the colorless torment in the weak light from my window. I kept lying back down and trying to convince myself it was a dream, unable to sit still for more than a few seconds before jolting upright again to stare at the painting. It took me almost half an hour to finally get out of bed and turn the lights on. I laughed out loud to see the shadows retreat, and the portrait sleeping peacefully in the casket with his eyes closed once more. I still slept with the light on the rest of the night though. In the morning, his eyes were unmistakably open once more.

I didn't blame Jack's painting. I blamed myself for being blind like he always scolded me about. I called my mother and told her about my weird dream on her voice-mail. 'Grandpa Jack is in pain', I told her. I would have said more, but I felt stupid and hung up shortly after.

I didn't actually hear the screaming until the second night, and by then it was already too late.

Sometime in the early morning—I was out of bed and halfway across the room before I was even fully awake. The sound ripped me from my bed so fast that I didn't even realize it was coming from the painting. There was enough light to see Grandfather's features twisted in agony.

My downstairs neighbor started pounding on the roof. That only seemed to make the screaming louder. The thrum of blood in my ears matched the beat, then raced past.

I tried to run, but my door handle wouldn't turn. I didn't struggle long—to stand by the door I had to be right next to the portrait and the sound was excruciating.

Next I pulled the painting from the wall. Hanging beneath it was a second painting—one I'd never put there. One of the disfigured ones with its lumpy flesh supported wrong from underneath. I saw this as a sign, although I was too freaked out to guess at what. I hung the screaming painting back to cover up that abomination.

Re-secured to the wall, I started to retreat toward the window. I never made it more than a step before a firm grip grasped my wrist and pulled me back. One of Grandfather's hands no longer ended at the canvas. Cold pale skin, its nails digging into me, relentlessly dragging me back toward the picture as though through an open window.

Now I was screaming too. Someone started hammering on my door. I tried to brace myself against the wall with my feet. The pale hand shook for its effort, but it was still stronger—inch by inch pulling me into his coffin. I almost wriggled free when his second hand shot out—this one catching me by the throat—to haul me forward at an alarming rate.

I was so close I could smell him. Not the old spice cologne he always wore. My face pressed against the canvas, it smelled like rotten meat. Then I was through—I clenched my eyes shut, helpless as his cold arms wrapped around me.

It was quiet on the other side. I couldn't even hear my heart anymore. The surrounding pressure was gentle, like being encompassed by cool water or even a heavy fog. A moment later and the sensation was already retreating. I opened my eyes to find myself standing in my bedroom, facing the portrait on the wall. Hands folded across his lap, eyes closed, at peace just like it ought to be.

I spent the next half hour profusely apologizing to my neighbors. I'm lucky I didn't get locked up. After that I called my mom, surprised to find her in tears.

"Are you okay? Where are you?" I asked.

"I'm okay. Dad's okay. I visited him in the cemetery this morning. It's stupid of me, right?" She paused to sniffle and blow her nose. "Do you think he knows?"

I told her I think he was pretty pleased about that, and that it made me happy too. I don't know what would have happened to me if she hadn't.

LIFE BEFORE BIRTH

HAVE YOU EVER BEEN IN A CAR ACCIDENT?

I'm not asking about a scrape or a fender-bender. I'm talking about the screech of rubber skidding so hard that you can smell it burning. When the airbag feels like a cinder block, and the blizzard of glass and shredded metal is a thousand super-heated needles searching for your skin. Every bone in your body feels like it's been replaced with twice the weight of lead, the aching throb so deep that you can't even feel it right away. And the scariest thing isn't even all the blood, even though that's sprayed across every inch of twisted metal that used to be the inside of your car—the scariest thing is not knowing where it's all coming from. You could be missing a leg and you wouldn't even know it. There's so much adrenaline pumping through your system that you can't even be sure whether you're alive or dead.

And then you remember your kid who was sitting in the back. Your twelve-year-old son on his way home from school, sitting in the passenger side because he liked to have a clear view of the speedometer. The side where the SUV T-Boned your car, crumpling it like a tin can to pin his little body within the car's deformed chassis. And when the ringing in your ears finally starts to die down and you hear the crying, you're so relieved, because as long as he's still alive, everything will still be okay. And it takes you a few more seconds to realize the heaving, weeping sound is actually coming from you, and that your little boy hasn't moved or made a sound.

That's how it happened for me, anyway. It took two minutes and forty seconds for the ambulance to arrive, which I guess is pretty incredible in the big scheme of things. I was surprised when I heard a paramedic mention the number though, because I could have sworn it was at least an hour. I guess when Einstein was coming up with his theory of relativity he neglected to mention the effect of waiting to find out whether your son is alive or dead.

My son Kevin did survive though. He suffered a concussion and was knocked unconscious, but there wasn't any permanent damage. The news was such a blessing that I couldn't stop laughing when the doctor told me. His mother took a week off work to take care of him, and I really thought that everything was going to be okay. At least until the night after the accident when Keivn asked me:

"You know how on cartoons they get hit and see stars?"

"Yeah sure." I was trying to put him to bed, and he always asked a lot of questions whenever he was looking to stay awake a little longer. "I didn't see stars though, did you?"

"No. I saw something else," he said.

"I'm not surprised." I drew the blankets up to his chin. "You got hit pretty hard. The doctor said your brain wasn't getting oxygen for a while, and sometimes that makes people see things—"

"Dad, I think it saw me too." He was barely peeking out above the covers, but his eyes were huge and quivering.

"Well all that matters is that you're safe now. Your mother and I aren't going to let anything—"

"Dad, where were you before you were born?" he interrupted again. I frowned at him, hesitating. I don't think this one is addressed in the parenting handbook my wife picked up at the thrift store. "I saw the place I came from. And the thing that made me. I didn't like it."

"What was it like?"

Kevin shivered, pulling the covers a little higher so that only the top of his head was showing. "It made me feel small," he whispered. "Like a little seed falling off a big tree."

"That doesn't sound so bad. Trees are supposed to spread their seeds."

"Not this one. It was taller than anything you can imagine, with branches going from one side of the universe to the other. And there were faces under the bark, only it wasn't bark, it was skin—and they were screaming, or trying to, but it was like they were being suffocated by the skin, and—"

"Easy Kevin, none of that was real—"

"—and the roots were skin too, and they were squirming like worms, and there were babies in there, only they weren't born yet. But they were screaming too—"

"Kevin!"

The covers were all the way over his head now. He was breathing heavily and trembling from head to foot. I gently folded the blanket back to reveal his flushed face. He took a long breath, then said:

"It hates losing its children. Hates it more than I knew anyone could hate anything. It saw me, Dad. I'm not lost anymore, because it saw me, and it's not going to stop at anything until it takes me back."

I didn't know what to say. I kissed him on the forehead and told him it was a bad dream. He didn't look convinced, and maybe that's my fault. I didn't feel very convincing when I said it.

I talked to my wife about it for a long time that night. We eventually agreed that bringing it up would only keep it fresh in Kevin's mind. Best to just forget about it and hope he does the same.

He didn't speak another word on the subject for the rest of the week. He was sad and quiet, spending long hours by himself in his fort behind the house. I didn't intrude on his space or push him though. The accident was the scariest thing he's ever gone through in his life, and it was completely normal for it to take time to recover.

Then on Friday there was the note. It was written on the yellow legal pad in the kitchen we used for grocery lists. A single line in a messy scrawl that read: *I'm going back.*

"Honey? You need to go out again for something?"

"I don't think so. Why, do you need something?" she asked. She came around the corner and we both stared at the yellow paper. Of course, that was Kevin's handwriting. And we both stared a little longer as the same thought slowly bubbled to the surface of our minds.

Then there was a *THUD* upstairs, and that thought became a lot louder.

"Kevin? You okay up there?" my wife shouted. Then with a smile: "Remember when we couldn't get him to stop jumping on the bed—"

THUMP THUMP THUMP THUMP... Incessant, desperate flailing. We raced each other up the stairs, the sound getting louder and louder until we flung open his bedroom door—

And the sound was replaced by my wife's scream.

Kevin's limp body dangled from a rope, tied to a jutting piece of wood above his closet door. We rushed to take him down, tripping over the chair he'd stood on before he kicked it over. The thumping had come from his legs kicking the closet while he choked, and now they weren't moving, and time stood still again.

He never lost consciousness this time though. We were all crying by the time we got the rope from around his neck. I remember saying: "You're never going to leave us, do you understand? We belong together."

He held onto us so tight that it hurt, and he was trembling all over again. "I have to go, but I'm scared to go alone," he said.

"Never. Promise you won't go anywhere without me."

"I promise. I promise."

"Wherever you go, I'll be right there with you," I said, and he hugged me even tighter.

I don't know why he started laughing, or why my wife and I joined in, but I think it was just relief. Pretty soon we were all sitting on the floor together hugging and laughing about nothing, and then it was over. And everything was going to be okay.

We couldn't get him an appointment to see a psychiatrist until Monday, but he seemed more cheerful after that and I thought things were going to get easier from there. His appetite was flourishing, and he was watching his favorite shows again. I thought that was proof that he was back to his old self. I guess when we want something badly enough we'll look for any excuse to justify it being true. We only see what we want to see, even though it's the things we can't bear to look at that need to be seen most.

The next note came on Sunday afternoon. He wrote: I'll be at my fort if you want to come with me this time.

I didn't need to look for my wife or ponder the clue. I was out the door before the paper even drifted to the ground, sprinting as fast as I could for the woods behind the house. There was a hollow log that Kevin always used to play around. Over the span of years we'd both dug out the area below it to make his secret fort. On the outside it just looked like a decaying log, but below there's just enough space for two or three people to sit and hide. And all I could think about was his little body tucked away in that hole where no one would find him—about how long ago he might have written that line, and what he could have done to himself in that time.

I couldn't fit inside the log to slip down the way he did. He wasn't answering my shouts, so I didn't even slow down when I hit the decaying wood. It pulverized under my weight, spraying chips and dirt in every direction. Then I was on my hands and knees, hurling away rotten chunks and pounding on the ground until it gave way underneath me.

Kevin had expanded the fort a lot in the last week. I hadn't expected to fall so fast or so far—almost eight feet, I think. But Kevin was there, and he was alright, and that's all that mattered. As long as we were together, we'd get through this. I held him close, and he held me back, and everything was going to be okay...

But I didn't really believe it this time as the ground kept raining down around us. Kevin broke away from me and pulled a rope which I hadn't noticed before. The other end was connected to a plastic tarp sitting above the hole. I didn't understand what was going on until the tarp slid forward, dumping its huge payload of dirt directly on our heads. By then it was already too late. He'd buried us both alive.

The tarp must have been balanced on a slope or something,

because after that first pull the dirt kept coming. The torrent was so dark and thick that I had to hold my breath. I got a last flash of Kevin gritting his teeth and hauling at the rope, then he was gone, lost in the avalanche which sealed us together. I managed to catch his hand before the dirt trapped my arms against my body. I felt the pressure of it building around my chest, then up my shoulders, packing around my neck, finally covering my head completely.

The weight was so intense that I couldn't budge. I squeezed Kevin's hand and felt the pressure returned. He was holding onto me for dear life—for something dearer than life, which he'd thrown away so casually. But as the weight of earth above us increased, the pressure from his hand was fading, growing limp. I was lucky that I held my breath so quickly—my expanded lungs occupied a little more space and gave me a small pocket of air. I tried to breathe as shallowly as I could, but even with the slightest intake of air I could feel the dirt sliding in a little tighter around me, making it that much harder to expel my next breath. A relentlessly constricting serpent, its coils drawing tighter and tighter around my chest.

I was going to die. Kevin was going to die, and I couldn't save him. But at least he wouldn't be alone. All I could do was squeeze his hand and wait for the time it didn't squeeze back. I started feeling dizzy as I labored harder and harder for air. The burning in my lungs mounted until my whole body felt like it was going to explode, and then slowly, slowly it subsided. Or maybe it was still there, but I didn't feel it so much because my consciousness was drifting off somewhere else...

...somewhere else where it was still pitch black, but I didn't need my eyes to see the tree. That was what Kevin called it anyway, although I would describe it more like a neural network, a billion tendrils connecting and separating to span across an infinite sky. Where two or more branches met, I'd see a face trapped beneath the tendril's skin. All ages, all races, all expressing a myriad of human emotions. Some had jutting brows bristling with hair like a Neanderthal, while others I could have passed on the street without thinking twice.

But I understand why Kevin said they were screaming. There was a sound coming from each, an infinitesimally small note in the grand symphony which encompassed me. Many were screeching, thrashing against their confines and howling in pain. Others babbled in an unknown language, laughing or crying like raving lunatics. Still others were tranquil, softly speaking a single word or phrase over and over again, though these too seemed mad and meaningless. I scanned face after face looking for Kevin, somehow feeling that if only I could find him, then even now I could bring him home.

I don't know how long I searched these infinite faces, but I knew I was growing too weary to continue forever. I might have already seen him and passed him by without noticing; there were so many faces that they all started to blend together and look the same. I was no longer able to even untangle their individual voices, each raucous note replaced by the mighty roar of their combined chorus, rising and crashing like the sea.

I screamed for Kevin until my scream was all I was, my contribution devoured by the song until the two were one. The combination of our outpouring joined the music, together creating something awesome from the ugliness. All the chaotic dissonance of our senseless pain was an integral part of that greater harmony, though I'd never know it from focusing on any one of the mad faces individually. And though I couldn't find Kevin in their midst, I knew I must be hearing his voice somewhere in the chorus too. And somewhere far away in another world, I felt the ghost of small fingers squeeze my hand.

My wife had found the note and followed us to the fort shortly after, keeping her wits about her enough to call the police. When I regained consciousness on the ground, the paramedics told me I was lucky to still be alive. I told them they were right.

Forgive the poverty of my words which seek to capture something too great to be confined. That hole was the tomb where I died and the womb where I was born. And now that I have seen the tree, I understand why Kevin knew he had to return, just as I will someday when I'm ready.

They never found Kevin's body, despite excavating an area four times the size of the original hole. I never found his face in the labyrinth either, but I don't suppose that matters. Whether it laughed or cried or whispered to itself is irrelevant, because he wasn't any of the unfathomable billions of interchangeable faces. He was the song itself: beautiful, eternal, and never alone.

MY SOUL IS IN A PAPER LANTERN

DO YOU KNOW WHAT IT'S LIKE TO LIVE WITHOUT A SOUL? BECAUSE I DO.

It's like watching a romantic movie that's so perfect you find yourself falling in love with the character. Then the lights come on, and you suddenly remember that person doesn't exist. And even if they did, they would never care that you exist.

It's like running the wrong way on a racetrack. It doesn't matter whether you ever finish or not, because everyone else has already crossed the line and gone home. You've run farther than anyone else, your legs are agony and there's a fire in your lungs, but you're still running because you're afraid of the silence when you finally stop.

Living without a soul is sitting in the eye of the hurricane. Life is moving all around you, and sometimes it feels like you're part of it when it passes too close. But in the end nothing and no one can ever move you, and though the wind howls fierce in its savage glory and sweeps all the world from under your feet, you'll never know what it feels like join that wild dance. And that's okay. You tell yourself that at least you won't be hurt like all those other fragile humans burdened with their souls, but deep down you wish you could feel that hurt. Just for a moment. Just so once in your life you know there's something important enough to be hurt over.

I lost my soul when I was only six years old. My father didn't want me. My mother told me so. She said I was the reason that he left, and I believed her. I was in first grade at the time, and our class project was to make a paper lantern which was closed at the top. The hot air from the candle was supposed to lift the lantern, although mine wasn't sealed properly and couldn't leave the ground. I was getting really frustrated, and after the fourth or fifth attempt I got so mad that I actually ripped the whole thing to shreds.

My teacher—Mr. Hansbury, a gentle dumpling of a man with a bristly mustache, squatted down next to me and gave me the lantern he had been building. I was so mad that I was about to destroy that one too, but he sat me down and said:

"Do you know what I love most about paper lanterns? They might seem flimsy, but when they fly, they can carry away anything that you don't want anymore. You can put all your anger into one of these, and the moment you light the candle, it's going to float away and take that anger with it."

That sounded pretty amazing to me at the time. I settled down to watch him glue the candle into place, concentrating all my little heart on filling the lantern with my bad feelings. It started off with just the anger at the project, but one bitterness led to the next, and by the time Mr. Hansbury was finished I'd poured everything that I was into the paper. All the other class lanterns only hovered a few feet off the ground, but mine went up and up and on forever—all the way to the top of the sky. The other kids laughed and cheered to see it go, and my teacher put his hand on my shoulder and looked so proud, but I didn't feel much of anything. How could I, with my soul slowly disappearing from view?

I remember asking Mr. Hansbury if I could go home and live with him after that, but he said he didn't think my mother would like that. I told him that she would, but he still said no. I don't suppose it would have mattered one way or another though, because it was too late to take back what I did.

There's something else besides the numbness that comes when your soul is gone. I didn't see them the first night, but I could hear them breathing when I lay down to sleep. Soft as the wind, but regular and calm like a sleeping animal. I sat and listened in the darkness for a long while, covers clutched over my head; the breathing seemed so close I could feel its warmth billowing under the sheets. I cried for what seemed like hours, but mom didn't come, and I was too afraid to get out of bed. I don't think I fell asleep until it was light outside.

Mom was angry at me in the morning for keeping her awake. She'd heard me, but she thought I would give up eventually. I didn't get breakfast that day, and I didn't mention the breathing again. That was only the beginning.

I think a soul does more than help you appreciate the things around you. It also protects you from noticing the things you aren't supposed to see. And with it gone, they were everywhere. Beady eyes glinting from under the sofa, a dark flash at the corner of my eye, scuffling in the drawers, and late-night knockings on doors and windows. I never got a good look at them, but they were always watching me. I'd wake up in the middle of the night and feel their weight all over my body, pinning me down. Rough skin against me, dirty fingers digging into my nose and mouth. Worse still, their touch penetrated my mind, inserting thoughts so vile that I knew they couldn't be my own, although the longer they were in my head, the more difficult it was to be certain of that.

Did I want to insert a needle into my eye and see how far it would go? Probably not. Then why could I not stop thinking about it?

Were they making me think about beating my class-mates into bloody pulps? Or setting fires to people's homes to watch them weep on the sidewalk? Or was that all from me?

The first few nights I lay awake and cried to myself, but I soon learned to be more afraid of my mom than I was of the creatures. As much as I hated the shadows, they never hit me after-all. I wouldn't call it living, but I continued to exist for years like that. During the day I kept to myself: exhausted and numb. All colors seemed muted except for the glittering eyes which tracked me from unlikely crevices, all sounds muffled but for their scrapings and breathings. The only times I could really feel something was when I was lay awake in the darkness, but these were the times I wish I felt less. Neither screams nor silence brought any comfort from the intrusive probing, and my mind was flooded with persistent images of violence, self-destruction, and despair.

Over time I found a trick to help me get through the insufferable nights. I convinced myself that my body was not my own, and that nothing it felt could do me harm. The real me was flying safe somewhere, high up in the sky inside that paper lantern. And no matter what happened to my flesh—no matter what my flesh did to anyone else—that had nothing to do with me.

I kept everything below the surface as best I could until I was fourteen years old. By then I'd lost all ability to distinguish the origin of my thoughts. All I knew is that I wanted to hurt someone—hurt them as badly as I wanted to be hurt in return. I picked fights at school. I pushed my classmates around, and they stayed clear of me. I once drove a pencil into someone's hand when they weren't looking, grinding it back and forth to make sure to tip broke off inside the skin. I heard the creatures snickering at that, but it was a disdainful kind of laugh.

When I was called into the principal's office afterward, I was surprised to see Mr. Hansbury there too. The principal was all rage, lecturing me and stamping around like the Spanish Inquisition. Mr. Hansbury didn't say much. He just looked tired and sad. He didn't speak until the principal dismissed me, at which point he put his hand on my shoulder and leaned in real close to ask:

"Have you looked for it?"

I didn't have the faintest idea what he meant. I gave him a stare that a marble statue would find cold.

"Your lantern. Did you ever try to get it back?"

I told him to go fuck himself.

"I'm sorry for telling you to send it away," he added, gripping my shoulder to stop me from leaving. "I thought it would be easier than facing the feelings, but I was wrong. People can't hide from themselves like that."

The pencil was good, but it wasn't enough. My thoughts matched the sardonic tone of the laughter, mocking me for my pitiful attempt. As the creatures crawled over me at night and their intentions mingled with my own, I decided to bring a knife next time. I considered a gun too, but resolved that it wasn't personal enough. I'd rather look into one person's eyes when the blade slipped into them than shoot a dozen scurrying figures from a distance. And what happened to me afterward? It didn't matter, because the real me was safely floating in the breeze a thousand miles away.

It wasn't going to be at school this time. I wanted to take my time and not be interrupted. Instead I went out at midnight, the taste of those dirty fingers still fresh in my mouth. I didn't care who my victim was as long as they could feel what I was doing to them. My neighborhood was quiet at night and there weren't a lot of options, so I decided to head down to the 24 hour gas station on the corner.

Kitchen knife gripped between my fingers, cold air filling my lungs, goading laughter and applause from the creatures thick around me in the darkness, I almost felt alive there for a second. Just like I did with the pencil, but this would taste better. Holding the knife, I felt like a virgin on prom night with my crush slowly unzipping my pants. I wasn't in the eye of the storm anymore—I was the storm, and tonight would be the night—that I saw a paper lantern floating in the air, just a few feet off the ground. The shell was so filthy and stained that I could barely see the light inside. It was impossible for the fragile thing to have survived all these years, more impossible still for the single candle to have burned all this time, but I knew without doubt that it was my light by the way the creatures howled. They hated it with a passion, and would have torn it to shreds if I hadn't gotten there first. I plucked the lantern from the air and guided it softly to the ground, the shades screeching as they whirled around me, feral animals cowed by the miraculous flame.

Holding the lantern close, I found the note that was attached.

"I found this in the woods. Took a couple days to find it."

-Mr. H

I collapsed on the sidewalk, trembling for all the time I'd spent away from myself, blubbering and sobbing like an idiot until the flame guttered out from my tears. The howling creatures reached a feverish pitch, and then silence, all rising together into the sky with the last wisps of curling smoke from the lantern. It hurt like nothing I'd felt in years, but it was a cleansing kind of hurt. I didn't hide from it. I didn't send it away. I didn't drown it with distractions or fight its grip on me. I won't go so far as to say that pain is a good thing, but it is undeniably a real thing, and I'd rather hurt than send it away to live with the hole it leaves behind.

THE WORLD'S OLDEST TREE

"JUST BECAUSE YOU CAN'T SEE THEM DOESN'T MEAN THEY AREN'T REAL."

"How do you know?"

"Because you can feel them when they're close," I said. "The goose-bumps on your skin, even though it's not cold. The way the air tastes, and the dry lump in your throat. That's how they let you know they're about to strike."

"How do you get away?"

"No one ever has. You get about ten minutes after you notice them before they force themselves inside you. Then it's all over. Wait—did you feel something? Clara look at your arms! You've already got the goosebumps!"

My sister squirmed, thrashing against the seatbelt which suddenly looked like it was squeezing the breath out of her frail body. Her skin was bone-white, although that was hardly surprising since she never went outside.

"Mark stop scaring your sister," mom clucked from the passenger seat. "We're almost there, just hold on."

"Mooooom, I can feel them!" Clara howled.

I was doing my best to softly blow air on her from the corner of my mouth without her noticing it was me.

"Ghosts aren't real, Clara. You're twelve-years old—you should know better by now," my dad said without turning. It had been a long drive for all of us, and he was gripping the wheel so tightly it looked like he was ready to swerve off the road and camp in the first ditch we found.

"See? I told you." Clara crossed her arms in an infuriating display of smugness.

"Then how come dad's mouth didn't move when he said that?"

I'm almost ashamed to admit how much pleasure I got from her double-take. Almost. Then came the rapid, aggressive burst of tapping on the window and Clara actually shrieked. I couldn't stop laughing as dad rolled down the window.

"Camping registration?" the park ranger asked, face shadowed by his wide-brimmed hat. He glanced disinterestedly into the back seats to catch Clara giggling and smacking at me. She wasn't strong enough for it to hurt, and I was laughing too so I didn't bother defending myself. Mom looked tired, but peaceful.

"Thank God. I thought we'd never get here." Dad handed the man an email printout.

"Long drive, huh? Where you folks from?" the ranger asked.

"California. I tried to tell them we have our own forests, but Clara was heart-set on seeing the great quaking aspen."

"Welcome to Utah then. You won't be disappointed. Did you kids know that the Pando is the oldest and biggest life form on the planet?"

"I did!" Clara raised her hand, flailing it around like an eager student. "Although each tree is only about 120 years old, they're all connected to the same root network which has been alive for over 80,000 years, stretching over 105 acres."

"Just 80,000?" The park ranger smirked. "I've heard it's more like a million. We're not sure exactly, but there's a good chance the Pando was alive before the first human being walked the earth. Pretty incredible, huh?"

"Yep! I wish I could live that long," Clara said. Mom and dad exchanged furtive glances.

"It's not about how long you live." Mom's voice cracked, and she had to take a long breath before she restarted. "It's about what you do with the time that you have. And I for one am grateful for every second we get to spend together as a family." Dad squeezed mom's hand. It must have been hard too, because their interlocked fingers were trembling. The uncomfortable silence which followed only lasted a moment before the park ranger handed us a pass and waved us on our way.

It's no secret that my sister is sick. Mom and dad don't like to talk about it, so I didn't know exactly what it was. She spent a lot of time in the hospital though, which seemed stupid to me because she was always weaker going out than she was going in. I've asked her about it before, but she just shrugged and said, 'they'll figure it out.' I didn't like the way her face looked when she said it, so I didn't ask again. Seeing her scared like that wasn't any fun.

It was almost dark when we got to the campsite. I helped dad setting up the tent while mom unpacked the car. Clara just sat on a log and stared at the sunset, which seemed really unfair to me, but it's not like she'd be much help anyway. The light was weird here—even after the sun went down, it didn't really get dark. The twilight felt like it went on for hours, and the air was so quiet that time must have frozen. I was half-hoping Clara would pick up on the weird atmosphere and start believing in my ghosts again, but I think she'd forgotten all about them. Maybe she was never even afraid in the first place, only putting on a show for my amusement.

"Can you hear them?" Clara asked when I went over to call her for dinner.

"Who?"

"The trees. They've been waiting for me for a long time."

I didn't buy it. She was just trying to creep me out as revenge. "What are they saying?" I asked anyway.

Clara's pale skin glowed in the enduring twilight, almost as white as her eerie smile. "It doesn't speak with words. It's more like feelings. Images. Ideas. The 'Trembling Giant' is angry. Slow, purposeful, smoldering, anger, like a glacier carving a hole in a mountain range. And it needs me to set it loose."

I wish she wouldn't smile like that. "Dinner's ready, come on." I turned back toward the fire in a hurry, not wanting to give her the satisfaction of seeing me shudder. Glancing back over my shoulder, I could still see the glow of her little teeth piercing the gathering dusk.

The next day was miserable and dull. I wanted to go out hiking and explore the forest, but Clara was too tired and mom insisted we didn't leave her behind. The whole point of this trip was to spend time together as a family, she said, so we were just going to do activities that we all could enjoy. So there we were, surrounded by spectacular natural beauty with adventure and discovery hidden behind every tree, while we sat in the dirt whittling sticks. Singing songs. Weaving baskets, watching the world drip by one excruciating second at a time.

"The baskets are fun! Look how nice your sister's is turning out."

"Can I make a really big one?" I asked.

"Of course! You can make whatever you want."

"Okay I'm going to weave a coffin then. You can just bury me wherever."

"Don't even joke about that," my father grunted.

"Or better yet, I'll make one for Clara. If she's too sick to do anything fun, then she might as well—"

"Mark!" Mom that time. I'd crossed a line, and I knew it, but I didn't care. I was bored out of my mind. I missed my computer and my friends. I hated all this lovey-dovey family time. They always took her side about everything and gave her whatever she asked for, but if I ever wanted something I was just being selfish.

"I'm going to be in the woods if anyone needs me. As if."

I heard Mom start to chase me for a second, but Dad stopped her to interject: "Stay close, okay? Don't get lost."

Getting lost didn't seem like such a bad option at the moment. White-barked giants stretching as far as I could see, with mazes of fallen trees and branches that I could use to build forts. Lush grass and ferns to run through, craggy rocks to climb, meandering streams to jump—I can't believe the rest of them sat 8 hours in the car just so they can keep sitting around here. I marveled at the natural grandeur as I walked, mesmerized by the idea that this huge forest was all a single living thing. I decided to dig with a stick to get a look at the connected roots, but the ground was hard and the going was slow.

This would have been a lot easier if I'd had some help. When Clara and I were little, we used to do everything together. She was like my side-kick, always enthusiastically following me around leaping to attention whenever I had a mission for her. What was the point of playing games with yourself when no one was there to cheer your victories or mourn your defeats?

My frustration at the futility of the dig was quickly mounting, but I used that feeling as fuel to ram the stick down even harder. Out of breath, sweating and aching, I thrust the stick so hard that it snapped in two. I don't know why that made me so angry, but it did. I dropped to my hands and knees and started digging with my fingers, hurling rocks and dirt clods around me in every direction. My fingers were accumulating cuts and scrapes, and I was about to give up when my hand suddenly broke through a thick clump of roots to reveal a hole in the ground.

Dirt and pebbles rained down the hole to disappear in the darkness below. It must have been deep too, because even with my ear to the ground I couldn't hear anything land. Unwilling to return and admit defeat, I spent the next few hours widening the hole and trying to find a way to climb down. By the afternoon I was so filthy that I was practically indistinguishable from the earth I churned through. My fingers were openly bleeding in places, and the beating sun frowned down with disdain at my efforts. None of that mattered though, because I'd opened the hole wide enough to slip inside the yawning darkness.

I climbed down the network of roots which were matted as densely as a net. My phone's flashlight prodded the darkness like a needle in an elephant, utterly underwhelming in the massive space I suddenly found myself within. The hidden cave was a converging point for the tendrils from innumerable trees which merged into larger roots, joining again in turn to weave great networked tapestries which dwarfed the thin trees above the ground. I continued climbing downward along the widening roots, tempted to hide down here all day and freak out my family.

Below the cave, my route terminated in a small circular space, not much larger than my own body. It felt like being inside an egg: completely encapsulated by the roots which were matted so densely now that they formed an impenetrable wall of wood. It was so quiet down here that I could hear my heart throbbing in my ears, my labored breathing a hurricane which fractured the stillness.

'Can you hear them?' my sister had asked last night, wide-eyed and serious.

Up above under the wide open sky with my family eating dinner? That question was child's play. But here in this hidden kingdom under the earth? I placed my hand on a massive wooden column and felt what she was talking about. This could have been growing before humans existed. It could have been touched by forgotten Gods or aliens who walked the Earth before history began. Or perhaps the Earth itself was living through these mighty pillars, lying dormant but for the quiet seething anger which slowly burned through the millennium.

The root was warm to the touch, and as I felt it, it was unmistakably feeling me in return. I had the unnerving feeling that a sound too deep for my ears to register was silently screaming around me. The feeling became more intense the longer I held on. I saw a fire in my mind's eye, running in infernal rivers from the depths of the world to drown the cities which infested the land like festering rot on clean skin. The root was getting hotter under my touch, and as much as I tried to clear my head, the thoughts returned—the decaying towers, the teaming crowds aimlessly running, the rivers of blood which flowed down crumbling streets.

I ripped my hand away and let go, panting for breath. This was better than ghosts. This was real. And all I could think about was showing it to Clara and watching her freak. I scrambled back up the roots, pulling myself hand-over-hand onto the surface to run the whole way back to the campsite.

"What in the world—" my mother started.

"Where's Clara? I want to show her something."

"She went to lie down for a little while. How did you get so filthy?"

But I didn't wait. I sprang into her tent, practically dragging her to her feet while my parents protested from behind.

"Just for a second, okay? You can sleep anytime, but this is what we're here for."

"Mark don't you dare bother her—"

"It's okay, mom," Clara said, dragging herself out to flinch beneath the sun. "I'm here to spend time with Mark too, right?"

There it was again. Mom and Dad holding hands, clenching so tightly they shook. That didn't matter though. All I could think about was Clara's face when I showed her my secret discovery. Our parents offered to come with us, but I figured that would destroy the whole fun of the secret. I was pleasantly surprised that Clara was so willing to go—it seems like she didn't want to do anything anymore.

"You heard it too," she said the moment we were alone.

"Not heard. Felt."

"This isn't a trick, right? You're not just making fun of me because I believe it?"

"When have I ever tried to trick you?" I put on my best facade of shocked-innocence. She snickered.

"How about when you wrote 'soap flavor' on the ice-cream box so you wouldn't have to share?"

"That's an isolated incident."

"Or when you told me the cactus had soft spines like a cat's fur?"

"I didn't think you'd just slap it."

She laughed again, and we walked on in silence for a bit. She was obviously struggling, but she was just as obviously making an effort to hide it, so I didn't say anything. It wasn't much farther anyway.

"Up there, right around that grove. Anyway if I trick you so much, then how come you still believe me?"

She shrugged, catching my eyes for a second before turning to look where I was pointing. "I guess I don't know how many more chances I'll have to be tricked. I want to make the most of it while I still can."

I didn't know how to respond to that, so I kept walking.

"That's why we're here. You know that, right?" she asked.

I kept staring straight ahead.

"This might be our last chance for the whole family to be together before I..."

"It's over here," I interrupted, squatting down beside the hole. I expected her to say something sarcastic or to complain.

"Give me a hand, okay?" She didn't even hesitate. Feet first, she began lowering herself down. I helped keep her steady while she climbed. I kept my eyes on our hands so I didn't have to look at her face. I fully understood what she was saying, and I didn't want her to say more. I didn't start climbing after her until her feet touched the cave floor.

"You're right. It's stronger down here," she said.

"You haven't seen anything yet. Come on."

I continued leading to the point where the roots terminated in the enclosed root-egg. There wasn't enough room for both of us to fit in the perfect nest, so I helped her climb in while I waited in the larger cave. Her fingers grazed the roots in silent reverence, hand jerking back from their warmth. That little smile glinted in the darkness, stretching into a euphoric grin as she touched the wood again.

"You feel it?" I asked. I knew she did, but I had to ask anyway because the silence was so heavy down here.

She simply smiled and closed her eyes. The sound of my rushing blood filled my ears again. I had to keep talking.

"What made you think it was calling for you?"

She wasn't the one who answered though. It was that scream again, too deep to hear, but I felt the echo in every vibrating root. It came from everywhere—all the mighty forest bellowing in silence, all the unknown depths of the roots, all resonating with a single, persistent, throb. Even outside of the egg I could start to feel the colossal intent seep into my mind. Incessant, irrepressible thoughts, so vivid I might as well be seeing them with my eyes. Imagery of burning rivers bubbling up from the Earth to exhaust themselves in the open air, leaving behind an abyss so deep that it must pierce through the core of the planet.

"Clara? What's going on? What do you see?" Even shining light in my face, I could barely see it. All was fire and the bellowing howl, mounting in pitch just enough for me to actually hear the low rumble like an earthquake.

"Clara, you have to get out of there. Something is going to happen."

"I know. I'm making it happen." The voice sounded so small and distant next to the enveloping presence. "We both need each other. "I need its enduring life, and it needs a body guide its will."

"Clara where are you? Quick grab my hand!" I fumbled to reach down to her, but the visions were too intense for me to see straight. My raw hands kept butting up against the roots.

"Tell mom and dad that I didn't die. That I'll never die."

Why couldn't I find the opening? I'd been standing right over it a moment ago.

"Tell them I'll be with them in the forest, even when they think themselves alone."

It took me going down on my belly to finally realize what had happened. It wasn't that I couldn't find the hole—it's that the hole didn't exist anymore. The roots had moved, fully sealing Clara inside the earth.

"Clara! Can you hear me? Clara get out!"

"I am out, Mark." The reply was so faint. "No more tricks between us. You're the one who should be running."

I'm not proud of the fact that I ran, scrambling back up the roots to pull myself onto the surface. Some might call it cowardice, but I know the certainty in her voice, and I trusted her more than I trusted myself in that moment. Even above the ground I could still feel the silent scream, so low and powerful that my entire body vibrated. Panting for breath on the surface, I started to scream with everything my ragged lungs would allow. I don't know how long this went on for, but by the time I stopped, the forest was silent again.

The earth wasn't shaking. The visions had cleared. All except for the hint of Clara's face outlined in the bark of an aspen tree.

AM I DREAMING, OR AM I THE DREAM?

I've decided that it must be one or the other. How else could I explain seeing the same person everywhere I went?

He's impossible not to notice with his long gray mustache waxed to a pinpoint. Bushy eyebrows caught in a perpetual explosion, floppy white hair that looked like it was having an argument with the head. He doesn't always speak to me, or even look at me, but for the last two years he's always been there.

He first appeared as a substitute teacher when I was in my junior year of high-school. He introduced himself as Mr. Brice, although there was a long hesitation before he gave his name as though he couldn't decide what he wanted to be called. His voice wasn't right either—I remember him spending half the class switching accents, his speech collapsing occasionally into a variety of foreign languages before he caught himself and readjusted. The class found him "dapper" and charming in his fine tailored wool suit, and I didn't initially suspect him of anything more than being eccentrically addled.

The next day he was working in the cafeteria. Substitutes go where they're needed, I suppose, but oddly none of my classmates seemed to remember him. They remembered that we had a substitute teacher, but everyone was quite sure that it wasn't him. He gave me an extra scoop of chili and winked at me, muttering in an English accent: "I won't tell if you don't." I don't think he was talking about the chili.

Mr. Brice spent the next few weeks rotating throughout the school. One day he was the janitor, next he was a guest speaker, or even the principal himself. I quickly learned to stop bringing up the phenomenon when it became obvious that I was the only one who noticed. Mr. Brice was learning too—it didn't take long before his speech stopped fluctuating, and his clothing adapted to nondescript khakis and a polo shirt.

I tried questioning him more than once, but the man stubbornly adhered to the role he'd currently assumed, pretending he knew me only as well as the character he played. At the same time, there would always be little winks or enigmatic phrases thrown in which conveyed our peculiar intimacy. I caught him alone one day when I'd forgotten my calculator and had to double back for it. Mr. Brice was on the phone, casually reclining with his feet flung up on his desk. I distinctly remember the words:

"Of course he's caught on, but he isn't frightened yet."

He winked again when he met my eye. I stood in abject confusion while he politely disengaged from his phone call.

"Were you talking about me?" I asked.

The feet came down with a stomp.

"All the time," he said, leaning forward to fold his well-manicured hands demurely on his desk. He cocked his head to the side, studying me intensely. "You preoccupy most of my attention nowadays, but I mustn't get too attached to you."

"What the hell is that supposed to mean?"

"You don't belong here. I don't want it to hurt when I have to get rid of you."

"Um..."

He coughed. Then the infuriating wink. "What I mean to say is: the teachers can't go home until the last student leaves, so run along."

I snatched my calculator without another word. The whole situation was so unnerving, and I couldn't think of anything to respond. Mr. Brice blatantly picked up his phone again as I left.

"He's just leaving. No, I don't think he'll run yet. Where could he possibly go where I couldn't find him?"

I didn't see him at school much after that, but he was always somewhere, always watching me: on a bench reading the newspaper, or bussing tables, or working behind the counter at the gas station. I never confronted him, although I did try taking a picture of him a few times. The pictures would work, but only for a day. When I looked back at the photo after that, everything else would be the same except for Mr. Brice, who would invariably be replaced with the real person —the same person that everyone else remembered being there the whole time.

Like he said, I wasn't afraid yet though. The situation enthralled me for a few weeks, but after that it simply became part of life. And as long as Mr. Brice was there, my life was being steered in a particular direction.

Mr. Brice the school counselor took the liberty of submitting my application to a science program at Stanford University where he felt I would excel.

Mr. Brice the college administrator overlooked my mediocre grades in favor of my exceptional essay, which I never remember writing.

Mr. Brice the restaurant manager fired me when I mentioned wanting to wait a bit on college. He said he didn't want my life here interfering with my "future opportunities". I almost hit him when he winked that time. More than all his other meddling, that one really got to me. I was fired right on the spot in the middle of my shift with two co-workers watching. I just felt so angry and helpless and alone. I wanted to scream at him and tell him that I won't play his game anymore, but that would just make me look like the crazy one. I wanted to tell him that he didn't control my life, and that I wasn't afraid of him, but of course he already knew that to be a lie.

"Go quietly now, won't you?" he said. "You don't want an incident on your record."

"Why not?" I was conscious of all the eyes on me, but I had to say something. "Since when has anything I've done made a difference?"

"Oh but it can. Not to you maybe, but I'd hate to think of how other people might be affected by your stupidity."

"Are you threatening me?" I said it loud enough for the whole restaurant to hear. Five seconds of silence can feel like a very long time, and I gloated the whole while. He wasn't embarrassed or defensive like I thought he would be though. He glanced dispassionately at the surrounding patronage before taking two long strides toward me —close enough for me to feel his breath on my face.

"Yes. I'll threaten you, if that's what it takes."

I hadn't expected that. Neither had anyone else around us. One of the waitresses made a nervous giggle, but it was cut unnaturally short.

"I'm doing this for your own good," Mr. Brice added. "Don't test me."

We stared off for a moment before his phone started ringing.

"You're a piece of shit," I told him as I left.

He just smiled, speaking into his phone: "Please calm down. Nothing has changed. We own him, and he knows it."

I lingered by the door to listen in, but he'd already hung up.

Both of my parents were fired on the same day. Neither were given more than a superficial reason. I suppose I should be thankful that it wasn't Mr. Brice the serial killer that visited them instead. I'd gotten so used to his ubiquitous presence that I never really stopped to think how much power he had over me. Over everyone. I fantasized about trying to kill him for a while, but immediately thought of Mr. Brice the policeman and Mr. Brice the judge who would find me wherever I went.

The mood was really dark around my house for the next few days until I received a full academic scholarship in the mail. Considering their recent terminations, my parents made it clear that they wouldn't be able to help me with my tuition. They told me that I'd be an idiot not to accept it, and of course they were right.

It didn't seem like a bad life that he had planned for me. I was being handed opportunities that other people could only dream of, but it wasn't my life. If I just gave up without a fight, then who knows where it would end? Maybe he wanted to use me to build a new bomb, or design a weaponed virus. If I gave into him now, then I'd be surrendering my whole life to him. Trying to confront him again seemed too dangerous, but whoever he kept talking to on the phone must know what was going on. I just had to steal it and see who had called him while I was being fired.

This wasn't exactly a simple matter. I couldn't break into his house, because he could be anyone or anywhere. I had to lure him to me, and that meant doing something which threatened to destroy his plan for me. As long as he controlled the situation, it seemed like any criminal offense or outrageous act could be covered up by the people he posed as. It was overwhelming how powerless I felt, but with or without him, I could never control how other people acted. I just had to focus on myself—the one thing he couldn't take away.

I chose the top of a bank for this purpose. I was able to climb up pretty easily because of the adjoining buildings, and it had a nice flat roof that was high enough to do some real damage if I jumped. I stood up there for a long while, watching a street so familiar and mundane, yet so surreal and incomprehensible that I felt like a visiting alien. As the wind whipped around me I wondered whether I would still jump if he didn't show up to stop me. Would my death be a victory over him? Or was it the inevitable conclusion that he had always led me toward?

A hand on my shoulder meant I never had to find out.

"Took you long enough," I said without turning. I stiffened my shoulder under his grip. I wanted my tension to be obvious. I wanted him to really believe I would do it.

"It's a hard climb for someone my age. Couldn't you have found something a little lower to jump from?" I could almost hear the wink in his voice. His hand tightened slightly, but I pulled away—the toe of my shoe now over the edge.

"I'm not here to negotiate. I want you out of my life."

There was a long silence. I glanced behind me—Mr. Brice was dialing a call. "Hello hello—I have a bit of a pickle," he said into the phone.

I didn't waste my chance. Pinning his free hand against my body, I spun to snatch the phone from him. He lurched back, but I dove after him. A quick spin as he tried to shield the phone with his torso—hands buffeting each other out of the way—then another lunge and I had the phone. I wrapped my whole body against it, hurling myself to the ground to protect it. His arm was still tangled up in mine though, and with the turn he slipped straight out into the open air. Those few seconds watching him tumble were the longest of my life. I turned away before he hit the ground, but I still heard the sickening crack.

"Who is there? What's going on?" the voice in the phone. My voice, strained and weary, muffled and distorted, but unmistakably mine.

I didn't have time to decipher this. I couldn't decipher much of anything, except that the world was coming to an end. A man collapsed in the street, causing a small turbulence of panic around him. Then a second, and a third—everyone crumpling into discarded bags of meat. The buildings were dissolving into so much dust, and the light of the sky bled and ran like water color. A moment later and the building beneath my feet gave way, tumbling into blackness. I woke on a narrow cot, holding a phone in my hand. I tried to jerk upright, immediately regretting my decision as my tether of IV lines dragged inside my veins.

"A few more years and we would have had a cure." Mr. Brice's voice, but not Mr. Brice. The thing over my bed was more akin to the dissolving world I just witnessed than any human being I'd ever seen. Skin in constant dissolution, warping and reforming before my eyes.

"Am I dreaming?" I asked.

"Not anymore."

"You—you did this to me—"

"I spun the dream. A dream about the life you could have lived. And if you were to discover a cure in that dream, you'd wake up and still remember it. You'd be able to get better again, but now—"

I couldn't look at the creature. I turned away to look down the length of my body. My emaciated arms. The outline of knees as sharp as blades beneath my blanket. That was even worse.

I'm not writing this as a warning. There isn't a lesson here—although perhaps there is some merit in trusting one's dreams, no matter how outlandish. No threats or looming dread. I'm simply sharing my story because the dream spinner has left me. I'm alone, and angry at myself, and so very frightened. I'm going back to sleep in the chance I dream again, but if I do not wake, then I suppose what I'm really writing this for is simply to say goodbye.

OUR SHIP SAILED OVER THE EDGE OF THE WORLD

THERE WASN'T A GIANT WATERFALL SPILLING ENDLESSLY INTO SPACE, IF that's what you're wondering. Only a damn fool would think the Earth is flat. Besides, I figure we'd run out of water pretty fast that way. The things we've seen though—the things that seen us back—well if they belonged in this world, then it must mean humans don't. I guess it's easier for me to tell myself I sailed right over the edge into some new place entirely than accept that those creatures are here with us.

Let's get our facts straight first. I know a lot of folks use fishing as an excuse to get wasted where nobody's around to judge them. They're the people who see four hundred pounds of flabby porpoise and swear they were visited by the fairest lady to ever trade her cooch for a tail. Not me. I'm stone-cold sober and proud of it. My buddy Jason—yeah he likes to knock back a few when we're out on the water, but he's not the one telling the story, so that doesn't mean shit.

Meet the Iron Cucumber—our pride and joy. 22 foot cuddy cabin that we bought together for our fishing trips. Last weekend was supposed to be like any other; we had our cabin stocked with our gear, an ice chest full of deli meats and beverages, and minds keen on pretending the city life was just a recurring bad dream. During the week we both worked as financial analysts at a bank, but by Friday we'd have trouble hearing all that blather over the rising call of the wild.

"We're basically werewolves," Jason had said on one of our trips. "Everyone we know sees us in our suits all day and assumes that's what we are. But that's just because they've never seen us under a full moon."

"So when the full moon comes you sit in a different chair and put a hat on?" I'd asked. "Hide yo' children. This one's feral."

"Say that to that thrashing 160 pounder I wrestled to the ground."

"160 pounds? Congratulations. To your wife for losing all that weight."

Jokes aside, Jason is a badass. He's got to be over 200 pounds himself, but he's 6'2", and with his bristling beard and those tribal tattoos running up his forearms, I've got to admit he looks a lot more dangerous than I do. He's a wizard at boating too—it was his idea to get the thing in the first place. He sniffs the wind and makes some crazy accurate guesses about the weather. Says he came from pirates on his father's side, with maternal gypsies to boot. I know for a fact his family were potato farmers from Ireland, but I never told him so. Point is that I know he's a lot of talk and bluster, but if we were going to war, then I'd want him as my captain. I guess that's why I never doubted him when he said, "Something unnatural about the air tonight."

Not as far as I could tell. There wasn't any breeze, and everything smelled like salt and fish and BBQ potato chips to me. I still nodded sagely, staring off into the vastness of the black waters.

"Tastes like oil," he said, spitting into the waves. "Like we're inside a giant machine that's turning all around us."

"If you didn't want to be a cog in a giant machine then you shouldn't have gone into banking," I said.

I expected a sarcastic quip back about how he 'ain't no tool'. It was unnerving to see him just staring off into the darkness, a slight shudder running down his massive frame.

"I suppose you're right," is all he said.

I don't know if it was just his mood, but within an hour I thought I began to feel it too. It was almost like hearing the screeching metal of vehicles colliding on the TV, then muting it and watching the silent picture. Just seeing it was enough to clearly imagine the sound, even though it was perfectly quiet. Our conversation was falling flat, so I brought out a book to read to distract myself from the unsettling sensation.

"There weren't any clouds when the sun set," Jason said, still staring vacantly into space.

"That's good, right? Clear sailing weather."

"So where are all the stars?"

He was right. Almost 9 PM and pitch black without a single bead of light. This far from the city they should be spectacular.

"Maybe the clouds moved in after the sunset?" I asked.

"With what wind?"

Quiet again. I shrugged and turned the page.

"If I had to die anywhere, I'd rather it be out here," he said after a long pause.

"What the fuck, Jason?"

"Think about it," he said. "Of all the ways you could go. Getting cancer and having your bedroom turned into a jail cell. Or Alzheimer's and forgetting your family and even yourself. Maybe a nuclear holocaust. I'd rather it happen out in nature when I'm still my own master."

"You're just saying that because I'm here with you. Look Jason, that's sweet and all but I don't think I'm interested in a relationship..." my words trailed off in the heavy silence. Even that couldn't lighten his mood. He sighed and dropped down to his sleeping bag on the floor. "You out already?"

"Yeah, I don't know what it is," he said, climbing into the bag. "I'm just going to sleep it off. Things will be better in the morning. And if they're not... well wake me before it happens."

"Before what happens?" But he didn't reply. I tried to put it out of my mind and keep reading, but I couldn't keep my focus. After about 30 minutes of re-reading the same page I got so frustrated I threw the book straight over the side of the boat. It felt good. Sitting there in the stillness listening to the gentle waves and riding the rhythmic sway I started to calm down. For a moment, anyway.

"There wasn't a splash."

"I thought you were asleep," I said.

"When you threw your book overboard. I didn't hear it hit the water."

Shit, neither did I. And I should have, right? It was really really quiet out there. I got up and peered out where I'd thrown it. Blackness. I turned on my flashlight and scanned to see if it was still floating there.

"Jason—you're going to want to see this."

I turned around, but he was already on his feet. He joined me at the side, and together we stared out at the emptiness beyond.

"Jason?"

"Yeah, I see it. I mean, I don't see it, but I see it."

"Yeah. Okay. Just making sure."

The water was gone. The whole ocean. We were sailing on inky darkness—like a black gas which twisted and bubbled in nebulous designs. Deep within the cloud there was thousands of tiny pricks of light, almost like stars. Jason leapt to the controls.

"What are you doing?"

"Turning the boat around."

"What's the matter? I thought you were okay dying out here?" He just glared at me. I know it was in bad taste, but I was freaking out and humor is like a defense mechanism for me. Jason brought the engine to life, but it began immediately making such a horrendous noise—like a car throwing up—that he immediately killed it again.

"No water," he grunted. "Can't run without water."

"At least we found our missing stars," I said. I would have done a more convincing job of playing it cool if my voice hadn't cracked in the middle.

"I don't think those are stars."

Back to the side of the boat—he was right. Of course he always had to be right. The lights were moving. Delicately but unmistakably moving, like fireflies drifting through a heavy mist. I watched transfixed as one began floating closer toward the boat.

"Catalina Harbor, this is the Iron Cucumber." Jason was speaking into the radio, but I couldn't turn away from the light.

Short static. "Catalina Harbor, this is a distress call. Repeat. This is a distress call. Over."

"Jason you need to see this." He gave me a distracted wave. The light was about the size of a baseball now. I couldn't tell how close it was, but it was clearly moving this way.

"Iron Cucumber, this is Catalina Harbor. Is your ship sinking? Over." Jason stared blankly at the receiver for a moment.

"Repeat—" the radio began.

"Yes, we're sinking. Please send help right away. We're approximately 14 miles west of—"

"Jason!" I shouted. "It's got a body!" I couldn't tell what exactly. It was nothing but a silhouette, mostly concealed by the bright light which had grown to the size of a basketball.

"Please repeat. 14 miles west of—" the radio began.

"Never mind. We're okay. Sorry about the confusion. Over and gone." Jason switched the radio off.

"We are definitely not okay. What the hell?"

Jason gave a mad grin. "I'm not sending another human being into this. We wanted an adventure, right?"

"This is not an adventure. This is a bad trip. This is the end of the world—this is—"

"This is the call of the wild," Jason said. He raised his head to the empty sky and let off a chilling wolf howl.

"Give me that radio—now!" I lunged for him, but he chucked it across the boat. I winced as it skidded along the floor, hoping to God it hadn't broken. I sprinted after it.

"Times like these are when you find out what you're made of," Jason said. "How do you feel about going for a little swim?"

I reached the radio. It was still intact. I turned it back on and spun to see Jason leaning way out over the boat, his whole torso over the side.

"Catalina Harbor—this is the Iron Cucumber—over." I shouted into the receiver. Then holding it against my chest: "Jason don't you dare—"

"Look buddy," the radio crackled, "I don't know what kind of game you're playing, but harassing an emergency line is a serious offense. Over."

"This is not a game. We are in immediate distress. Over."

"Iron Cucumber, is that right? Over."

"Yes sir. We're located—Jason where the hell are we? Jason!"

Jason leaned a little farther, and then he was gone. He slipped overboard without a sound, straight through the black mist.

"The Iron Cucumber is still in the harbor. Spot 427, right between The Goliath and Sister Beetle," the radio said.

"Excuse me?"

The radio went to static. I let it slide from my fingers and rattle to the ground. The place where Jason went over was so bright I could barely look at it. The light must have almost reached the boat, but I was too afraid to go to the edge and look.

"Jason?" I shouted. "Jason are you there?"

The light was beginning to recede. I couldn't stand it anymore. I went to the edge to look down, and—

Fingers gripped the railing. I'm not ashamed to say I shrieked and fell on my ass. A moment later, and Jason had climbed back on board. I didn't have time to say anything. The second he had his footing, he slugged me across the face and I blacked out.

I woke up screaming.

"Chill dude, we're almost back." I was in my sleeping bag, and Jason was sitting next to me. I recoiled immediately, pressing myself against the wall of the boat. "You okay? I thought you had a stroke or something."

"The water was gone. The lights—"

He laughed. "Man, what a relief. Just hold tight, okay? I'm going to get you to a hospital."

"So you didn't see anything weird out there?"

"Just you having a fit like a seizure or something in your sleep. You want a hand?"

"No, don't touch me."

"Okay man, you just rest. We'll call the hospital as soon as we're in cell range."

I didn't call the hospital when I got back though. I told him I was fine and made an excuse to get away. I called the Catalina Harbor instead. I asked them if they received a distressed radio call from the Iron Cucumber, and they said yes.

It wasn't a dream. It wasn't a fit. I'm not making this up.

So what the hell happened over the edge of the world? And what was it that came back in the boat with me?

IT WASN'T A HIT AND RUN. I REVERSED TOO.

I'M WEARING THE WRONG SUIT. THIS ONE HAS A HOLE IN THE BACK. I forgot my phone charger at home, but it's too late now. I shouldn't have packed so much—I won't have time to check my bag. I never should have booked such an early flight in the first place. And I REALLY shouldn't have hit that pedestrian.

It all happened so fast. Accelerating through the blind corner in the pre-dawn twilight, I congratulated myself on beating the light. I didn't see him until I was a few feet away. I still didn't know what happened until I heard the crack and lurched from impact. He disappeared under the hood of my car and I slammed on the breaks, but it was too little and way too late. The car skidded to a stop about a dozen feet past where he went down.

The flight didn't exist anymore. My job didn't exist. Only my breathing did—great heaving gasps that I had to consciously force to keep myself from passing out. I could see his crumpled body in my rear-view mirror, but I was too scared to even get out of the car. I must have sat there for at least a minute, just staring at the smeared trail of blood. The unnatural angle of his right knee—the shoulder that flopped uselessly out of its socket—and finally the twitch of movement as he began to crawl.

I wish I could tell you I was too numb to know what I was doing, but I was thinking very clearly when I threw my car into reverse. It wasn't about missing the flight anymore. It wasn't just the insurance, or the medical bills, or the court cases that would come of this. My whole life was balanced on the edge of a knife, and a mistake like this was all it would take to ruin me.

I wish I didn't catch his eyes in the rear-view mirror when I hit him again. It wasn't surprise, or pleading, or even fear I saw there—just raw accusation. He knew he wasn't going to walk away from this. He knew exactly what I was thinking—exactly how selfish and cowardly I was. In that moment, I think he knew me more truly than my parents or my closest friends. The rest of my entire life didn't matter because the person who hit him a second time was who I really was.

And the third time. And a fourth. And the fifth. Back and forth over the body. It was almost light now, but it was still early enough for the street to be deserted. I pulled into an automated car wash at the end of the street. I ordered deluxe. That's where the numbness came—I didn't think a single thought as I sat in my car and watched the water jets and soap bubbles. Then I drove off, swearing to myself that nothing ever happened.

I still made my flight (miraculously). I had to run through the whole airport. My heart was beating so fast when the security looked at me, although of course it was absurd to think they knew what happened. The whole regimented travel routine coaxed me back into the illusion of normalcy though, and by the time I reached my boarding gate I'd half convinced myself that it never happened at all. I was just stressed and worrying about nothing. It was just a bad dream, but now I've woken up and it was time to go on with the rest of my life.

It still felt like I was dreaming though. I didn't walk. I drifted. Finding my window seat, I stared at the runway and marveled how surreal it looked. Airplanes defy all natural instincts for what is possible. All our technology does.

"Mind switching seats? You can have a window," I heard from the aisle. I was lost in thought though, oblivious to the outside world.

"Thanks a bunch. I just wanted to sit with my friend."

The shuffling of bodies, all moving in an orderly fashion. No one batted an eye at the absurdity of the whole show. Any kid can get behind the wheel of a five thousand pound unstoppable killing machine. If someone saw that hurtling toward them a few hundred years ago, they would have thought it was a demon straight from hell.

The sound of folding paper. "You keep up with the news?" the man next to me asked. I shrugged and kept staring out the window. Intrusive images of that unnaturally angled knee kept bursting into my mind, but I forced it out again. What if there was still blood on my car? I didn't have time to check that thoroughly.

"These politicians," my neighbor continued. "Absolute disgrace. Even the good ones—they don't care about who they're hurting. They're just afraid of being caught."

That made me look. Twice. And a third time. The man I'd hit this morning wasn't looking at me though. He was just calmly reading the paper. Now I know what you're thinking already—that it was my guilt making me see his face on this unrelated stranger. It wasn't just a passing similarity though. No wounds, no blood, no dislocated arm, but it was him alright. And when he looked up at me and smiled, it was the eyes I'd seen in my rear-view mirror.

The plane lurched, and I gave a little gasp. We were moving. Taking off. I unbuckled my seatbelt and started to stand, but the stewardess was quick to scold me back down. I couldn't think of an adequate reason for why I had to get out of there, so I just sat back down instead. That was stupid of me. I should have made up a medical condition or something, but I guess I was still in shock. It wasn't long before we were in the air and it was too late anyway.

"That's the worst thing about it for me," the person I killed this morning said. "Lack of conscious. If you're going to do someone in, at least show some respect. Say a prayer or something. But just doing it cold like that—" he gestured at his paper, but I didn't look. "It really boils the blood, you know?"

"Excuse me, I have to go to the bathroom." I started to stand again, but he grabbed my arm and dragged me back down to my seat.

"Seat belt sign is on. You're a grown man. Show some self-control."

I nodded, numbly buckling myself back in.

"I'm sorry," I mumbled.

"Sorry for what?" he asked.

I shrugged.

"Go on. Say it."

"I'm sorry," is all I could muster up.

"No you're not. You're just like the people in the news. You're only sorry you got caught. How long do you suppose this flight is?"

"Um, about 3 hours."

"That's plenty. You've got three hours to finish me off." He was looking me dead in the eye.

"Or...?"

"Or it'll be my turn. And one man to another, you have my word," he leaned in real close here, "I'll get it right the first time and won't need to back up."

"What the hell are you?"

He just grinned. The seatbelt sign went off, and he stood up to stretch. As he did so, something fell out of his sleeve and onto his vacated seat. I reached out and picked it up—a sharpened plastic shiv. He winked.

"I've got to use the bathroom. You take care now."

By the time he reached the end of the aisle I'd began to process everything. He wanted me to try to kill him again. Why? It didn't matter. Was he bluffing? I don't have much experience with immortal zombies, but my guess is they can do pretty much anything they set their mind to. It was one thing on a dark road without any witnesses, but on a secure and crowded flight without any escape?

But he'd given me the shiv, and he was alone in the bathroom right now. That couldn't be a coincidence. This was my one shot, and I was going to take it. Concealing the weapon, I moved to the bathroom at the end of the aisle. All those eyes on me—they're just passively tracking movement. They don't know. No one suspects anything.

Then to the bathroom door—it was unlocked. I took a deep breath and opened it.

He was sitting on the toilet, his pants around his ankles, grinning up at me. When I was in the car, it took me a long time to work up the nerve to back up. This time I didn't even hesitate. I lunged at him, driving the plastic straight into his heart.

He barely flinched. I let go of the shiv, horrified to see it buried in his chest, even more horrified to see myself doing it. He calmly wiped his ass and pulled up his pants while I watched. Then he pushed past me, moving to exit the bathroom. I couldn't let him get away. I grabbed the shiv and stabbed him again, but he wrapped his arms around me and locked me against his body.

"Good luck turning your back on this one," he grunted as I struggled against the implacable grip. Together we tumbled out into the aisle—and this time all those eyes really were on me.

"Help!" the man screamed, appearing to notice his injury for the first time. "This man's trying to kill me!"

My hand on the shiv, the wound in his chest—there's no playing innocent there. I dropped my weapon and put my hands in the air. The man writhed on the ground, screaming and carrying on even though I knew he was fine.

"You're a liar!" I shouted as someone grabbed me from behind. "It's just an act! Can't you see he's faking?"

I swear I saw the man wink as they wrestled me to the ground, but I didn't fight back. But how the hell am I supposed to explain that in court?

Attempted murder. That's what I'm on trial for. As part of my guilty plea, my attorney advised me to tell a full account of what happened. That's what I'm doing, because I know it's still less than I deserve.

THE MISSING CHILD SPEAKS

I DON'T HAVE KIDS OF MY OWN, SO I CAN ONLY IMAGINE HOW terrifying this must be for my neighbor Amy Galligan. I didn't know her well, but we've chatted a few times in the apartment mail room—her about the difficulties of being a single mother, me playing up my shipping job at Amazon to make it sound like I'm a big shot. It's a monster of a city though, and there are so many people with so many problems that I was hardly even phased when I saw the missing poster of her four-year-old daughter hanging around the building.

Taken from a public playground at Fairbanks Park.
*Any information, please call 818-***-*****

"Maybe she tossed it," I remarked casually to my buddy Dave.

"Tossed what. The kid?"

"Yeah, or flushed it or something, I don't know. I know the woman, and she bitches all the time about how she has no life of her own anymore. Seemed to me like she would have been happier without it."

"It's not an IT, man, she's a baby girl. And you can't flush a four-year-old—what the fuck?" Dave and I knew each other since grade school, so it amazed me that I could still get a rise out of him with dark jokes like that. "Anyway, why would she put up missing posters if she didn't want the kid?"

"Duh, it's so she won't look suspicious." That was Sammy, Dave's girlfriend. Slim, beautiful dark hair, and snarky as a goth in church—I don't know how my goodie-goodie friend got so lucky. I pointed at her, then tapped my nose in what I hoped to be the universal signal for 'she knows'. Dave just looked bewildered and flustered.

"No one would do that to their own kid. The moment they're born, they take a part of your soul with them. It's not just like you're split in half either—they've taken all the best parts of you. All your innocence and hope and wonder at the world that eroded from you over the years—it's all right there in your arms, promising a better life than you could ever live for yourself. And when you're looking at them, all those holes in your soul that you didn't even know where there are filled back in. For the first time in your life, you know that you truly matter."

"Dude, you don't even have a kid," I said.

"So what? I'm human, aren't I? I know what's what."

Meanwhile I swear Sammy was humming the tune to Family Guy's 'Prom night dumpster babies' song. I think my heart just did a back-flip.

"Screw you both." Dave bounced off the couch in agitation. "I'm going to go check on her and see if there's anything I can do to help."

"Seriously? You don't even know the lady," I protested, feeling a little flustered myself.

"Yeah, what gives?" Sammy chimed in. "I thought we were going to play paint-ball today."

I could handle Dave's anger. I even found it funny. If I'm being honest, maybe I was even a little jealous and wanted to torment him. That sad, pitying look he gave us though? That cut deeper than I'd care to admit. I guess Sammy felt the same way because a few moments later all three of us were standing outside of Amy's apartment.

Dave knocked first.

"Excuse me, Ms. Galligan? It's your neighbors."

Nothing.

"Are you sure she's home?" Sammy whispered.

"Yeah, I heard her toilet like five minutes ago. Thin walls." I matched her hushed tone.

"Oh, I didn't know she had twins," Sammy said. I almost burst a lung trying not to laugh.

Dave pressed his ear against the door. I expected another death glare from him, but he just turned around and grinned.

"It's okay. They must have found her. I hear the kid talking," he said.

We were about to go when the door opened behind us. Amy was standing in the doorway—bird's nest hair, loose bathrobe, face puffy with fresh tears and anxious stress—even Sammy didn't have anything to say about that. A little girl giggled from somewhere inside her apartment.

"Is your daughter...?" Dave began.

Amy shook her head and wiped her nose with the back of her hand. She turned around and walked inside her apartment, leaving the door open. Dave followed without question. I didn't move until a few seconds later when Sammy entered.

"There's lots of boxes, mommy." The slightly tinny voice was coming from an Amazon Echo Dot sitting on a coffee table. Beside it were scattered a halo of used tissues. "It's too dark though. Mommy, where are you?"

"It's okay Lilly," Amy said, her voice cracking. "I'm going to be there soon, just hold on."

Amy looked at us pleadingly, and we stared back in stunned silence.

"How long has she—" Dave began.

"About an hour," Amy cut him off. "She said someone took her from the park, and she doesn't know where she is."

"Was it an Amazon van?" I asked. Dave gave me another disapproving glare, but it melted as Amy nodded. "I think so. Lilly said it was black and orange."

Sammy was on her phone, typing furiously.

"Police?" Dave asked.

Sammy shook her head, showing us her screen a moment later: a picture of Lilly with a plain white background.

"This is her, right?"

"Where did you find that?" Amy asked urgently.

Sammy hit the back arrow, returning the screen to an Amazon product page. I would have laughed if I hadn't seen Amy's face.

Lilly Galligan.
$1,495. Used. In stock.
4.2 / 5 stars. 10 Reviews.

"4.2 stars though," I said, trying to lighten the mood. "At least she's got—"

Glares all around. I didn't finish that thought.

"Baby, can you hear me? What else do you see?" Amy demanded.

It wasn't Lilly who answered though. It was just Alexa's generic, robotic voice. "Would you like to place an order for Lilly Galligan now?"

"Come on, isn't anyone curious to read the reviews?" I asked. "Like, what are they going to say? 3 stars, can't color within the lines?"

"Shit, dude," Dave said.

"Yeah, seriously. Not the time." Even Sammy agreed.

"None of you are any fun," I said. "I put a lot of work into this. The least you could do is play along—"

I was ready when Dave took a swing at me, and I managed to back-peddle out of the way. There was a lot of yelling—some hysterical sobs from Amy—then Dave chasing me half way around the room before they gave me a chance to explain.

"She's at a warehouse, okay? God, what babies. Can't anyone take a joke?"

That time I did get punched. It's okay though—I took it like a man. They all insisted I drive them there right away, which is what I was intending to do all along, anyway. This will be the first time I've ever tried to sell adults, so I wonder how much I'll get for these three.

ARE YOU HAPPY NOW?

HAIR TWINED BETWEEN FINGERS. DIRT BLOODIED INTO PASTE. COILED muscle, panting breath, and a broken smile.

"What are you?" I'd shouted down at him.

"I'm me."

I hit him again—hard enough for the bones in my hand to rattle against each other. I don't know why it made me so angry that he was still smiling.

"I want to hear you say it! What are you?"

"Too much. I don't want it, I don't want, I don't—"

Again—the pain in my hand was triumph. The kid would have been flat on the ground if I wasn't still holding him up by his hair.

"Just say it. That's all you got to do. Admit what you are."

"I'm happy."

I dropped Chase to crumple in a heap. The boy was laughing, blood spraying from his mouth as he did. Exhausted, I sat down next to him. He rolled back and forth, body rigidly locked in the fetal position. He was taking great gasps of air and choking on his own blood, laughing all the while.

"God damn it. You're literally insane," I panted.

Chase chocked again. The coughing didn't stop this time. I helped him onto his knees and slapped his back to help clear the airway. He rewarded me with a giant bloody smile.

"I would have stopped if you just said it," I said, my voice calmer. "Why are you so stubborn?"

"You want me to say I'm autism," he slurred. He was hard enough to understand without a mouthful of blood.

"Autistic," I corrected. "I want you to tell the truth and stop pretending you're normal."

"I never pretended. I never normal—pretended normal." His breath was coming easier now. I couldn't look away from the long line of viscous blood which hung from his lip without quite falling. "Not many people are happy. I'm special like that."

We both laughed, although I don't think we were laughing at the same thing.

For the first few weeks I knew Chase, I hated his guts. All the special attention he got—everyone doing stuff for him and congratulating him for accomplishing absolutely nothing—for that big dopey grin he didn't deserve—I thought it was all just a big act. I hated that he wore clothes like a normal person and sat in class without doing any of the work. I thought I could beat the truth out of him, and I guess I did. The truth was that he really was happy—maybe the only truly happy person I'd never known.

"I know I'm autism," he told me later in his customary lurching speech. "I know what it means—I'm autism. I don't play around—play pretend."

"Then why don't you ever say it?"

"I do. I just say it last. If I say it first, people don't listen to the rest. They think they already know me."

I stayed quiet while we walked home. He was rolling his sleeves up and down his right forearm. Up and down. Then both down. Then both up. He never stuck with one tick very long. The next moment he was on his tip-toes, tottering along behind me. Then he was loudly humming some made-up tune, or flapping his arms like a bird, or spitting straight in the air and shrieking with laughter as he tried to dodge the falling drop. Whatever he was doing seemed to absorb him completely—so much that when I spoke again he jumped in surprise to find me still there.

"You're too busy busy," he said, even though he was the one doing everything while I just walked. "That's why it's—why you're not happy."

"I'm not even doing anything," I said.

"Too many things," he insisted, almost shouting it. I looked around to make sure no one else was around. I didn't want anyone to think we were friends. "Not nothing. You're looking at ten things. Thinking about twenty. Thirty forty fifty—not real things. Old things. New things. Could-be-things and shouldn't-be-things."

"So what? You're the one always spazzing out."

His whole face furrowed in confusion. Then he smiled.

"I just do one thing with my whole heart."

I was getting frustrated. "That's not true. In the five minutes we've been walking you've done like a hundred different things."

He shook his head, his grin widening. "Just one thing. All my heart —just one thing. Then when I'm finished, I do another."

"And that really makes you happy? It doesn't bother you that you're different?"

He didn't answer though. He'd stopped to pet a bushy plant as if it were a dog.

"I'm not waiting for you," I said. "I'm going home."

"The plants can't walk."

"I'm not talking about the plants—"

"Or drive cars. Or make friends," he rambled. Despite myself, I stopped and waited to hear where this was going. "They're different too. And some have flowers and some have spikes and some have flowers—"

"You already said flowers," I interrupted.

"Because some have lots," Chase declared, unperturbed. "It would be stupid if they didn't grow though—just because they were different. Everything grows—is different. Everything dies. Everything dies." He grasped the bushy plant he'd been petting with both hands and ripped it violently by the roots. A moment later and everything was in the air—stems and leaves and clods of soil all raining around us while he laughed and danced through it.

"You're retarded," I said.

Chase grinned. "So are you, but it's okay. We're still growing."

He wasn't so talkative the next day in school. He had a fresh bruise under one eye. I know that shouldn't have made me so angry after what I'd done to him, but it did. I asked what happened, but he didn't feel like talking.

"Tell me who did it," I demanded. "I'll make sure it doesn't happen again."

He shook his head, not looking at me. I tried to grab him by the shoulder and turn him my way to get a better look, but he yelped and darted into the corner of the room. He pulled out a notebook from his bag and began writing furiously, not looking up as I crept closer. If someone was hurting him, then I wanted to know. I liked the idea of getting into a fight with someone—like it was my penance for what I've already done.

I snuck a peak at what he was writing. Chase was halfway through the notebook, and I figured it was some kind of journal or something. I got too close again though, and Chase started shrieking. The teacher assumed I was picking on him and gave me detention on the spot. It was so stupid—when I was ACTUALLY trying to hurt him we got along, but now that I was trying to help I got in trouble. I shouted at Chase, telling him to explain that I was on his side. Chase didn't look up though. The only result was the teacher grabbing me by the arm to march me all the way to the principal's office.

"Boys will be boys—" I heard the principal say through the door. I waited outside on a hard plastic chair for him to finish his meeting.

"Chase is being tormented! You don't understand how hard it is to take care of a—" came a man's voice. I stopped kicking the wall to listen.

"Perhaps a public school is not the safest environment for—"

"It's your job to make it safe. If anything happens to him—"

"Mr. Hackent, please. The teachers will always do their best, but they can't be everywhere at once. What happens before or after school—"

I opened the door. Sudden silence. The principal in his sweater vest and the man I can only assume was Chase's father in a suit, both staring at me.

"I can keep an eye on him to and from school," I volunteered immediately.

The principal looked uncomfortable. He was well aware of my history of fighting. I guess he thought it was more important to placate the angry man sitting across from him though, so he nodded after a moment.

"That's settled then," he said. "The teachers will keep Chase safe during school, and now he'll be safe on the way too."

Mr. Hackent growled at me, his eyes narrowed in suspicion.

"What about at home?" I asked, staring straight back.

"What happens at home is none of your business," Mr. Hackent replied, standing up rigidly. "If anything happens now, at least I'll know who to blame."

The bruises didn't go away though. There was a fresh one at least once a week. Chase didn't want to talk about it, but at least he was talking about other stuff again—everything except what he wrote in his journal.

"One thing—your whole heart—one thing at a time," Chase said. "If you let that one thing be something bad, then that bad thing is all there is."

"Just ignoring something doesn't make it go away. If someone is still hurting you—"

I stopped because he wasn't listening anyway. He was just playing with his ears, not looking at me. Folding them back and forth. Back and forth.

"I don't ignore it," he said after a long moment.

"Huh?"

"I just don't take it with me," he insisted. "I write it down, then I leave it behind. Fists only hurt once. It's not too bad, and then it's over. Thinking about it hurts more—hurts longer. Most things are like that—it's the thinking about the thing that hurts more than the thing. So just stop thinking about it."

"Are you happy now?" I asked him.

"Always happy," he said, although he didn't smile that time. "I just got to focus on growing."

He didn't look at me very often, but he did this time. Right in my eyes, still staring while he hid his journal behind an electrical box. He put a finger to his lips, hissing a loud SHHHH before turning to walk away. He could have hidden it anywhere, but he was doing it right in front of me because he trusted me. I entertained the thought of just taking it to try to find out the truth, but now it seemed more important to prove I was his friend.

I hate how much sense he made at the time. I hate how easily I let it go.

I started seeing Mr. Hackent at the school more frequently. There'd always be shouting as soon as the principal's door closed, and I wasn't the only one who noticed. Pretty soon kids started talking, and someone must have spoken up about seeing me beat up Chase that one time. After that I was forbidden to walk with Chase, or even talk to him in the hallway.

The bruises didn't stop though. They weren't happening at school, and they weren't happening on the way to and fro either. I kept getting called into the principal's office. I tried to explain that it must be happening at home, but no one believed me. I started getting really angry at Chase. I wanted him to tell people the truth, but he couldn't handle the pressure. Detentions turned into suspension, with threats of permanent expulsion if Chase didn't stop getting abused.

It wasn't my fight. That's what I told myself. The little idiot was going to be happy no matter what happened, and the only thing I was doing by getting involved was making things worse for myself.

I let it go. I stayed the hell away from him—didn't speak to him—didn't even look at him. Even when he tried to talk to me, I just walked away. I thought no one could blame me if they saw that I wanted nothing to do with him.

It didn't stop me from blaming myself though. The lights and sirens were on my block a few days after I cut contact. I was taken down to the police station for questioning. There was so much going on that I couldn't even process it. I just remember rolling my sleeves up and down. Up and down. Trying not to think. Up and down, with all my heart. Because the moment I stopped, I know I'd hear everyone talking about the autistic boy—that's what they called him on the news, not even using his name—the autistic boy who took his own life with a razor blade. I'd hear about the incessant bullying which drove him to it, and hear his father blathering about doing all he could.

But I know Chase would never do that. He was happy. He was growing. And nothing could have stopped that except someone pulling him up by the roots.

The first thing I did was retrieve Chase's journal. There were a hundred things I could have done with it to prove what really happened, but I only picked one. One thing at a time. One thing with all your heart, and for me, that was revenge. Mr. Hackent is a dead man.

It took a few days snooping around his house to find a reliable way in: the broken grate which let me slip into his basement from the outside. I'd wait until I saw him leave for work in the morning, then I'd sneak upstairs to his bedroom. Over the next week, he'd find quotes from Chase's journal cut out and left around his house.

He doesn't like hurting me. He just can't help it. - on his bedside table.

Dad wishes I was normal. I wish he wasn't. - taped onto his bathroom mirror.

He wants me to go, but I have nowhere else to go. - on his leftover eggs in the refrigerator, ketchup soaking through the paper like blood.

It was working too. Every day Mr. Hachent left for work, he looked a little more tired. A little more on edge. On Thursday he skipped work entirely, and when he left Friday morning, it looked like he'd been wearing the same clothes since Wednesday. When he got home that night, this is what he found.

Are you happy now?

It wasn't a note though. It was spray paint this time. On every wall. Every counter. On the ceiling and across his bedsheets.

Are you happy now?

I heard him shouting the words when he came home. Screaming at the top of his lungs, the sound distorting as he ran from room to room, seeing it everywhere.

Are you happy now?

Neighbors reported a gunshot that same night. Rumor had it that he spent several hours ranting about ghosts to his family before it happened. The police concluded that he'd been driven to madness over the death of his son, which I guess isn't too far from the truth.

One thing at a time. And now that I've finished what I set out to do, I've got to keep myself busy. Really busy—incessantly jumping from one project to the next. I need to always be living, always growing. Because I know when it gets too quiet I'll have to stop and think, and I'm afraid of the moments when I have to ask myself:

Am I happy now?

SHE LOOKS LIKE A FUTURE VICTIM

How do killers and rapists choose their next victim? Does it have to do with some repressed childhood memory, fueling a blind hatred toward a particular type of person? Or is it just something they see in the moment: the shape of a body, or her pretty face stirring the blood into an undeniable throb? Whatever it is, I understand why he chose my co-worker Casey. It's hard even looking at her without letting your mind wander. It's not that she's overtly sexual or provocative or anything—it's more the way she moves, graceful and flowing to the point where even waiting tables looks like an intricately choreographed ballet.

It was at the end of our shift the other day when I noticed this customer staring at her. He'd been there for almost an hour, and he still hadn't ordered anything except a coffee. He didn't have a book or a phone or anything either—he was just fixated on her, tracking her every movement with his hungry eyes. Scruffy coarse beard, leather jacket, snake tattoo winding all the way down his hands—I wouldn't want him staring at me. I tried to warn Casey and offered to drive her home (she lives right around the block), but she didn't seem very concerned by him.

She should have been though. The second she walked out the door, the scruffy customer was on her heels, making zero effort to hide his single-minded fascination. I'm not one to be paranoid or anything, but there was a desperate urgency as he followed: a predator stalking the last few feet before the chase is on. Better safe than sorry—I hopped in my pickup and trailed them around the corner.

Casey glanced over her shoulder, and she must have seen him because she started walking faster. The man matched her stride for stride, almost breaking into a run the last few yards before she reached her apartment. I parked on the street until I made sure she got in safely. The building needed a key to enter the lobby, and watching the man rattle on the locked door it was obvious he didn't live there. I watched him pace restlessly for a minute before he began to circle the structure. My instincts hadn't lied to me yet; he was still trying to find a way into the building.

I got out of my car to watch what he was up to. I wasn't thinking about personal danger. All that mattered was that Casey was safe—that and her thinking of me as a hero for looking out for her. I lost sight of the guy for a few minutes after I turned the corner though, and I had to circle the whole building again before I realized what he was up to.

He was climbing the metal exterior stairs of the fire escape. He must have jumped from the top of a dumpster to reach the platform. A black ski mask was pulled over his face. This was getting serious. I should have called the police at this point, but I was still entertaining this fantasy about charging in to save her, and my nerves were on fire with the thrill of the hunt. I clambered onto the dumpster and made a wild leap, action-music playing in my head as I hauled myself onto the metal platform. I shouted at him to stop, but he was already four floors above me and disappearing into an open window.

How much could he do to her in the time it took me to climb four stories? I didn't want to think about it. My last fight had been in grade school. What the hell was I thinking? It was becoming way too real, way too fast, but I'd already committed this far and I couldn't turn back now. I raced up the rattling metal stairs with a sound like a herd of elephants. There was a scream—Casey's scream—but the air I inhaled had turned to daggers and I was already going as fast as I could. Reaching the window he entered by, I dove inside, utterly out of breath and ill prepared for whatever was waiting for me.

I was in a bedroom. Casey was stripped to her underwear, face down on the bed, hands roughly tied behind her back. The man was looming over her—that's all I needed to know. I grabbed steel reading lamp from her desk and smashed it two-handed into the back of his skull. I wish he wasn't wearing the mask just so I could see the look on his face as he crumpled on the ground.

"Hey baby? What was that sound?" she asked, muffled against the pillow.

I was still trying to catch my breath and couldn't respond. It gave me a moment to take in the whole scene: the Valentine's chocolates on the desk, the fuzzy pink ropes which tied Casey's hands, the fact that she wasn't struggling or trying to get away. How had he known this was her room from the outside anyway? Unless...

The truth hit me so hard that I wanted to crumple on the ground next to her boyfriend. Or even better, knock me out the window so she never saw me or figured out what happened. Absolute panic as she began turning her head in my direction. Mind-numbing, terrified, dry-mouthed panic as I dropped to the ground under the bed.

"Well? I'm waiting!" Casey said, wiggling her butt.

I could only think of one solution. I ripped the ski mask off her boyfriend's unconscious body and put it on, and I stood up.

"Please don't hurt me!" she wailed at an unexpected volume. Did she see through my disguise? "I'm all alone, Mr. Intruder Man! What are you going to do to me?"

I couldn't answer or she'd recognize my voice. I couldn't run because she'd already seen me. And seeing her tied up in her underwear like that, practically begging for it... well if my mind wasn't already numb from panic, then that would have been enough to purge the rest of my thoughts. I was in absolute despair and euphoria at the same time as I climbed on top of her, feeling the curve of her body squirm against mine in an erotic and fantastic nightmare.

Is it still rape if she wants it? If she loves it? If she's begging for more? The sex was phenomenal—the best of my life—and I can tell she felt the same by how she welcomed me into her and moaned. I was really starting to get into it when I heard another, deeper moan. She must have thought it was from me because it made her go even louder.

But I knew better. It was her boyfriend on the ground, starting to wake up. There I am, frozen mid-thrust, her desperate for more, now listening to her boyfriend waking up. Oh my god oh my god oh my god—I leap off and leap straight through the window, completely naked from the waist down. A second later there's the most ear-splitting scream, joined by a confused bellow. Casey appears at the window a moment later, still naked, watching me flying down the steps and leaping onto the dumpster below—sliding off in my panic to plaster flat on the ground.

Thank god I was still wearing the mask. I hope she leaves her window open again tomorrow night.

THE EXORCISM OF AN ANGEL

THERE IS NO GREATER CURSE THAN THE POSSESSION OF A DEMON, NOR greater honor than the visitation of an Angel. God has blessed our home with his presence, and I am nothing but grateful for the miracle which has occurred. And yet I tremble as I write this, because through this trial we have learned one lesson most truly of all:

"His delight is not in the strength of the horse, nor his pleasure in the legs of a man, but the Lord takes pleasure in those who fear him."

Psalm 147:10-11

To fear God does him as much honor as to love him, for both are equal expressions of belief.

God does not give us the choice of which laws to follow. The comforts of modern life have seduced men into a pitiful state of moral lassitude, but our family does not compromise on our beliefs. Righteousness can be feigned for the sake of impressing one's neighbors, but the truth of our souls cannot be hidden from God.

"I do not permit a woman to teach or to have authority over a man; she must be silent." -1 Timothy 2:12

But the insolent girl would not be silent before my husband. Not until I struck her. First she howled, then she whimpered, and then she was still. How beautiful the fear of God had made my child.

Elizabeth was only six years old when she turned from the path. She spoke when she was not addressed. Lies flowed from her mouth as naturally as truth, she refused to pray, and she showed no shame in drawing blasphemous monsters and images which did nothing to glorify God. My husband, Luke, and I prayed for her every night, but the Lord knows that a child understands the weight of a cane more keenly than any word.

"Foolishness is bound in the heart of a child; but the rod of correction shall drive it far from him." -Prov 22:15

Her high-collared dresses hid the marks, and for a time Elizabeth showed enough respect for her parents not to speak against us. I should have listened to Luke and not sent her to that public school where her mind could be further polluted by the unfaithful. Her rearing was impeccable, so there's no other way I can explain the filth which began spewing from her mouth.

"I don't want to go!" she said last Sunday morning while I dressed her for church. "I hate him! I hate God!"

"God loves you," I tried to explain, but she wouldn't listen.

"No he doesn't. God hates me too."

"Why would you say such a thing?" I asked.

"Because he made you my mom."

We didn't go to church that day. After Luke heard what she said, she was in no condition to go anywhere. The Lord knows I wept as much as Elizabeth did. It couldn't go on like this, I told myself. Luke thought that she would learn in time, but I wasn't strong enough to endure her lessons. I cleaned my daughter's wounds and made her comfortable, but her blood was still on my hands when I prayed that night.

"Where did we go wrong?" I begged from the quiet. "Oh God, if you truly love us as we love you, send us an Angel to grant us the happiness we deserve."

I could see the light through my closed eyes, and I knew the Spirit was with me then. I felt his warmth on my hands and face. I dared not look, or speak, or even breath, afraid to disrupt the miracle in progress. For one divine moment I knew my prayers were answered and I was in heaven. The next moment, I heard Luke shout "Fire!"

Smoke was billowing under our bedroom door. The hallway was an inferno—flames gutting between the floorboards, climbing the walls, igniting the pictures and the wooden crucifixes pounded into the walls. I staggered towards Elizabeth's room—coughing and falling to my knees to crawl under the smoke. Luke grabbed me under my arms and heaved me toward the front door, but I kicked and fought him the whole way.

"Elizabeth! She's still in there!"

"The Lord preserve her," Luke said, uncompromising as always. I was dizzy from the smoke, and I wasn't strong enough to fight Luke off. Before I knew what was happening, I was panting and heaving on our front lawn while the house burned.

"Elizabeth!" I'd screamed through my strained throat. "Elizabeth where are you?"

Luke wouldn't let me go back in. I was screaming and crying hysterically, but he forced me to the ground and held me there until the fire department came. If Elizabeth was crying for us, I couldn't hear her over the roaring flames. Maybe she stayed quiet though, more afraid of us than the fire. Luke prayed while the firemen battled the blaze. I didn't, knowing my prayers had already been answered. This is the happiness we deserved.

Three strong men entered the house when the exterior had been doused. Veterans in full gear with masks and oxygen tanks. Elizabeth had nothing, and sore as she was from her punishments, I don't know if she could have escaped that house even without the fire. Three men exited the house, their arms empty.

Elizabeth was barefoot and walking unassisted between them. Her face was clear, unmarked from soot, her breathing slow and even. Her skin was pure white, unmarked by injury or burn.

"A miracle," Luke had said.

"A miracle," the firemen were quick to agree.

"A curse," I wasn't brave enough to reply.

We all stayed in a hotel that night. Luke was so exhausted from the ordeal that he slept soundly, but I couldn't help but lie awake and listen to Elizabeth whispering to herself. She was traumatized, my reasoning said. She was trying to process what happened, and she needed me to hold her and tell her it's going to be okay. I almost got up a dozen times in the night to comfort her, but each time my muscles locked from some nameless instinct as old as fear itself which begged me not to approach the mumbling girl.

"Elizabeth is a good girl. A good girl," I heard my daughter whisper. "Elizabeth will not punish them."

I pretended to be asleep, trying to match my husband's deep breathing. I couldn't get enough air though, and my involuntary gasps must have betrayed me because Elizabeth would sometimes sit rigidly upright to stare at me in the darkness. I watched her through slitted eyes, not daring to move.

"Elizabeth prayed too, you know," the girl was obviously speaking to me, but all I could do was lie there and keep breathing. "Do you know what she prayed for?"

I clenched my eyes tight. I felt so stiff that I might as well be dead. I didn't hear anything else, but I was too scared to look. A full minute before the silence became too loud, and when I opened my eyes again, the girl was standing right beside my bed.

I jerked upright, hopelessly tangling the covers in my surprise. Luke woke with a start and flailed around the nightstand until he turned on the lamp. "What is it? What's going on?"

Elizabeth was back in her bed, rigidly upright, just staring at me and smiling. I forced a smile in return.

"Nothing's the matter. We're all okay now. Get some sleep Elizabeth."

Luke grunted and turned the lights back off, rolling his back toward me.

"Goodnight Lady," Elizabeth said. I don't know how many hours it took me to fall asleep after that, but I never saw Elizabeth lie down the whole time.

Over the next few days, the insurance inspectors concluded that it was an electrical fire, although there was so little information in their report that it seemed more like speculation to me.

Elizabeth hasn't given us any trouble since. She's mild and dutiful in her behavior and her prayers. She still loves to draw, but the serene passionless faces she repeats over and over are far more disturbing than the monsters she used to decorate the pages with. Luke couldn't be happier of course—he's got the perfect little angel he's always wanted. He doesn't seem to realize that we've always had an angel, or that somehow she didn't make it out of that fire.

She's watching me as I write this, smiling and swinging her feet, but I don't care. She may even read it if she likes—it doesn't matter. God already knows there is more divinity in an imperfect child than all the angels in heaven. I worship him with my fear now, so if that truly pleases the Lord, let him hear me and send my daughter home.

But she's giggling now, so perhaps he has other plans in store for me.

NOW HIRING. LAST THREE EMPLOYEES KILLED THEMSELVES.

TWELVE WEEKS LOOKING FOR A JOB AND THINGS WERE GETTING desperate. I'm talking water-and-electricity-off desperate, with the landlord playing my door like a drum.

I called my way through entire directories of offerings, often not sure what I was interviewing for until the morning of. I'd get three or four meetings on a good day, but nothing stuck until the excessively tan man from Mello Corp shook my hand.

"You've made a good decision," Cameron had said, pulling me in a bit too close. "Employees at Mello Corp are like a big family. They all stay for life."

I wish I'd gotten a chance to clarify what my actual responsibilities were. I just saw a salaried position and a plush dark-wood office, and that was good enough for me. It didn't help that Cameron only described the requirements in vague generalities about loyalty and teamwork. Even the liability forms didn't help—just a flash of an official letterhead and it was whisked away, leaving me nodding and smiling.

Truth is that I don't have much respect for office jobs. I figured a week lying low and Googling things would teach me everything I needed to know. So far so good—few days in, and I'd spent it all coasting around chatting with people. I was given some menial cleaning tasks, and a few organizing and carrier jobs, but mostly I was free to just watch and learn.

It seemed to be a delivery company, although they only shipped one product. No-one ever mentioned what the product was, and I didn't want to betray my ignorance by asking. Few dudes in their late thirties said they'd been here over 15 years each though. First and last job they'd ever take. The two women working the phones were both 10+ years, and another guy upstairs said he'd been here over 40.

Cameron wasn't joking about the commitment. The funny thing is though, no-one seemed the least happy or boastful in announcing their sentence. There wasn't any small talk in the break room, no affectionate nicknames or the inside jokes you'd expect with such long camaraderie.

All eyes were sullen, tracing patterns in the uniform carpet. Muffled voices, drudging steps, smiles that gave up before they started.

"I don't get it," I casually threw out to one of the guys. "Why does everyone stay so long if they don't like it here?"

"They don't all," he said, not quite meeting my eyes. "Last three with your job killed themselves to get out early."

I gave him a big grin, sucking up to show I appreciated his joke. His deadpan face betrayed nothing. My grin slowly faded as we sat together in silence, him shuffling one foot against the other. Then he left, and I was left standing wondering what the hell was going on.

I can't imagine myself in this gloomy place for 10, let alone 40 years. I resolved to keep applying to jobs and only work here until I found something better. Besides, I sort of enjoyed the thrill of the hunt, and this place was snooze-ville.

I wish it had stayed that way. Few days later and I was making my first outside delivery. Blank cardboard package, about the size of a cake. I was bored waiting to receive it, then bored waiting in traffic. I was bored when I rang the doorbell, and bored when she opened the package. And then something started buzzing. And it wasn't boring anymore.

Wasps were flooding into the air, and they resented their captivity with a vengeance. The sound magnified within seconds until it was all I could hear in every direction. I did what any sane person would do: scream like a little girl and run as fast as I could without looking back. Only I did look back—about a hundred feet down the driveway by my car. The buzzing had all stayed at the house around the woman.

She wasn't screaming anymore. Her throat had swollen shut, bulbous swellings covering her face and neck. She still flailed around with her arms and legs, but the movements were getting more sluggish with every vain stroke. The things were crawling through her hair, up her dress, even into her open mouth.

I've seen allergic reactions before. There was a kid in my middle school who ate a peanut and turned into a balloon animal, but it was nothing like this. I don't know if the wasps were purposefully stinging the same spots around her face and neck, or if that's all I could see, but the swellings seemed to stack on top of each other, one grotesque swelling budding off the last.

First things first, and I vomited. Then I wiped my mouth, got in the car, and made sure all the windows were rolled up. By then my phone was ringing:

"Now you really are family," Cameron's voice was a ray of unwelcome sunshine through a dreary morning.

"You knew? What was inside, you knew about the—"

"They're magnificent, aren't they? Put someone's scent in the box, starve them a little, and then that's the only one they'll hunt."

"You're absolutely insane. I know where you work. I'm calling the cops, and—"

"Smile for the camera, won't you?" he interrupted.

"Huh?" I looked up and down the street. A blinding flash. One of the guys from work was standing outside my window with a camera. He gave me a thumbs up and took another picture.

"That will go well with the live video," Cameron said. "Combine that with the signed confession you have plotting and executing her murder—"

"I didn't sign—"

"Are you really sure?"

It didn't matter what I tried to say. It was caught in my throat anyway.

"You have a break until 1, then two more deliveries in the afternoon."

The phone cut off.

Well I'd love to explain more, but my break is almost over and Cameron is very clear that he doesn't like lateness. Maybe I'll leave early instead, like the others.

SGT DAWSON'S WIDOW DESERVES TO KNOW HOW HE REALLY DIED

DEAR MRS. DAWSON,

My name is Frank Tiller, and I was with your husband when he died. I don't know how to contact you proper, but the sergeant once told me the two of you used to read stories like this, so I figure you might find these words too. He used to read to you while you drew pictures from what's happening, isn't that right? He said you weren't scared of nothing though—didn't matter how dark it got, your laughter was a light to follow. I don't suppose you're laughing much these days. I know I'm not.

Two gunshots, one in the chest, one in the stomach. He didn't abandon his position, not as long as he could provide cover to give the rest of us a chance away from the ambush. That's what they told you, wasn't it? I was shocked when I read the report, but I suppose I understand why they lied. That's a hero's death they gave him. They knew you wouldn't question it, and really that's all they cared about.

Pardon if I'm overstepping my bounds ma'am, but if I were you I'd want to know the truth, even if it weren't so pretty.

The report said he died May 22nd, but you have to understand that this begun on the 13th when our squad encountered a land-mine. It detonated beneath the front left tire of our LTATV jeep with a sound so loud I only felt it. I was thrown clear when the jeep went into the air, but Sergeant Dawson got the worst of it in the driver's seat. What metal hadn't disintegrated had melted and run like candle-wax, leaving a crater in the car like a meteor just punched through.

Nobody could have told you how your husband walked away from that with hardly a limp, just like nobody could say he was the same afterward. Doctor said it was an acute case of PTSD, but I see what PTSD looks like every time I look in the mirror, and it didn't feel nothing like that to me.

I don't know how to right describe it ma'am, but when the sergeant talked, I felt like he was calling from the bottom of the deepest of deep wells, like he wasn't here at all but just a little echo that started a long time ago.

Sometimes he'd look right at me and say something like, "Frankie what you got waiting for you back home?" and we'd talk like a bunch of geezers on a park bench with all the time in the world. He was like that when the Captain came in—sober enough to be approved for his position again.

Captain wouldn't have been so quick if he saw Dawson at his dark times. He'd forget who I was, or who he was, wandering lost and scared until I found him and brought him back to his quarters. Other times he'll be screaming at a wall, really going at it, red faced with the veins bulging in his neck and spit flying like a drill sergeant.

Every day it seemed the dark side was a little more the only side. Even when he had it together, he'd forget my name or say something which betrayed how fragile his mind was. Once real loud in front of everyone in the barracks he ordered me to "Climb to the moon on the finest of ladders", his voice sing-songing like a lune.

The Captain didn't see it, but the rest of his men did. I'd hear them making fun of the sergeant behind his back, taunting him for his wild intellectual and personality fluctuations. Your husband only made it worse, ordering a man to grow a beard, or demanding to know why the King of England was so late in arriving. He was a laughingstock behind closed doors, and sometimes the doors weren't even closed.

Other men gave me shit for not joining in, but on my word I

wouldn't do that. If the sergeant asked me to jump I'd ask how high, and if he said it was to the moon, then I'd give it my damn best. Count all the bricks in the barracks—it was 16,444, and I didn't leave until after midnight.

You see, I knew your husband was still in there, somewhere nobody could reach him anymore. He was the same man who had saved my life on more than one occasion, and I would follow him to whatever end. I thought that if he noticed I was listening—really listening, then he'd find his way back. If he knew he wasn't being judged or looked down on or forgotten, he'd have a reason to return.

God ma'am, those days scared the hell out of me. I wasn't just scared for the sergeant who seemed to keep getting worse, I was scared for myself. The only way I used to sleep at night is trusting the sergeant was going to keep me safe, and these days even pills couldn't settle me down.

I didn't give up on him. I want you to know that. Every damn impossible thing he'd say I'd look in the eye and say "Yes sir!" Everything except one—the night of May 22nd. The night he grabbed me by the shoulders and looked me in the eye, the night he really knew me, when he asked for me to take his life.

"I feel something bad coming, Frankie," he said. "Like my soul needs to take a really bad shit that's been brewing way too long."

I told him not to worry about it. We all feel like that all the time. He chuckled a bit, but he wouldn't lay off.

"I want you to put a bullet in me. Two to be sure. Something's coming Frankie, and I don't want to be around when it gets here."

The next question out of his mouth was how much would it cost to buy India. I told him I'd need some time to research it, and he let me go for the night.

He had no right to ask a question like that (not the India one). I didn't deserve to be put in this position where I had to just walk away in shame. Maybe the rest of the men were right, I thought. I ought to have called the medical officer and gotten him locked up a long time ago, for his own safety and everyone else. I just couldn't bring myself to admit he was already gone.

That's why I'm taking responsibility for what happened ma'am, and it's why I'm writing you this letter now. The sergeant wasn't wearing nothing but his skin when the midnight shift caught him sneaking around the base. I know for a fact that neither of the soldiers fired a shot before they were both dead, without even a chance to set the alarm.

There's a lot of different accounts after that ma'am. Some say he had fur growing down his sides and a mouth like the inside of a butcher's shop. Others think he was high on amphetamines or something, so much that he didn't feel no pain—not even remorse for the men he killed.

All I can tell you with certainty is what I saw with my own two eyes. That was the sergeant burying his head in a man's chest cavity like a starved dog. And when everything was all over, seven body bags were stacked against the far fence, his being one of them.

One in the head, one in the chest, two to make sure. I guess on that count the army told the truth. Just what the sergeant ordered. But I was a damn fool for not listening to him sooner, and there's six fine ladies who are going to have a man in uniform knock on their door holding a flag, just like how it happened to you.

What they didn't tell you though—what they didn't want to tell anyone, but I damn near forced it out of them—was that the sergeant was cold long before I shot him down. 8-10 days, that was their best guess, putting the actual death closer to the 13th. Nobody knows how your husband walked away from that, and it's my theory that he never did.

UGLY LITTLE LIARS

EVERYONE I KNOW IS AN UGLY LITTLE LIAR. I CAN SEE IT CARVED INTO their skin, open wounds gaping and sucking endlessly at the empty air. I can see it in their grotesquely swinging club foot, or the jutting disfigurement of their face. If they could see each other's ugliness, they would never leer and grin at each other the way they do. They'd never even leave the house, too ashamed of the truth of their soul that only I can see.

I used to be frightened of everyone when I was little. I thought I was the only boy in a world of monsters. Then came the day when I was in pre-school when my teacher (bulbous nose like an overripe pimple and sticky yellow pools for eyes) asked me if I'd taken Sally's pudding cup. I looked straight into that tremulous pimple and swore up and down that I didn't even like pudding. My hand itched all the while, the sensation mounting to an intense burning by the time I'd finished. I started to cry, so the teacher decided I was telling the truth and moved on.

I did lie though. The scar on my hand is proof of that. It looks like someone took a red-hot knife and twisted it in the flesh between my thumb and index finger. I tried to show the teacher, but even with a magnifying glass she couldn't see anything there. Neither could my mom. It didn't take me long to learn it was better not to talk about it at all. I don't know what makes me different, but I can tell you with certainty that I learned quickly not to lie.

Most children are pretty clean. Teenagers are generally the messiest, because their wounds are freshest. By the time they reach their 20s and 30s, most of that is just a latticework of old scars, dried and hardened to show their dishonesty is mostly left behind.

Of course there are the outliers too. The perfect skin of an angel drifting through a crowd. I like to watch them when they don't know I'm looking, as if their purity somehow redeems the rest of the filth they've submerged themselves in. On the other side there are the true monsters—the ones who don't even look human anymore. The bigger the lie, the bigger the mutation. I always keep my distance from those when I can help it, as much to avoid getting nauseous as for my own safety.

There's one particular instance I'd like to draw attention to though. I don't often see fully grown men with such profuse, dripping wounds. It wasn't the milky pus dripping from his eyes that bothered me most though, or even the blood which spilled from his suit pants to leave glistening pools wherever he walked. He was the first person I've ever seen with a second head, the second "neck" bridging off the first, composed of nothing more than a network of unconcealed veins and arteries. The second head looked much like the first, even wearing the same heavy horn-rimmed glasses, although the second face never smiled—stark contrast to the perfect teeth of the perpetual grin beside it.

I was just finishing a delivery to the hospital when I spotted him exiting the building. (Great job, delivery driver. Not much chance for people to lie when you're only asking their name). Ordinarily I'd just cross the street to avoid the ghastly figure, but his singular deformity made me stop and pause. The second head was staring right at me, almost as if it knew I could see it. The blank face betrayed nothing however, and I was about to get in my truck when the two heads spoke in unison.

"Come along, hurry now. Before anyone sees you leave!"

A half-dozen colorful children paraded from the hospital, close on his heels. They looked like they're dressed for a Mardi gras or something—decorative hats, scarves, rainbow beads and flamboyant masks. The misshapen man made a show of looking left and right as though playing a game, and all the children played right along, some even tiptoeing as he led them toward his black SUV.

"That's it, everyone inside. I'll keep you safe, don't worry about a thing."

A hole opened in the forehead of the original before my eyes. An inaudible gunshot which pulverized the skin and left a crack in the exposed skull beneath. I stood in shock for several seconds—several seconds too long. The SUV was already on the road by the time I got behind my wheel. It was none of my business, right? I'm glad I didn't say that out loud, because of course that was a lie. I might be the only one to know who that man was inside, so of course it was my obligation to follow.

I laughed at myself for the first few minutes in pursuit. I was being paranoid. There's a perfectly reasonable explanation for this. Then the SUV took a sharp turn onto a dirt road, and suddenly I wasn't so sure anymore.

The crumbling farmhouse they pulled up to was another red flag. High chain-link fences surrounded the property—the only new thing in the place. Two of the upstairs windows were boarded up, and the whole property stank like a corpse. I didn't want to raise suspicion, so I parked a ways back along the dirt road. I watched as the man parked inside the chain fence, locked it behind him, and then began to herd the children around the back of the house. I snuck forward through the dry reeds, keeping low and trying to get close enough to catch another lie.

"What's back there?" one of the older girls asked, 12 years at most. Old enough to be rightly suspicious.

"You have nothing to be afraid of. I won't let anything hurt you."

Something ruptured on his back underneath his shirt. A thick yellow and red liquid began to stain the inside.

"Come on, tell us!"

"What's your best guess?" both heads replied.

"A birthday party!" one of the younger boys squealed.

"Amazing! That's exactly right."

The stain was rapidly spreading, the wet shirt clinging to lumps like boils beneath.

I didn't waste any more time trying to be a hero. I called the police, and an officer promised to be directly on his way.

I couldn't just sit around and wait though. I had to get closer, but the chain fence had been padlocked behind them. The second head was watching me as the group rounded the corner of the building. I was already pacing along the perimeter to look for a way in.

I heard the first scream. A few seconds later, more shrieks swiftly joined in. I leaped onto the fence, desperately trying to haul myself up. The links were too small to get my foot into though, and I wasn't strong enough to climb with just my fingers. I heard the man's roaring laughter and I redoubled my efforts, this time trying to dig underneath. I managed to bend part of the unsecured links at the bottom, churning through the loose soil to make some room.

I strained my ears, but all the children were drowned out by the loud carnival music which began to play. I vaguely heard another shriek climb its way through the noise. A few moments later and I'd widened the hole enough to wriggle through on my stomach. After that it was just a mad dash around the building, dreading what I might find, and even more terrified of lingering long enough to hear one more child scream.

I almost ran head-first into a donkey who didn't look the least apologetic for being in my way.

"Hey mister can you help me up?"

I stared down at the little boy trying to clamber up the stoic donkey's leg. I hadn't noticed he was bald while his hat had been on.

"This isn't any ordinary petting zoo," the disfigured man was saying, his bloody back to me. "These are magical animals. All you have to do is play with them, and you're going to feel all better."

The second head was looking right at me. It coughed a great mouthful of blood onto the ground. Another shriek—coming from two girls chasing after a pair of chickens. One of their headscarves unraveled as they ran, revealing a second bald head. The stench was even stronger here, although that wasn't too surprising considering all the animals.

"And the plants that grow here—they're magic too," he was saying. "Everyone gets a carrot. They'll make you grow up big and strong."

The second head was coughing so much blood that the skin was visibly dehydrating, shrinking down like a prune.

"I don't want to grow big! I want to stay little!" one of the girls wailed.

"That's okay too. Go ahead and take a bite. You'll never grow up at all."

I waited for the next wound, but it didn't come.

I left the way I came, crawling under the fence. The police car was already parked outside.

"What's the situation? Where's the kidnapper?" the officer asked me.

"I was wrong, I'm sorry. He isn't a monster."

"And the kids?"

"The kids are all going to be fine," I said, already feeling the red-hot burn radiating up my leg.

I used to think lies were the worst thing in the world. That they turned people into monsters. The real monsters—they're just as fine hurting people with the truth as they are with lies. Truth and lies—those are facts. Those we can see and know. Ugliness isn't created by the subject though, it's created by the perceiver in passing that judgment, and I'm the only ugly one here today.

MESSAGE IN A BOTTLE

Last year my wife Janis and I were walking on the beach near our house. We've been married almost twenty years and still hold hands wherever we go, so my first awareness of the bottle was when she started racing ahead and dragging me across the sand.

"Hey Matt! Look at the size of that shell!" she said, simultaneously blocking my view of it as she ran. "Oooh wait. Is that what I think it is?"

"Probably. Assuming you think it's a piece of trash."

Janis let go of my hand to drop to her knees, allowing her skirt to pool around her on the sand. "It's not! It's a treasure!"

"It's probably some homeless man's piss pot."

Anyone who has been married knows exactly what look she gave me. Sort of a 'I've known you long enough that I don't have to pretend you're funny anymore' look.

It really was a beautiful bottle though, despite the erosion and clinging barnacles countless years had stained its surface with. It seemed to be made of some type of ceramic, and the fat base was surrounded in intricate geometrical designs. A leering face was carved into the neck, and a moldy cork with a pungent smell was wedged in the top. Janis wasted no time trying to pry it open with her nails.

"It looks like something that might have been on an old ship," she said, grunting with the effort like an offended farm animal. "How can you not be excited by this?"

I shrugged, looking out to sea. "I like to save all my excitement for the big things. Like weekends and pizza night. Speaking of..."

But she had it opened now. She'd turned it over to shake the contents into her outstretched palm. I expected a rush of water and nothing else, but the thin rolled parchment which slipped out was immaculately preserved. Janis unrolled it and studied the page. The wonder in her face gave way to amusement, then incredulity, her brow continuing to furrow into a bitter anger.

"Well don't leave me hanging! What's it about?" I asked.

"I don't know. Ask your girlfriend." She shoved it against my chest and turned to stomp back toward our house without another word. Bewildered, I opened the letter and read:

Dear Matthew Davis,
I miss you. I need you. How much longer will you make me wait? If your love endures as mine has done, what keeps you away from me?

"Janis? Honey?" I called, unable to tear my eyes away from the note. The paper—the bottle—even the smooth archaic penmanship, all seeming ancient and untampered with. So what were the chances that it would be addressed to someone else with my name?

My wife was already gone though. She didn't talk to me until late that night when I finally got frustrated enough to snap at her. It was either a coincidence or a practical joke played on me, neither of which were my fault. She wasn't convinced, but at least she opened up about her fear that I was cheating on her. She thought that someone hid the note near my house where I would find it as a romantic gesture. Eventually she came around, but it was an uneasy peace at best.

And it only got harder from there. There was another bottle almost every morning, wedged in the sand at the high tide line as though it had washed up overnight. Sometimes my wife would find them, other times I would. I posted pictures online of a few of the bottles, and the closest match I was able to find were potions used by 17th century alchemists. That seemed like an important clue to me, but all my wife ever focused on were the notes.

The ocean ends, though we do not see it. The summer fades, though the sun seems unassailable in the sky. Only our love will never grow old. I will not give up on you Matt.

Or

How long has it been since we've made love? Do you still remember what it felt like to be with me?

Janis did her best to play it off as a joke, but I could tell that it was getting to her. She kept making excuses to spend more time alone, and when I pressed her to talk about her jealousy, she'd only treat it like an accusation and get defensive. We'd start fights over nothing, until by the end of the night we were screaming at each other and the next morning not remember why.

One night all it took was me coming home late from work and she was yelling before I even opened the car door. I couldn't take it anymore. I just slammed the car into reverse and left without a word, driving down to the beach to be alone. All the bottles were arriving within about a hundred yard stretch, so I resolved to spend the whole night there until I caught whoever was really leaving them.

Despite living within walking distance of the ocean, I'd never spent any time there after the sun went down. It's amazing how alien a familiar place can feel when the night closes in. The gentle rhythm of the waves seemed less innocent somehow, like I was listening to some colossal creature slowly breathing beside me. The reflection of the moon cast strange shapes into the water, and the cresting of each black wave seemed like it was being distorted by unseen creatures just below the surface.

I maintained my silent vigil until just after midnight when the moon was masked by a thick layer of clouds. My phone had run out of batteries, and it was so dark that I don't think I would have seen someone drop the bottle ten feet away. It would have been completely black if it weren't for the reflection in the ocean. I was getting ready to give up, or at least go back to the car and look for a flashlight, when a thought occurred to me.

If the moon was completely obscured, how was its light still reflecting from the water? The longer I stared, the more sure I was that the light wasn't a reflection at all: the soft luminescence was coming from below the waves. I raced back to my car to check for the light, but I didn't find one. There was a snorkeling mask in the trunk though, so I took that instead and returned to the beach.

I stripped to my underwear and took a step in. The water was ice around my ankles and I almost turned around, but the light was even stronger now and I was drawn like a moth to the flame. By the time the water reached my knees, my feet were so numb that I couldn't even feel them. The light was moving too, twisting and dancing like a living thing, one second drawing close, the next leading me out a little deeper.

Deep breath before the plunge, and I flung myself into the oncoming waves. The cold water closed over my head, but the thrill of my discovery made it feel like liquid energy washing over my body. The light was coming from a woman, shining out through her translucent skin. She was gracefully twirling through the water, her slightest movements propelling her more easily than a practiced stroke. At first she looked like she was swimming, but as I drew closer it quickly became apparent that all the movements were wrong.

Her elbows and knees moved in unnatural, double-jointed arcs. Her neck appeared to have no bones at all, and it turned fluidly to track me independently of her turning body. In her right hand she carried a bottle, just like the kind that had washed up on shore. If my mouth hadn't been full of water, I might have screamed. I also might have said, "Hello Janis," and she might have said, "I've been waiting for you."

I don't know how long I followed her for. She'd let me get almost close enough to touch her before drifting back just out of reach. I was mesmerized by the light and couldn't resist trying to get a better look. If it weren't for the eldritch radiance and the strange movements, I would have sworn it was Janis, and I thought if I could only get close enough to catch her then I'd know for sure.

I was getting tired though, and stretching for the ground and feeling nothing I suddenly realized how deep I had actually swum. I surged to the surface in a panic. The lights of houses on the shore were so far away that they looked like stars. I spun helplessly in place, trying to get a bearing of where I was, when a hand grabbed my ankle. She didn't try to yank me down. The caress was gentle, but as soon as I tried to pull away, her grip tightened. I felt her fingers climbing up my leg, the incessant pressure building like a constricting snake slowly strangling its prey.

I tried to start swimming back toward shore, but the more I fought against her, the harder she pulled. A moment later and I was underwater again, bending double to vainly pry her hands off with my fingers. Water was flowing into my nose and mouth at this point, the bitter salt igniting my throat and flooding me with fresh waves of panic. The more I panicked, the harder I fought, and the harder I fought, the deeper down I was dragged. The last thing I remember was Janis wrapping her whole body around me, her limbs and spine completely encompassing me as though she had no bones at all. I remember the icy waters giving way to numbness, then the suffocating pressure giving way to oblivion.

It was early morning when I woke on my back on the beach. There was a bottle still clutched in my hands.

Can you forgive me? it read. *I forgive you. As long as you visit me every year, I can wait a little longer for you to be mine again.*

Even when I went home, it didn't feel like home anymore. I found Janis' body lying in bed with nothing but an empty bottle of Jack Daniels and two empty containers of sleeping pills. I was sick of notes, but there was one left for me to read on the night-table.

I saw you with her in the water, and I'll never forgive you.

It's been a year since my wife died. Maybe when I go back down to the water to visit her again, she'll finally understand.

It's only her that I've ever loved.

ILLUMINATING THE DARK WEB

July 1st, 2018

A FACE IS STARING INTO THE CAMERA. SANDY HAIR, MID-TWENTIES, male, somewhat reminiscent of a squirrel in his rabid mannerisms.

"The big day is finally here. This is our first time testing out our new SPYDER bot on the dark web, and we're both pretty excited. We've only got a week left to iron out the bugs before Kevin has to defend his thesis, but I don't anticipate any problems. Kevin is nervous as hell, but the kid is an absolute genius. He's still configuring his TOR network and VPN, so I'm going to catch everyone up who are just joining the stream now.

"Typical web crawlers haven't been able to explore the dark web because they can't index specific inputs like forms or authentication pass-phrases. I'm mostly here for moral support and don't understand it completely, but Kevin's SPYDER bot has machine learning algorithms which have been training the last few weeks to learn a new adaptive method of keyword selection.

"You hear that derisive snort at my oversimplification? Yeah that's Kevin. Say hello Kevin!" The streamer looks off camera.

Off camera voice: "Shut up Brian."

"Whatever, fuck you too, man. Based on the training results, we should be able to index a couple thousand pages a day. Google only reaches 16 percent of all available websites, so that means it's going to take us approximately... forever to get through it all with our current computing power. This is just a proof of concept though. All we're using at the moment is Kevin's old laptop that his dog Crinkles practically smashed. The power chord was stretched across the room and this little bulldog comes barreling right through—"

Indistinct grunt off camera.

"Hold on, it looks like we're good to go. If all goes well, then in a couple of months you're going to start reading about how the dark web ceased to exist because of our little SPYDER. I'm going to end the stream now to let it get started, but join us again tomorrow to explore all the cool stuff we found!"

July 3rd, 2018

The sandy haired man is back. There are bags under his eyes, but he's as enthusiastic as ever.

"Hey guys, it's me again. Sorry for the delay, but we hit an unexpected bump. SPYDER was doing great and had already logged a few hundred sites when it abruptly stopped with this weird error. It keeps telling us that it has already indexed everything. Kevin is able to manually direct it to keep finding new sites, but as soon as its automated it just says it's finished again.

"Kevin is practically ripping his hair out, but it's not like this has been a complete waste of time. We did discover a brand new, never-before-seen color that I'm pretty sure didn't used to exist. All Kevin had to do was put on a white t-shirt a week ago, then eat nothing but BBQ chicken wings and sweat out the sauce."

The camera starts to pan to the left. An unseen hand shoves it back into place.

"Anyway," Brian rambles, "it looks like we might still be awhile, so—"

Off Camera Voice: "Got it. I don't understand it, but I've got it."

"Well whip me red and call me apple sauce, because it looks like we're back in business."

Off Camera Voice: "What? That's not a saying. Nobody says that."

"Kevin Kevin Kevin, you have GOT to get out more. People are saying that like ALL the time. So what was the holdup?"

Off Camera Voice: "It's all linked. Look at this—a drug marketplace, an anime-forum, a counterfeit producer, some dungeon-porn—"

"You have my attention."

Off Camera Voice: "It's all referencing the same destination. SPYDER stops indexing because it thinks the whole dark web is this one site. I'm going to try to get in..."

"That relates to a joke I know. So a drug lord, a weebu, a conman, and a pornstar all walk into a bar..."

Off Camera Voice: "This isn't a real joke. Just shut up, I'm trying to concentrate—"

"—and the barman says, 'what are you guys doing together?' So the drug lord says—"

Off Camera Voice: "They've all got something to hide."

"Even the pornstar?"

Off Camera Voice: "It's gotta be a blackmail thing. These guys must be tunneling into other websites to get info or hold them ransom. But there's no way they can be everywhere. Every single site SPYDER finds... shit. Shit-mother-fucking-bitch-sticks."

"Oh like that's a real saying."

Off Camera Voice: "They're on my computer. I have no idea how they traced SPYDER back, but the mouse is moving on its own. It's typing an address into TOR..."

"What are you doing?"

Off Camera Voice: "Popping out the battery. The power button isn't working."

"No don't!" The streamer dives off camera. Bumping noises.

Off Camera Voice: "Dude give that back!"

The streamer returns in front of the camera holding a battered old laptop. "Nah man, this is what the people are here to see! Let's find out where these hackers are trying to take us."

"I swear to God, Brian." An overweight torpedo wearing a blotchy shirt of unclassifiable color hurtles across the screen. The streamer's chair tips over, and both men go down. The laptop is left in front of the camera where a long line of seemingly random letters and symbols are typing themselves into the address bar of a TOR browser.

Indistinct muffled swearing.

The website loads. A countdown timer starting at fifteen minutes begins to tick down. Kevin and Brian stick their heads up over the desk in unison to stare at it.

"At least shut that damn camera off," Kevin says.

"Only if you'll let it countdown so we can see what happens," Brian replies, swatting away Kevin's hand which stretches for the laptop.

"God, you're such an asshole. Whatever, fine, just shut it off."

The sandy man begins to wave, but the screen cuts off halfway through.

When the stream returns, the timer reads 15 seconds. The angle is weird, as if the camera is in his lap hidden beneath the desk. The looming Kevin is pacing and muttering to himself in the corner of the screen. Brian surreptitiously leans over the camera and gives a thumbs up, mouthing the letters OMG. The timer hits 0 and stays there.

A dog starts barking somewhere in the distance.

"Are you happy now?" Kevin grunts. "Give it back, okay?"

There's a knock on the door. A single knock—loud and deliberate. The barking intensifies, snarling, growling, all hell breaking loose in its little world.

"Not really," Kevin whispers.

A second knock. Then a third, each about three seconds apart.

"You get it." Both men say at nearly the same instant. They stare at each other until the next knock.

"This is your fault!" Kevin wheezes in a voice halfway between a whisper and a shout.

"Yeah, yeah," he replies. He approaches the door, the camera angle still at waist height. Then in a louder voice: "Who is it?"

"Are you still recording?" Kevin hisses. "Unbelievable."

The screen is filled by the door as Kevin gets closer. He's right up against it, so he's probably looking through the peek-hole. CRASH—a sound loud enough to max out the speaker volume. The door explodes inward in a wave of splinters. The screen shakes erratically, and there's nothing but splinters and lances of light and screaming.

A gray-skinned hand streaks across the camera. If you freeze the frame, you'll notice that the skin looks more like coarse cloth, and that there is stitching running up and down the fingers.

The stream cuts off.

July 10th, 2018

Brian has turned the stream back on. His face seems paler. His skin is breaking out, and his hair hangs in greasy strings around his face. He's sitting at a bare table in a concrete room. The lights are dim, but there's a large man standing in the back of his room. His hands are folded motionlessly in front of him.

"Um, yeah, hi guys. This might be... my last broadcast for a while." He glances back at the figure in the corner, but there's no movement. Back to the camera: "Kevin's okay. I mean, he's different, but he's okay." He glances back to the corner of the room, but the figure still hasn't budged. Brian's shadow shifts with his movement, and for a moment the stitched cloth/skin of the person in the corner is visible running all the way up his arm.

"I guess they had something like SPYDER. They were only tunneling into websites on the dark web, anyway. I guess those kinds of people could disappear without as many questions being asked. They wanted my followers to know though..."

Brian swallows. He looks behind again. Then a sudden burst of movement—grabbing the camera and dragging it up to his face. "Close your browser now. Shut off your computer."

The figure in the back has started to move. Great, lumbering steps, charging forward.

Brian's words are a breathy rush. "It only takes fifteen minutes for them to find you once they've established a connection."

The cloth hands seize Brian from behind and drag him off camera.

"Don't do this Kevin!" He shouts. "How long has your browser been open already? Just shut the damn thing off!"

There's a heavy THUD. A heavyset face appears in front of the camera for a moment. The human eyes look strange embedded within the cloth. Stitches run down either side of the face along the jawline. The cloth might just be sewn to the skin, but it fits so closely to the anatomy of Kevin's face that it looks more like the cloth has replaced it.

The stream cuts to black, replaced by the last few seconds of a depleting timer.

ME, MYSELF, AND I PLAY GAMES TOGETHER

WE ALL HAVE THE SAME GOD, AND HIS NAME IS CHANCE. AND WE'RE ALL praying every second of our lives.

If only I had jumped a little higher when skateboarding, then I wouldn't have clipped the barrier and hurt my ankle. If only I hadn't hurt my ankle, then I would have been on the soccer team with my brother and sister. If only I hadn't stayed home instead of going to watch them practice. Then all three of us would have died driving home one Tuesday evening, and I wouldn't have to sit wondering why I'm still here.

Were we close? Triplets have that tendency, yes. We were practically identical, enough so that dad couldn't even tell which of us was the girl when our hair was covered. We were each other's shadows for twelve years, sharing clothes and toys and doing almost everything together until the day I learned to do everything alone.

Nelson, aka Nelly, was the smart one. My sister and I would take credit for his grades as if they were proof of our identical genius, even though we never did as well. Teresa was a gentle soul who was most easily identified as the one with the cat on her lap. Now the cat sits with me, always mewing softly to echo the empty longing we both feel.

My mother survived the collision with the drunk driver, but she hasn't been the same since. Sometimes she'll call me by the wrong name, not realizing her mistake until halfway through the conversation when she'll suddenly freeze and fall quiet. Then she'll close off and become guarded, looking at me as if I was a stranger.

One such occasion happened a little over a week after the accident. I was passing through the living room to the kitchen when Mom called out to Nelly, asking for a glass of water on his way back. I didn't correct her, but Nelly did.

"I'm busy, ask Teresa," he said. He said it with my mouth, not having one of his own anymore.

That snapped mom back into awareness. She realized her mistake at once and the hoarse strain in her voice returned.

"I'm so sorry," she said. "I know you aren't Nelly. It's just —"

"I am too Nelly. I'm just busy." I didn't mean to say the words. I certainly didn't think them before they left my mouth. But neither did I choose to turn around and head back upstairs even though that's exactly what I did.

It was surreal to watch my legs move on their own, almost as if I was sleepwalking through a familiar dream. The cat rubbed against my legs at the base of the stairs, and I automatically reached down to pet it, marveling at her unusual affection.

"Whose a kitty kitty kitty? You're a kitty kitty kitty!"

It's not the type of thing I'd normally say, but then again, I wasn't the one saying it. That was Teresa, and by the way the cat sat down on my feet and rolled onto her back to be scratched, I knew the cat understood that too.

I raced up the rest of the stairs and slammed the door behind me. I couldn't understand what just happened, and I needed to be alone to clear my head. But I wasn't alone at all, because Nelly and Teresa were still with me.

Nelly thought it was tremendously funny how furiously I gasped for air. I know because I could hear him laughing as clear as if I was wearing headphones. The cat began to meow outside the closed door, and Teresa wanted me to open it and let her in. I'd already begun to turn the doorknob before I realized what was happening and forced myself to stop.

"It's no fair if you don't let us have a turn too," Teresa scolded. "I would have let you if it had been the other way around."

"We'll take turns," Nelly offered. "We can each do every third day, or if you'd rather, we can break it up hour by hour."

"As long as you don't try to make me waste my turn on sleeping," Teresa said. "Eww, does that mean you two are going to make us kiss girls and stuff? 'Cause I wouldn't make you kiss a boy."

The knock on the door made me jump. I still hadn't caught my breath—if anything I was breathing harder than when I'd been running up the stairs.

"Do you want to talk, or...?" My dad's voice trailed off from the other side.

But Nelly and Teresa hadn't stopped their chatter inside my head. They were having a heated debate about what to do about sharing boyfriends and girlfriends, and with dad talking through the door, I couldn't make sense of them. I could tell that dad was worried though, because he kept trying to push the door open. Nelly and Teresa kept getting louder and louder, talking over each other until they were almost shouting and—

"We're busy!" I screamed to be heard over the din.

The pressure on the other side of the door vanished. Nelly and Teresa went quiet. There was a long pause before Dad said, "Okay, yeah. Sure. Just know that we love you very much and..." Pause. "... and things are going to get easier as time goes on."

But he was wrong. Things got much, much harder soon after.

Laying awake that night, we all came to the conclusion that it would be best not tell anyone there were three of us. We agreed to take turns by the day, on the condition that we could overrule big decisions by a two-to-one vote. Of course Teresa protested saying the boys would team up against her, but she was quickly overruled by Nelly and I and so the rule stood.

Besides, we quickly realized that any two of us could quickly overpower the third, rule or no rule. If Nelly wanted to sneak downstairs and eat a bowl of ice-cream, I could stop him as soon as I realized what was happening. But if Teresa decided she would like some ice-cream too, then there was nothing I could do to prevent the two of them from lurching my body out of bed and crawling downstairs through the darkness.

The other unsettling realization was that while I could stop one of them from taking control, I could only do so with a conscious effort. In such cases my muscles would lock up as if performing a static exercise until gradually one conceded, or the third broke the tie. If one of them moved suddenly without announcing their intentions however, then I wouldn't realize what was happening until I had already watched myself move.

This arrangement came with a number of advantages. We unanimously agreed to let Nelly take our tests for us, and we gave him a little extra time so he could study and do our homework too. I was also able to join the soccer team as soon as my ankle was strong again, and my new teammates were amazed to see that I already knew all the drills and shots without having practiced a day in my life.

It all ran quite smoothly until the day at soccer practice when one of my teammates pulled us aside and pointed to the bleachers. They were mostly empty except for a scattering of parents huddled together on the front row.

"Isn't that Mr. Thrope? Morgan's dad?" my teammate asked, gesturing to a rather fat man with a baseball cap pulled low over his face.

"Who is Morgan?" I asked. I would usually hear Nelly and Teresa whispering to each other even when it wasn't their turn, but they were both completely silent now.

"Donno, he's in an earlier grade," my teammate said. "But his mom is the one who hit your mom's car, right? I think she's in jail now."

"What's he doing here if his kid doesn't play?" I asked.

The coach blew the whistle though, and we all had to jog back to our positions. I spent the next half-hour making a mess out of every shot because Nelly and Teresa weren't helping out. It's the quietest they'd been since they first spoke.

I covered by pretending that my ankle was hurting again and sat down to rest. Mr. Thrope immediately got up and started walking toward me. I tried to leave, but found my muscles stiffen and lock me in place. My brother and sister still weren't saying a word. I waited frozen as the man stepped into the second row and sat directly behind me.

"Hey kid. You were looking good out there," the man said.

"No I wasn't," I replied.

"Maybe, doesn't mater. We all have those days where things don't go as planned, eh?"

I swung my feet beneath me and kept my eyes on the field.

"We all got some days we wish we could take back," the man continued, his voice unsteady.

"It wasn't your fault," Teresa spoke through me, turning us to face him.

"I know I know..." He'd removed his hat and was crumpling it with his hands. His face was twisted and quivering. "It's not about whose fault it is. I'm just sorry it happened, that's all."

"How old is Morgan?" Nelly asked.

"He's ten. Going to be eleven next month."

"Do you love him?" Teresa followed seamlessly.

"'Course I do. And I love his mom too, even though—"

"And you'll miss him when he's gone?" Nelly prompted.

The man furrowed his brow and said nothing. I tried to turn back to watch the field, but Nelly and Teresa were both pulling the other way. I must have looked quite odd inching closer to the man in short, jerking motions.

"What's sorry supposed to do?" Teresa asked. "If you didn't do it, then you can't apologize. If it didn't happen to you, then you can't sympathize."

"You're not really sorry," Nelly added. "Not yet."

The man gave us a queer look and put his hat back on. "I didn't have to come here, but I did. I'm trying to be good to you."

"I'm not the one you should be worried about," I said. I felt cool and dangerous watching the color drain from his face. Then his scowl returned, and he walked away, muttering something that sounded like 'psycho' under his breath.

I didn't feel nearly so impressive after he'd gone. I was scared.

"Morgan really has nothing to do with it," I told my siblings.

"Neither did we," Teresa said. "Neither do you." I'd never heard her voice so low and angry.

"I veto it. I won't let you hurt him—" I said.

"Two against one," Nelly cut in. Teresa said nothing to disagree.

~

WHEN THE LUNCH BELL RANG THE NEXT DAY, I DIDN'T RUN FOR THE door like I usually do. I stayed seated in my class until all the other kids had gone. I felt my mouth open and heard the words come out as though in a dream.

"Is Morgan in your next class?"

Mrs. Wilmore nodded, not looking up from the papers on her desk.

"He told me to tell you that he won't be making it today. He's got a doctor's appointment."

My teacher looked at me from over her glasses. "Tell him to bring a note."

"Yes ma'am," Teresa said. "I think it's pretty serious though. He might not be back for a while."

Mrs. Wilmore thanked me and went back to her work. I was slow to leave the room, trembling with each step as I fought against the irresistible betrayal of my limbs.

"I'll warn her. I'll warn him—I'll tell on you, and someone will stop you," I said internally.

"Go ahead and try," Nelly replied cooly.

"Mrs—"

My throat might as well have turned to stone. I couldn't even swallow. I tried to turn around, but my progress from of the room was relentless.

"It won't do any good to tell," Teresa told me soothingly. "They'll think you did it. And they'll punish you."

We'd already spotted Morgan in the lunch room. He was waiting in line for pizza at the counter.

"I don't care. This isn't right. Teresa, I know you wouldn't—"

"Shut up. Seriously, just shut up," Nelly interrupted.

My hand was reaching out to Morgan. He was a small boy, even considering that he was younger. I could clearly feel the bones in his shoulder where I lay my hand.

"Your dad is waiting for you outside," Nelly said out loud. "He said it's about your mom, and that you should hurry."

Morgan turned around and looked at me with eyes that looked too large on his small angular face. I don't know which bothered me more: that he was scared, or that I could feel Nelly and Teresa loving it.

Morgan willingly left his place in line and followed me through the empty hall. "Not that way," Nelly said. "He's waiting behind the school."

One of my hands was still on Morgan's shoulder, steering him out of the building. The other was clenched in my pocket. It was holding something smooth and cold and hard. I don't know what it was, but I'm sure I wasn't the one to put it there.

I couldn't force words through my lips, but I could still plead with the others inside. "Don't you think he's been through enough? With his mom in jail—"

"Shut up!" Nelly screamed internally. "You don't know anything. You don't know what it feels like to die. You don't know where we went, or how hard it was for us to come back. You don't even know how much it hurts watching everyone move on like we never even existed."

Morgan glanced at me and my face smiled back, showing no sign of the internal conflict. He tried to shrug my hand off, but my grip tightened as we neared the exit.

"We need this," Teresa agreed solemnly. "You wouldn't understand."

"This isn't you," I begged as we stealthily crossed the carpet. "I know you'd never hurt a fly—"

"The one you know died," Teresa replied sternly. "You don't know us anymore."

"Where is he?" Morgan asked as we stepped outside.

"Funny, I bet that's what he'll say too. When he comes to pick you up after school," Nelly said.

My hand withdrew from my pocket, the hard object still clutched inside. I don't know how they got a butterfly knife. Morgan was even more surprised.

I wish I could tell you that we were able to talk through it. That I made them understand that one death does not pay for another. I wish I could have gone all the way back to that day I was skateboarding and never hurt my ankle in the first place. Then all three of us would have died, and Morgan would have still been alive.

When my brother and sister died, I thought that loneliness was the worst feeling in the world. I'd give anything to feel the peace of loneliness again, but I don't think I ever will. Nelly and Teresa are still giving me turns though, and I'm using mine to write this.

I'm sorry Morgan.

I'm sorry Mr. Thrope.

I forgive you Mrs. Thrope.

Nelly and Teresa are getting loud again, and my fingers are having trouble typing. I guess I'll be spending my next turn writing another apology to the next ones we hurt.

PUTIN DOESN'T LIKE MY FATHER

NONE OF MY FRIENDS WILL LISTEN TO ME ANYMORE, AND I DON'T KNOW who else to tell. I don't have any ghost sightings to report, and there aren't any monsters under my bed, but I'm not afraid of that sort of thing. I'm afraid of what's happening to my family, and even worse, that everyone sees it happening but does nothing. It feels like drowning at a pool party, struggling and shouting and begging while all my friends silently watch.

It started a year ago with Dad's YouTube channel. He used to work as an aide for a political leader (A.N.), but then the campaign started traveling and Dad decided not to move. My mom is a teacher, and she tried to get him a job at her school, but he wouldn't have it.

"Мертвые не сражаются. Я мертв?" he used to say. Dead men don't fight. Am I already dead?

Papa is not the kind of man you can argue with. His voice is low and measured, rumbling out of his barrel chest like he's patiently explaining some irrefutable law of the universe to a child who isn't expected to understand. He always seems exhausted, grunting and groaning when he has to stand up or do anything, but you only have to see his eyes to know there's a bottomless reserve of spirit that could march him through an endless winter night.

He kept contact with all his political friends, and whenever they'd uncovered corruption or scandal, they'd tell my father. They were too afraid to mention it over the phone, not daring to speak above a whisper even in person. I'd sit at the top of the stairs out of sight while they talked though, and all those things they were too afraid to even think out loud would be spoken clearly on papa's show.

First came the letter. Polite, formal, from the Ministry of Communications. I'd picked up the mail and opened it because I was impressed by the official government stamp. I thought Dad had won some kind of award for his show. He didn't smile often, and I wanted to be the one who made it happen.

Instead, I found a generic letter informing papa that his channel was in violation of slander laws and needed to be closed. It thanked him for his "attempt at public service", even listing a variety of other "safe" topics that he could talk about instead. That same night, after everyone but papa had gone to sleep, we were woken by a splintering-crashing sound. We found papa standing in the living room holding a brick, staring out our broken window, his bathrobe fluttering in the freezing wind like some kind of battle flag. Mom was horrified, but papa was grinning from ear-to-ear.

"Они только пытаются заткнуть вас, если вам что-то стоит сказать." They only try to shut you up if you have something worth saying.

It was another four months before the next incident. My older brother was expelled from the University. They told him that they'd received multiple anonymous reports about his disorderly and rebellious behavior, but he swore up and down that he never did anything. We all thought that he was covering up something until that night when a second brick came through our window. The message couldn't have been clearer, but neither could papa's response.

His influence was expanding. He had several investigators reporting to him at all hours of the day and night. Over 10,000 subscribers. Every day a new video, a voice of reason cutting through the miles of red tape and political side-talk. Turning on the TV or reading the newspaper, it was impossible to tell what was real. Papa says uncertainty is a seed which grows into fear. That must be true, because I didn't know what was going to happen next, and I was afraid all the time.

Mom lost her teaching job shortly after. The school said that parents were concerned she wasn't sticking to the syllabus, instead feeding her own propaganda into the class. No one had ever complained to mom about it, and she said she'd never so much as mentioned politics (she taught math). She tried to get an appeal with the board, but after the meeting there were tears in her eyes and she wouldn't say a word about what happened. She'd taught at that school for the last 21 years. There wasn't another brick that night, but there didn't need to be. In the morning I found her teaching award from the governor in the trash, along with a carefully folded Russian flag.

Papa didn't stop, and no one asked him to. Not even when he started receiving death threats in the mail. He was arrested twice, first taking him at the grocery store for spreading libel. He was only gone a few days that time, but when he came back, he was more insistent than ever. He was working on something big. Something that would change Russia—change the world, even. Wherever someone in power feared what the truth could do to him, things would change.

They didn't give him the chance though. The second arrest happened at our house with someone knocking on the door. They didn't even bother to tell him why he was being arrested that time, but he didn't resist. That made me angry. Someone coming into our house and dragging him away from his family—he always told me he was a fighter. The silent, willing man who they marched into the night didn't look like a fighter to me.

The harassment only got worse while he was gone. Friends and neighbors who had known us for years stopped talking to us, turning the other way when we said hello. People at school treated me like I had an infectious disease. There was a rumor going around that my father was an anarchist. I heard everything—about his treason, his hatred for Russia, even accounts of how he raped and killed someone.

Defending him only made it worse for me, but I couldn't help it. I hit a boy in the mouth when he kept telling me I had to go to the station and suck someone's cock to get papa out. I wasn't even sure I wanted papa to be released. That's what I was thinking sitting outside the principal's office, waiting to be expelled like my brother was. I wanted papa to disappear—to have never existed at all. I was so angry that I almost stormed off right then, but I'm glad I didn't because I was able to hear what the principal was saying behind his door.

He was talking about my father. The person he spoke with sounded like he was giving the principal orders.

"Уничтожьте его семью," he said. Destroy his family.

Then the man starting listing things off, as calm and clear as though he was ordering food at a drive-through.

"Скажите ученикам, что его сыновья тоже предатели." Tell the students his sons are traitors too.

"Его дом должен быть сожжен." His house must be burned.

"Его жена должна быть изнасилована." His wife must be raped.

All done before next week when papa was to be released. The principal didn't even hesitate.

"Будет сделано," he replied. It will be done.

I didn't wait for the door to open. I ran home—7 miles, but I didn't stop once. I wasn't even angry anymore. I understand how pointless it is being angry at something that big and powerful. It would be like cursing the ocean for its waves. I also understand why papa was so compliant with being arrested. You can't fight something like that. It was fear, not anger, which kept me moving—desperately trying to think how I could explain this to Mom, and where we could sleep tonight where they wouldn't find us.

That fear—that numbing, helpless, lonely fear—was all I had to keep me company while I ran. And when the pain in my side came like a knife between my ribs and my legs trembled as I lifted them from the concrete—that fear was stronger. I just kept marveling at how powerful a thing fear can be—stronger than pain, or loyalty, or even human empathy. I thought it must be the strongest force there is in the world, and that must be why the government uses it to control us.

The fear that right and wrong don't matter when you are one and they are many. But it's a ridiculous fear, because the cowering people are the ones who are many. And it seems to me the government must know that too; they only try to frighten us because they are frightened of us. They're scared of us not being scared anymore. And how do we stop from being scared?

Papa said uncertainty grows into fear, so we must leave no doubt. I warned my mom and brother, but neither of them have left yet. They're helping me sort through papa's notes and recordings. We're going to find what he was working on when they took him. We're going to find what they were so afraid of, and we're going to release it to the world.

There's no uncertainty about it anymore. I'm not afraid, even though I know I will be arrested or killed for this. And when the word gets out that uncertainty will be gone from the people too. We are many and they are one. And it is their turn to be afraid.

THE TAKING TREE

MY EARLIEST MEMORY OF GRANDMA ELIAS WAS A SUNDAY MORNING AT her house. The eggs were firm and golden and the hash-browns were burned, just like they were supposed to be. Everything at Grandma's house was exactly right, all the way from the Christmas lights which never came down to her little corgi Muffins who followed her like a shadow. It was time for church, but I didn't want to leave.

"How come Grandma doesn't have to go to church?" I asked.

"She already knows all that stuff," my mother said, forcing me into a jacket like meat through a grinder. "You still have to learn though."

Grandma stuck out her tongue and waggled it about behind mom's back. I wasn't amused. It wasn't fair.

"Don't you want to visit God?" I asked Grandma.

"God doesn't live in a church, silly," Grandma Elias said. "He lives in that crab-apple tree in my backyard. Would you like to meet him?"

"Yes! Can we mom? Instead of church?"

I recognized mom's expression from the time she accidentally drank sour milk. "Absolutely not. Please don't joke about that kind of stuff, Elias. You know how impressionable they can be."

Grandma shrugged and winked. "I was counting on it. Another time then."

She didn't mention it again though, and I forgot all about the God in her apple tree. The subject didn't come up again until years later when I was in the 10th grade. Mom was in the hospital to remove some ovarian cyst, and I'd been left at Grandma's for a few days while she recovered. Every morning I'd wake up to find Grandma kneeling beside her apple tree, digging around its roots. I assumed she was just pulling weeds or something until I caught her burying a row of sealed Tupperware filled with leftovers.

"Is that for God?" I asked, suddenly remembering what she'd said when I was young.

"Yes. I wanted to thank him for looking after your mother."

"So it's like a prayer?"

She shook her head. "Is that what they teach you in that dusty old Sunday school? No, you must never ask God and for anything. You must only thank him for what he has already done."

I watched as she carefully patted the soil into place.

"Is he going to eat it?" I asked.

"What are you asking me for?" She moved to put her hand on the tree and invited me to do the same. I did so without thinking, but jerked away immediately. The bark was warm and pliable like rough skin. My fingers were still tingling, almost vibrating as though a whisper, too deep to decipher, still echoed through my body.

Grandma Elias just laughed and turned to go inside. Somehow I didn't feel like staying there alone.

Mom was released from the hospital shortly after, but a few days later she started getting sharp pains and had to go back in. No-one told me what was going on, but that alone made me know it wasn't good. I made a point of setting my alarm for the crack of dawn so I could watch Grandma digging around the roots of her tree. I waited until she left to investigate and see if there were any treats I could steal.

The first thing I uncovered were the Tupperware. They were all empty. Absolutely clean, like they'd gone through the dishwasher. I figure she must have traded them out for her latest donation, so I kept digging into the newly disturbed earth. The soil was damp here, but I kept going until I uncovered a patch of golden fur. Muffin was buried under the tree.

I was trembling from head to foot while I slowly covered up the little body again. It wasn't just the horror of what I found either; I could feel the vibrations emanating from the tree. The bark was so hot to the touch that it almost scalded me, but I forced my hand to remain to feel the hum of the presence. Not quite a sound, not quite a thought, but something suspended between flooded my senses.

I wasn't myself in that instant. I was looking through Grandma's eyes as she sat on her bed, hands clasped and shaking. I was in a hospital room watching a daytime soap opera on the television in the corner of the room. I was a hundred people doing a hundred things, thinking a hundred thoughts, dreading a hundred futures, and then it was gone. It was just me standing before the tree, panting for breath, staring at my swollen red fingertips that still stung from where they'd touched the rough skin.

I was scared and confused, but I didn't speak of it to anyone. Grandma didn't say a word about why Muffin wasn't in the yard anymore, and I didn't ask. She seemed to be in a better mood afterward though, singing or whistling to herself wherever she went. Then a few hours later we got a call from the hospital—that it had been a false alarm and that mom was already on her way to pick me up. For the first time, I was only too happy to leave Grandma's house.

A couple years later and I'd left my hometown to go to college. I got swept up in the daily dramas of life and didn't look back. Not until I visited again Junior year to help Grandma Elias start to pack up her home. She'd grown too old to look after the place herself, and she'd decided to move into a facility. All the conversations had been light and optimistic as though this would make her life so much easier, so I wasn't prepared for the shock of seeing her again.

The electric wheelchair was the first surprise. My family isn't exactly open about their problems, and nobody had told me that her arthritis was so bad that she couldn't even walk or open doors anymore. Her face was dried and loose, and her eyes were deep and sunken. I looked up the place she was moving into, only to discover it wasn't a retirement home at all: it was a hospice. My mom still kept talking about all the friends Grandma would make there, and Grandma said she was looking forward to the activities and the company. They were living in stubborn denial, and I couldn't take it.

"The only thing I'll miss is my garden and my tree," Grandma said, looking around her old home. "It's not like I can get down on my knees and dig anyway though, so I suppose it's for the best."

Luckily I knew where God lived, and I was sure he'd intervene. A small bribe or offering wasn't going to cut it though. It had been a life for a life when my mother was sick, and I was ready to pay that price again. The more I thought about it, the more sure I was that I could follow through. This wouldn't be a thank you gift though, and I had no intention of being subtle and simply hoping for the best. In other words, I felt that it had to be human, the most valuable thing I could think to offer.

The digging took a lot longer than expected. I came back with a shovel that night. Grandma Elias hadn't moved out yet, but I was comfortable in the familiar darkness and didn't make too much noise. When I finished the hole, I'd go find some drunk coming home from the bar and knock him out. Push him into the hole and cover him up. No one would ever know—not even Grandma.

If Muffin was still here, then he would have set off the alarm by now, but I couldn't even find the little body anymore. I kept at it for a few hours until the hole was a little longer than I was tall. I hopped inside to test its depth and found the earthen walls rose almost to my chest. That should be plenty. I started to climb out again, grabbing one of the roots for support while I pulled myself up. The root was fire, and I let go immediately, reeling backward to nurse my injured hand. I overbalanced and was about to fall, but something lashed out of the darkness to snatch me around a flailing arm.

I stared in dumb shock at the root twined around my arm for several seconds before the burning began to penetrate my long-sleeved shirt. The intensity of the heat was increasing by the second. I scrambled in the opposite direction, trying to hoist myself out of the hole without touching the tree. I barely got two steps before another blast of heat penetrating my ankle and dragged me to the ground. Back up to my knees, but an irresistible weight flattened me back to the ground. The heat of the roots withdrew, but the weight was increasing by the second.

Dirt and rocks were raining around me so hard it felt like a hail storm. The roots were sweeping all the piled earth directly on top of me. I managed to raise myself onto my elbows and knees to create a small air pocket, but I could go no farther. The last of the meager starlight quenched above me, and I was buried alive. I could still hear the muffled sound of the dirt packing in tighter above me for a little while, but it was becoming fainter and more distant by the second. Another sound was replacing it, the same vibrating whispers I'd heard all those years ago.

Part of me was still braced on my hands and knees in the darkness, but I hardly noticed anymore because I was also sitting on a hilltop and staring at the stars with a beautiful girl warm against me. I was sleeping in a bed—a hundred bodies in a hundred beds, all breathing slow and regular. And every passing second made me aware of a hundred new people, experiencing their bodies and hearing their maddening cacophony of thoughts. I was grieving, and celebrating, in ecstasy and agony, all so real that it might as well have been my own body experiencing these things.

It kept going. Faster and faster until the part of me that was buried under the tree was so insignificant that I hardly remembered it. Within moments I must have been every man, woman, and child on the planet, all their experiences mingling into a single omnipresent hum of consciousness. I felt myself being born in ceaseless explosions of sensation, and just as often did I feel myself die, snuffing out entirely. But each coming and going didn't matter, because I could feel the hum everywhere and in everything, eternal and immune from the fluctuations of its composition.

The feeling didn't last. One by one, then in hundreds and thousands at a time, those minds closed to me. My awareness was shrinking again, and my shaking body buried underground and my shallow breaths were becoming more real. Soon I had but one mind, one body, one life, and one desperate urge to not let this slip away like the others. I began to wiggle back and forth, using my small opening to continue displacing dirt above my back. I managed to make enough space to get my feet underneath me, and then the additional power of my legs helped to push upward through the earth. The air was thick and heavy with my own stale breath, but the higher I got, the less densely packed the soil was. My head was growing light, and I was afraid I'd pass out, but my hand broke through the surface and a clean cold gust of air filled my greedy lungs.

Inch by laborious inch, I widened the hole and crawled back onto the surface to lay panting on the ground. I thought I was alone until I heard Grandma Elias' voice only a few feet away.

"Well? Did you get what you asked for?"

I was too weak to do anything but lift my head. She was wearing a bathrobe, sitting in her wheelchair with her wrinkled hands folded demurely in her lap. She seemed as frail and ancient as ever.

"Asking doesn't work, does it?"

I managed to shake my head. I thought she'd be angry or disappointed, but she only smiled.

"When your mother was sick, I did something terrible. I asked God to make her better. She was going to get better anyway, but I didn't know that. I thought that if I gave up a life, then I could protect a life. The tree doesn't stop death though—it gives us something much more valuable than that."

"You're still going to die, aren't you?" I asked, unable to help myself.

"Does that frighten you?" she asked.

I said nothing. I'd felt what it was like to die. A drop of rain in the ocean, gone in an instant but still part of the whole.

"Me neither," she said, "and that is the true gift of the tree."

HAVE YOU SEEN THIS CHILD?

I DON'T HAVE ANY KIDS, SO I CAN'T REALLY IMAGINE WHAT IT WOULD BE like to have one missing. I do have a half-coyote dog who used to sneak out of the yard all the time though (Colonel Wallace), so I at least have a general idea how desperate and helpless it feels to have part of your life suddenly go missing.

Like grief, it comes in stages.

The denial: I just saw him a moment ago, I'm sure he's around here somewhere.

Anger: it's his own fault, bloody idiot. If he gets run over by a car, then I'm getting a turtle next time.

Bargaining: missing posters. Flyers in local groups. Calling every shelter in a ten-mile radius...

And so on, although I'm not sure any mother will ever fully reach the "acceptance" stage. Once they hit depression, it just loops back to denial and starts all over again. That's the feeling I got from reading the advertisement, anyway.

"Timmy Preston, age 7. Missing two weeks. Last seen in the Jefferson Heights playground. If you have any information on his whereabouts, please contact (818)-***-****. I never turn the lights off anymore in case it helps him find his way home, but the house has never been so dark. I'm not old enough to shake like this. Please have mercy on a grieving mother."

It was the first time I've ever seen a Facebook ad for a missing person, but I guess it makes sense. They allow you to target specific locations, and Jefferson Heights is only a few blocks away from my apartment. Next time Colonel Wallace finds a new angle to dig through my bushes, I might have to try that too.

Was I going to gather a mob and start combing through the city? No. There's too much tragedy in the world to chase down every wrongdoing. But that message really stuck with me, and so did the kid's photo: bright blue eyes, a sweep of blond hair, and a light drizzle of freckles. I took a screenshot on my phone just in case, then forgot all about it.

Until the next day. And the day after. And the one after that. I don't know how much money that lady was dumping into advertising, but that post never seemed to go away. Shit, now there's a sobering thought. The only thing worse than losing a kid would be draining the rest of your resources trying to find someone who couldn't be found. I once read an article about a woman who mortgaged her house to pay a private investigator to track down her daughter. The kid was never found, and the woman was driven to homelessness when she couldn't make the payments. I don't remember exactly what the quote was, but it was something like: "Do I regret it? Of course not. Getting me onto the streets will only make it easier for me to keep looking."

Well I still didn't search for Timmy. Not consciously anyway. I began walking my dog on a different route though—one that circled around Jefferson Heights and the surrounding neighborhoods. I didn't expect to see him, but that image was burned into my mind enough that I'd notice if I did.

I'd notice a blond kid with freckles peeking out over a fence. I'd notice how quickly he disappeared and ran back into the house, like he was afraid of being caught. I stood staring, not quite believing what I saw. An exact match of the screenshot on my phone—I called the number immediately, reporting what I found.

The woman on the other line was hysterical. She thanked me a dozen times. She said that was her ex-husband's house, although he denied ever seeing the boy. She told me she was going to call the police right away, and that I might want to get out of there if I didn't want to get involved.

I'm not ashamed to say I felt like the world's biggest hero for the rest of the day. At least until the evening news when I saw that familiar picture flash once more.

"Timmy Preston, abducted from his legal guardian," the local news reported. I turned up the volume, half-expecting to hear the woman thank me by name. "Taken from his backyard this afternoon."

I turned off the TV and just stared at the blank screen. I guess I'm still in the denial phase.

WHEN YOU DIE IN A DREAM

THE WIND PUMMELED ME AS I DOVE THROUGH THE LOWER ATMOSPHERE. My eyes were watering so bad that I couldn't see straight, although I don't know if it would have mattered considering how the landscape blurred from my speed. All I could distinguish was the looming wall of earth growing exponentially as I hurtle closer and closer, needle sized trees growing into a behemoth's grasping claws, until...

Right before impact, I wake up gasping. I've had that dream at least once every few months since I was four.

There are others too. I remember fighting in one of them. Some kind of a street brawl with dozens of swirling bodies dancing to choreographed violence. First I'll be pushing the other combatant back, then he'll push me, back and forth, back and forth. Until I'm about to land the finishing blow and he whips out a gun. I hear the sound, and see the flare of the muzzle, and my whole body tenses for a force it can't resist, but...

Right before impact, I wake up gasping.

So what would happen if I didn't wake up? Would I feel the bullet, like I felt the wind and the swinging blows? Would the dream dissolve into some unspeakable hellscape where I continue to experience the beyond? Or would I never wake up at all?

I finally got my answer thanks to a teenage girl who couldn't wait five minutes to text her friend back. Her left wheel slipped over the double yellow line, and her bumper clipped my car going 45 in the opposite direction. Before I knew what was happening, I suddenly felt the impact absent from my dreams all those years.

It didn't last more than a second. A wave of pressure too intense to be pain washed over my body. My face slammed into the airbag which felt like it was full of sand. All the light in the world constricted into a pinprick, the screeching roar devouring me until only a ringing tingle remained, and then silence.

I was out cold and didn't dream that time. I was pretty disoriented when I woke up in the hospital, but I remember grabbing the arm of a nurse and begging her not to let me fall back asleep.

"I know how it feels to die now!" I told her. Or at least I tried. My words were slurring, and I couldn't be making much sense. A moment later I felt a sting in my arm, and my vision swam.

The next thing I felt was the wind stinging my face and whipping the tears from my eyes. I was far enough up to see the curvature of the earth, but I couldn't appreciate the magnificent sight knowing what was to come. I could picture the impact so clearly now. Part of me knew I was still in the hospital bed, but I was so fixated on the rush that I couldn't convince myself it wasn't real.

This was a hundred times worse than the accident. Everything happened too fast in the car for me to be afraid, but this time I had a few minutes of excruciating anticipation. My stomach was a knot of snakes trying to strangle each other. The air flooding into my lungs was thin this high up, but it came so fast that I felt like I was perpetually caught between breaths.

I wanted to wake up so bad. I screamed the best I could, thrashing around and hoping that the nurse would notice my disturbance. I tried to convince myself that I could fly, but the rush wouldn't stop. I tried to spit, disgusted to feel the saliva dribble down my chin, unaffected by the surrounding torrent. I'm still in bed! This isn't real! But it felt real. And when my body was obliterated on the ground, I just knew that was going to feel real too.

Watching the ground speed toward me was torture. Closing my eyes and bracing for an unpredictable collision was even worse. I had a glimmer of hope when I heard the nurse speaking, her voice distant and muffled from the wind. A last desperate call for help, but I couldn't reach her. The muffled voice grew even fainter as it mingled with the city noises below.

No trees or branches to slow my fall. No water or soft earth to dampen the blow. Just concrete and asphalt for as far as I could see.

The landing was everything I knew it would be. I smashed through the roof of an apartment building, legs first. I felt my bones in my feet pulverizing to dust, but the shock wave was so brutal that I could feel my skeleton rearranging throughout my body. The roof caved in beneath me, and I tumbled through in a hail of broken tiles and splintered debris. There was a brief, horrible moment where my body knew it was dead but my brain hadn't caught up yet, and then...

Right after impact, I wake up gasping.

The clattering of the falling debris was still ringing in my ears, but it was over. Disoriented, I got up and staggered toward the bathroom. Even though I knew it was a dream, it was a relief to feel my intact body responding to my commands. At least it means I walked away from the car accident without too severe injuries...

The car accident. The hospital. But I wasn't in the hospital, where was I? I rubbed my eyes, finally noticing the giant hole in the ceiling of my apartment. And the twisted remains of a corpse on my floor. I almost threw up. Taking a step closer to inspect, I could no longer deny the bile rising in my throat. My dead body was lying in the middle of the room. In the distance, the blare of sirens cemented the absurd scene into reality.

I rushed to the bathroom and hurled in the sink. It took a few moments of heaving and spluttering before I was able to pull away and look into the mirror. I didn't recognize the face staring back.

THUMP THUMP THUMP—pounding on the door. I nearly jumped out of my unfamiliar skin.

"We heard an explosion. Are you okay in there?"

THUMP THUMP THUMP—my heart playing along. This was a

dream. I was still in the hospital. I had to wake up. The pounding on the door was getting louder, and I couldn't think straight. I ran to the balcony to get some fresh air, noticing that I was still over a dozen stories in the air. Someone was trying to force the door now, and I didn't have the stomach to stand over my dead body and attempt to explain the macabre situation. I swung my legs over the metal railing, and hesitating only a second, let myself fall again.

This time I'll wake up for sure…

The wind. The snakes in my belly. The scream of onlookers, and the full body immersion of pain. Next I knew, I was gasping for air. People were screaming all around me, so I started screaming too.

I heard a shrill, piercing shriek tear from my lungs. I clapped a hand over my mouth—a shriveled old hand, frail with a road map of bulging veins. I staggered away from the scene on the sidewalk against a stream of people. They're crowding to see the broken body of the poor fool who nose-dived from an apartment balcony a dozen stories up.

THUMP THUMP—my weary heart fluttering as I stared at my reflection in a car window. An old woman was staring back at me, her face distraught and confused. I watched one of her hands raise to her face and felt the leathery skin beneath trembling fingertips. THUMP THUMP THUMP—my heart going faster and faster, the strain of half-filled arteries vainly trying to keep up, then a sharp pain radiating through my chest. A heart attack this time, and I was dying again.

I had no disillusion about it this time. I continued watching my reflection for as long as I could stand until all color faded from my face and the pain in my chest had echoed into an all-encompassing throb. My vision swam, and everything started to slip away...

I've died twice more since writing that. If I'm careful, it seems like I can last a few hours before something gets me. Almost as if it's the will of the universe to track me down and snuff me out. I'm writing this to keep some record of what is happening while I still have a chance.

I think I always used to wake up because my brain had no experience of death to relate to. It's not really the impact waking you up at all, merely the shock of your scrambling brain saying "oh shit, what comes next?"

If you've led an easy life, I don't suppose you have anything to fear. If you've never broken a bone, or suffered a trauma, then the near-death experience is a safety valve that will shield from this revolving nightmare. But if you've suffered exquisitely in life and your mind knows how to retrace that dark path?

Even death won't be an escape.

DEAD DOGS DON'T DO TRICKS

THE BEST THING ABOUT DEAD DOGS IS THAT YOU DON'T HAVE TO FEED them.

The worst? Probably the smell...

That's what mom complains about, anyway. She thinks there's a gas leak under the house; she'd never let me keep Misty if she knew where the smell was really coming from. It was hard for me to keep a straight face when she called the company to complain, but I don't think she noticed my guilt. When mom is angry, she isn't very good with minor details like me.

This all started about two months ago. I wanted a dog. Dad wanted a dog. Mom didn't want dad. So we got a dog and called ourselves a happy family. Misty was a lean greyhound with a white patch on her chest like a plume of lace. I thought she looked like an alien because she was so skinny, but that was part of her charm. She was pretty skittish and didn't like being held, but she could always sense when I was feeling down and would run to plop her head in my lap.

Misty was the magic pill that was supposed to fix my family, and it worked for a while. Whenever anyone raised their voice, Misty would start scampering around or whimpering and the argument fizzled out. It didn't matter which side was right: if you scared Misty while trying to prove your point, then you've already lost the moral high ground.

My parents adapted. They learned to fight in a chilly monotone that was even worse than yelling. Misty could sense the tension in the air too, and I know it made her nervous. I tried telling my parents, but they insisted that they were speaking in ordinary voices and that I was imagining things. What could a twelve-year-old boy possibly understand about grownup matters or animal psychology?

Well here's something I learned: nervous dogs have accidents inside the house. A little damp spot on the carpet, sometimes a poop on the kitchen tile—no big deal, right? Wrong. It was the little extra stress that pushed my parents over the edge. Suddenly Misty took on a new therapeutic role as the household scapegoat.

Monthly bills higher than expected? Yell at the dog for being too expensive.

Dad sleeps in and doesn't have time for his morning walk? Yell at the dog for making a mess.

Family drifting apart? Yell at the dog for preventing a weekend getaway.

"Don't listen to them," I tried to tell Misty. She slept on the foot of my bed, and I could feel her trembling as my parent's voices filtered through the wall. "They're all bark and no bite. You'd understand if you were human like me."

The louder they got, the more she whined. Then doors started slamming, and the whine turned into a long howl. Mom ripped open my bedroom door and started screaming at us—Dad was in the living room dragging a suitcase toward the front door.

"Shut that thing up!" she yelled. "No wonder we're stressed, listening to that damn howling all the time."

He was leaving—fine, what do I care? But they had no right to treat Misty that way. Misty must have agreed too: the moment Dad opened the front door, Misty bolted. I'd never seen her move so fast, leaping straight over the couch like a flying deer. Dad dropped his suitcase and chased after her, and I was close behind.

The shouting was bad. The swearing was bad. The screech of tires on asphalt and the wet thud to follow were much, much worse. The little gray body was hauled out of the street, hanging limp in my dad's arms.

"Dead on impact," he grunted, dropping the body on the sidewalk. "She didn't suffer."

That was the first time Misty stayed still enough for me to hold her.

My dad was screaming at the man climbing out of his car. Mom was screaming at dad for leaving the door open. The driver was screaming at both of them. No one seemed to notice me burying my face in Misty's wet fur. I couldn't help but wonder whether they'd be acting the same if I was the one who wasn't moving. It was too much to handle—I dropped the stiffening body and ran blindly down the street in my pajamas.

My heart had never beaten so fast as when I sprinted away from that horror. And it never stopped so suddenly as when I heard the pattering feet behind me.

Misty was following me, gaining swiftly. I looked back at the arena illuminated by street lamps in front of my house. My parents were still yelling at the driver. Eyes back to the dog—the crushed face clearly stiff and dead. I could even see patches of exposed brain where the skull had caved in.

Misty didn't seem to notice. She just sat at my feet, white eyes staring at me, tongue lolling a little too far from the mouth to be fully attached at the base.

"We got to hide you," I said. In retrospect, I guess I should have been afraid, but at the time I was just relieved. I needed her, and she needed me, and everything else was someone else's problem as long as we didn't lose each other.

I looped around and let myself in the back door, my parents still arguing out front. I slipped Misty into my room and hid her under the bed. Then I lay on the floor to reassure her.

"Don't let mom or dad see you, okay? They wouldn't understand."

Misty seemed to nod, part of her jaw slipping loose for a moment as she did.

"You aren't hurting, are you?"

Misty shakes her head. I pat her, trying not to wince at the damp, cool skin.

"You understand me though. Hey, you know how to shake hands?"

She didn't, but it didn't take more than a minute for her to learn. By then my parents were coming back inside, so I jumped in bed and pulled the covers up. The door cracked open. I rolled away from the lance of light. The tension of hesitation, and then the door closed again.

I didn't speak a word about Misty the next day. Neither did Mom. Dad wasn't there, and neither of us mentioned that either. It's okay though, because I had a secret that I couldn't wait to get back to.

I spent a lot of time in my room after that. Or out after dark—any excuse to be with Misty. She never made a sound, and she never left my side. She'd always stare at me, prompt and ready for anything. Watching shows? She let me use her as a pillow. Late night bike ride? She was my shadow, a phantom just beyond the street lamps.

It wasn't just tricks she was learning anymore either. She mimicked everything I did. If I started brushing my teeth, Misty would lean up on the counter and lift her paw. She tried to wiggle into my pajamas when I got ready for bed, and when I whisper for her to hide, she whispers back.

"I hide," she'd say, each syllable laborious and strange from her mouth. "Hide and quiet."

It gave me the shudders the first time I heard it. Of course it was amazing, but listening to her struggling with the words made me think of a deaf person slurring things he can't hear.

"You don't have to speak," I told her.

The dog smiled, an unnatural expression which barred her fangs. "I will be... just like you."

I still loved Misty, but something changed after that. I felt like the more she understood me, the less I understood her. I also started catching her doing more things without me. I woke up in the middle of the night once to find her missing, although she was there again when I woke in the morning. Then once in the bathroom alone—she was just leaning on the counter and staring into the mirror.

"Happy face," she said, trying to smile.

"Angry face," she said, the expression only changing subtly.

"I love you... mommy... thank you... for breakfast," she said, working her way slowly through each word.

She wasn't just learning how to be like me. She was learning how to be me. I think that's the first time I was actually scared of her.

I couldn't exactly confide in Mom. She's been worse than ever since Dad left. She doesn't come home until late at night, and she's always ready to snap at the first thing she sees. So I just kept the secret to myself. And every day, I got a little more scared.

"Happy face," Misty said, and she really did smile. Her teeth even looked a little more human.

"Angry face," she said. I never noticed her having eyebrows before, but they were clearly furrowed.

This is about the time she started walking on her hind legs too. She fell over a lot at first, but within a couple of days she almost moved naturally. She wore a pair of my underwear because the elastic was the only thing that she could keep on. It bothered me, but I didn't tell her so. I didn't like it when she looked at me anymore. It felt too much like I was being studied.

This goes on for about two weeks before Dad comes home again. I lock my door as soon as I hear my parents talking in the living room. The tension in the air is like suspended electricity before a storm. That voice they're using—the strained, fake normal they used not to scare the dog—it's an explosion waiting to happen. It takes less than 30 seconds before the voices start to rise, and they begin talking over each other.

A silent lull—I press my ear to the door. Then I flinch as something glass smashes—a picture frame, maybe?

"Run," the voice under my bed whispers. Misty starts to drag herself out. I knew she was under there from the smell, but I didn't even recognize her. The joints were a little wrong, the face a bit elongated, but otherwise I might as well have been looking into a mirror.

"You're drunk," my mom shouts. "Get out and stay out!"

"Out of my own house? Goddamn idiot."

"Let go! You're hurting me!"

"The window," Misty urges. There's another smash from the living room. I can't make out the words anymore—the screaming is incoherent. I slide through the window and drop onto the grass below. Turning around, I see my bedroom door closing. Misty is nowhere to be seen.

"Mom, Dad. Please stop fighting." The voice distant, muffled, but unmistakably mine.

Three full seconds of silence. Then the screaming. Somewhere in that awful din, I heard my own voice say: "Can't you see what it's doing to me?"

I waited a full hour before going back in the house. My parents were in their room, speaking softly. Misty was waiting on the couch, grinning with human teeth.

I don't know if things are going to get better from here, but if they get worse... well Misty is looking out for me, and she's figured out some tricks of her own.

BLOOD GAMES

I WAS ALMOST FRIENDS WITH A MONSTER WHEN I WAS ELEVEN YEARS old. I would have preferred a human friend, but my family had just moved to a new city where everyone was cold and distant. My father promised that I would meet new people at school, but there were still a few weeks of summer and I had nothing to do.

Elisa Williams was the one I really wanted to be friends with. She lived next door in a beautiful gray house with a high-fenced yard. I used to sit with my back to the fence and listen to her playing and giggling; the sound bubbling up like music made for everyone but me.

I wasn't brave enough to introduce myself, but after a few days of moping around the house, my mother volunteered to do it for me. I stood behind her, carrying a basket of cookies while she knocked on the neighbor's door.

"Elisa!" The man who opened it looked like a poorly shaved bear. "Get over here and meet your new friend."

"We're busy!" came the shrill response from somewhere deeper in the house.

My mother marveled about the woodworking and craftsmanship and asked the age of the venerable structure.

"Now, Elisa!" the bear bellowed. "I know you're alone up there."

A short, angry sigh, like what circus lions must do before they're forced onto the stage. Then footsteps creaking down the stairs.

"I've got cookies!" I supplied hopefully.

"Elisa spends all day playing by herself," the bear said. "She's been so lonely since her mother passed. Some company will be good for her."

I thought about the giggling I heard through the fence, and I didn't understand how someone could have such a good time on their own.

Elisa appeared a moment later, her head hanging low in surly obedience. She wore shorts and long socks pulled halfway up her thighs: one bright green and the other purple. That's all I really saw, because I was so embarrassed that I couldn't look up from the basket of cookies I held out.

Elisa snatched the whole basket and briskly turned around again. I glimpsed a wave of black hair, curly like her father's, but not so wild. After a few steps she turned to glare over her shoulder with the resentful expression a vegan might give a BBQ.

"Well? Are you coming or not?"

I hadn't taken my second step before she cut in.

"Shoes off." I hasted to obey. "No, the socks stay on. What are you, some kind of barbarian?"

"No ma'am." I don't know why I said that, but I was scared of her and I didn't want to give her any reason to send me away.

Elisa seemed satisfied with the answer though, and she permitted me to follow her up the stairs toward her room. I felt like I was on solid ground until she said:

"We don't need any more friends. None of our games have room for a third person."

"Your dad said—"

"He isn't my dad. He killed my father and took me prisoner."

"Um—"

"Oh yes," Elisa said, pivoting her socked-heel on the wooden floor so smoothly that she seemed to almost float. "But that's okay, because sometimes he brings me little boys to eat."

I could only hope that my stunned silence was mistaken for composure. Elisa rolled her eyes and opened the door to her room.

"Just kidding. You're not stupid, are you?"

I was holding my breath, too afraid to even reply.

"I'm sorry. That wasn't a fair question. Most stupid people don't know they're stupid, and I suppose it's perfectly fine if you are as long as you don't try to perform surgery, or vote, or do anything a normal person would do," Elisa rambled.

The stairway and hall we passed were heavily decorated with framed portraits, hanging tapestries, and ornate tables littered with precious and intricate things.

It was a stark contrast to Elisa's room which had a simple metal-frame bed in the corner and a dark-wood cabinet on the other side. The walls were painted black, and the window was concealed beneath a thick curtain. There was nothing on the hard-wood floor to disrupt the monastic austerity.

"How do you play games without any toys?" I asked.

"We play blood games," she said sternly, stressing the plural again. "The kind that need magic to work. You do know about magic, don't you?"

"Yeah sure. Of course." I didn't want to say anything more to betray my ignorance. I reached for a cookie from the basket, but she slapped my hand away. I stood in disbelief as she ate one of the cookies herself.

"My mother taught me after she passed," Elisa said casually, moving to set the cookies on the cabinet. She retrieved something and turned to face me again. "If you want to play, then you'll need to give me your hand."

"What do you mean after she passed?" I tentatively stretched out to her.

"Now close your eyes."

She could have told me to jump out the window and I probably would have done it. She had the sweetest smile on her face, and the soft brush of her fingers tracing my palm made me blush. I closed my eyes and took a deep breath.

"Don't scream. Mother hates screamers."

I opened my eyes a sliver, just in time to see a metallic flash in the air. Elisa's grip tightened around my wrist while her free hand gouged a needle into the center of my palm.

I didn't scream exactly. It was more of a shrieking yelping sound, like a rabbit trying skydiving for the first time. I tore my hand away with the needle still in it, blood freely running between my fingers.

"Come back here!" Elisa shouted. "You're going to make a mess!"

We both dashed for the door. I hesitated to avoid running into her, but she pushed me aside and didn't slow until she'd slammed the door shut and locked it from the inside.

"You're wasting the blood. Give me your hand."

"No! You'll stab me again!" I gingerly pulled the needle out of the skin, prompting a fresh swell of blood. I felt dizzy.

"Baby." She snorted. That hurt slightly more than the needle. "You're already bleeding, so I don't need to stab you again as long as you play along. Here, wipe some on me."

She offered me the back of her hand. Bewildered, I rubbed a long smear of blood on her pale skin. Her dark eyes sparkled as she watched with eager fascination.

I almost took the opportunity to flee, but I couldn't resist asking: "How does blood magic work?"

"Mother said that when the world was young, all living things were connected and the same blood flowed from one to the next." Elisa plucked the needle from my fingers and pricked her clean hand daintily to draw forth a single drop of blood. "We started to fight one another though, and it got worse and worse until we had to pull apart into separate entities. We became so distant that we started taking different shapes, and some animals even preyed upon others until we forgot that we were ever the same. The blood is the only part of us that never forgot."

Using the nail of one index finger, she deftly traced a pattern in my blood. A circle, with a triangle inside, and a square inside that, and perhaps even a tiny pentagon within.

With deep concentration she pressed the single drop of her blood into the center of the design.

"Now what are you doing?" I asked.

She smiled, but the gesture seemed strained and unnatural, like a dog baring its teeth for a dog food commercial.

"Duh," she said. "I'm making magic."

And she was. The pattern of blood on her hand was glowing. Soft at first, but growing brighter in even pulses. My heart began to race with excitement, and the pulsing light increased to match its rhythm.

"What's it do?" I asked.

"I'm going to grow you a friend," she said. "That's what you want, isn't it?"

I wanted to tell her that I didn't need a friend anymore because I had her. But we don't always get what we want, even from ourselves. Especially from ourselves.

"Yeah sure. That's what I came here for," I said.

"Okay watch."

The light grew stronger, but I couldn't look away. The pattern was moving now. The triangle was turning within the circle, and the square within that, which moved in the opposite direction. And from the center grew a red stalk, like a time-lapse growth struggling through her skin to sprout and curl into the air.

Within a breathless moment the stalk had grown over a foot. The veins of Elisa's hand glowed beneath the skin like a network of roots. And from that strange plant, an even stranger fruit began to swell.

"What is his name?" Elisa asked.

"Um, how about Sid."

The fruit looked like an organ with a face. I didn't know what a fetus looked like at the time, but when I saw pictures when I was older I knew that's what it was.

"How big should he be?"

"I want to be taller than he is," I said.

Elisa smiled.

"What?" I said. "We'll be playing sports and stuff. I want to win."

"What does Sid like to eat?" she asked.

"Uh..." I glanced around the empty room, spotting the basket. "Cookies, I guess."

It was larger now. I could make out tiny blue hands and feet pressing against its transparent cocoon.

"And what does he love?" Her voice was fainter now, straining with exertion. Her glowing veins extended all the way down her arm now, and for the first time I realized the concentration on her face was mixed with pain.

"I don't know. I don't think I like this game. I don't want to play anymore."

"You can't stop now. What does Sid love?"

Elisa took a sharp intake of breath and grimaced. The plant had stopped growing, and the swiftly gorging fruit was about the size of a watermelon. How was it getting so big? Was it filling up with her blood?

"Stop it," I said. My voice cracked, but I didn't care. "Make it go back. Cut it off."

"It's not an it," she grunted. "His name is Sid, and he is already alive. You have to tell me what he loves, or he will be nothing but—"

"I hate it. I hate him. Make him go away, please."

"Hurry! You're part of the spell too. I can't do this alone," she said.

It wasn't a watermelon anymore. It was the size of dog and beginning to grow coarse fur. Now it was heavy enough that Elisa had to kneel and rest it on the ground. The hands and feet were becoming more defined and solid by the second. Its eyes fluttered once, and then opened to pierce me with pale sightless orbs.

"Mr. Williams!" I screamed. "Mr. Williams help! It's hurting her!"

Thunder on the stairs, but the wretched thing reacted to the noise and flailed its arms. One wild claw pierced straight through its encompassing sac and clawed the open air an inch from my face. Bright red fingers clutched the tattered opening and ripped it wide in a rush of blood. All at once Sid was free and on the ground, standing almost as tall as me.

Pounding on the door. It was still locked. "What's going on in there. Elisa? Are you okay?"

She lay panting on the ground. The blood was beginning to evaporate into a thick red mist. I choked and fell to the ground to avoid breathing in the heavy wet air. The tattered sac, the discarded dying stem, both withering before my eyes. Sid was crouched in terror, its matted blue fur showing through the evaporating blood.

"Open the door! Boy are you in there?"

I crawled across the ground to unlock the door. More pounding, louder and more desperate than ever. Out of the corner of my eye I saw Sid flinching at each resounding crash.

The instant I fully turned away from it to unlock the door, I heard Elisa scream. I pounded back the lock and the enormous pressure on the other side made the door spring like a trap.

The man was roaring, but it was too late. Elisa's stomach had been savagely opened. Sid loomed over her, digging through her stomach as though searching for something. When it turned to face Mr. William's onslaught, it was shoveling a bloody clump into its mouth.

Mr. Williams almost caught it, but it bounded away just in time. The bear man moved to the window to block its retreat, but he missed again when Sid lunged for the basket on the cabinet instead. By the time the man caught up with it, Sid had already fled through the door.

"It's my fault." I heaved for air.

Mr. Williams knelt above his daughter, clutching her soaked body to his chest.

"I could have shaped it," I said. "I could have told it not to hurt anyone. I'm so sorry."

"We need to get out of the house," he said.

I followed him downstairs though I knew it wouldn't return. The monster had been born with but one desire, and it would stop at nothing to get it. There was nothing left to satisfy it here.

A cookie monster was born that day.

THE STILLBIRTH LIE

"TIME OF DEATH: 10:27 AM."

Doctor Francis turned his back on the exhausted mother, the tiny body shielded in his arms.

The sound which escaped the mother's body was more like a wounded animal than a human: raw emotion without words. She reached toward the small bundle, but the doctor turns sharply and walks from the room.

"Let me see him at least! Just for a moment!" she cries.

"It would be too hard on you," the doctor says, pausing at the doorway. "Try to get some rest. You've had a long day." And he was gone, carrying the child with him.

I've been a nurse at Mercy Hospital for two years. I've seen more than my fair share of tragedy and heartbreak. I've seen grown men blubbering like babies, amputated limbs, inconsolable children with an incurable disease, but this was a first for me. I've never seen a doctor pronounce a child stillborn with a hand over its mouth to suppress its cries. The baby was still squirming in his arms as he carried the little boy from the room.

The doctor must have had a reason though, right? He noticed something was wrong, something fatal, and he thought it would be easier for the mother to bear this way. It just seemed so cruel. I had to confront him in the hallway outside.

"Where are you taking him?" I asked.

"B-1."

"The morgue?"

A feeble cry escaped the child's lips, but it was drowned out by the swelling wail from inside the maternity room. The doctor wrapped the tiny form in his lab coat and hustled off at a quickened pace.

"You can't seriously..."

"I could have you fired, you know." Doctor Francis said it as casually as though commenting on the weather. "All I'd have to do is tell the administration about that time you molested an unconscious person."

"That never happened. What you're doing now though—"

"Just your word against mine then, isn't it?" He stopped at the service elevator. The down arrow lights up. "And who do you think they'd believe? A lifetime veteran and beloved family doctor, or some sketchy nurse trying to save his own skin?" The elevator opened, and he stepped inside. He readjusted to tuck the bundled child under one arm.

I tried to enter with him, but he blocked my path.

"Don't be an idiot, okay?" he said. "You can trust me. I know what I'm doing."

"Yeah, because stealing a child and threatening an innocent witness is totally trustworthy behavior."

"This is for their own good. Them and their parents."

"Them? How many are there?"

Dr. Francis grinned as the door closed. The shifting light seemed to highlight his teeth into something like a snarl. The elevator whirred down. I helplessly mashed the down arrow, but there was only one shaft and I'd have to wait.

I sprinted to the stairs instead, racing against my own morbid thoughts. The door exiting the stairwell to the basement was locked. I fumbled through my keys. I'd never needed to go down here before, and I couldn't remember which one opened the morgue.

I heard a child cry on the other side. Was I too late? Was he already killing it? My fingers were shaking enough that even the right key wouldn't fit. Deep breath. Deep breath. Concentrate. Another cry, muffled and distant this time.

Then the key slid in and I flung open the door. The morgue was still and quiet. There was no sign of the doctor. I searched the room for several minutes, but the cold dead air seemed to mock the very possibility of what I'd seen. I probably would have given up and left soon, but a rattling sound froze me in place.

It was coming from inside one of the body drawers. It was beginning to open from the inside. I leapt across the room to hide behind an upright supply cabinet just in time before the drawer opened.

Doctor Francis crawled out and closed the drawer behind him. He straightened his lab coat, looked from side to side, and then proceeded to the elevator. The child was gone.

I waited until the elevator door closed behind him before rushing to the wall of drawers. Opening the one he crawled from, I immediately realized that it wasn't a drawer at all. It was a passage way.

Fresh wails from the other side prompted me to lie flat on my stomach and crawl through the tight metal space. The crying got louder as I went, until after about 10 feet I emerged into a room I'd never seen before.

Candles lined the walls with long lines of melted wax to mark their enduring vigil. Occult symbols were splashed on the floor in a dark liquid I preferred not to speculate about. And the cribs—a dozen of them arranged in a circle, each containing a frightened infant.

Thank God the cribs were still labeled with their medical charts. These children were all dead—if you believed the official statements, anyway. Their parents were all told that they were stillbirths.

How many heartbreaks and broken lives were there because of this profane room? It was enough to make me sick. I spent the rest of the day removing the children one by one, belly-crawling through the tight passage to bring them back up to the hospital and the world of the living.

The phone calls to the parents were bittersweet. I couldn't even begin to explain what happened. Some children had been down there for as long as a month, and the parents' shock at hearing they were still alive was absolute.

One tearful reunion after another depleted me to my very core. After the initial relief, the parents would start to ask questions that I couldn't possibly answer.

In the first meeting I tried to spin a complicated story about mixed medical records, but it sounded impossible even as I said it. After that I simply told them it was a miracle, and honestly that's what it felt like. By the time all but one child was sent home, I felt like an angel bringing the children back from the dead.

The parents of the last child were out of town, so I'd have to wait until they could get back. It was a little girl named Emma with a single soft blonde curl. She'd have to stay in the hospital one more night, and I volunteered to stay with her to make sure I was there when the parents arrived.

I'd alerted the security about doctor Francis, but all the commotion of the reunions afterward had driven him from my mind until that evening. I'd spun so many false tales to explain what had happened to the children that I hadn't even considered what the actual justification was.

I sat with Emma in the extra patient room where I'd be spending the night. She slept peacefully, soft little hands curled and still. Even if doctor Francis was insane, he must have chosen these children for a reason. He'd delivered hundreds of children over the last month, but he'd only hidden a few of them.

The hospital was growing quiet around us. The day staff were going home, and the lights in the hallway were dimmed. The peace was disturbed by a sound outside my room:

"Where is she? Where's Emma?"

"You're not allowed to be here, sir. I was told—"

"Nonsense, I work here. Where is she?"

"314, but doctor Francis—"

I tensed as the door swung open. I caught a glimpse of a security guard hurrying toward us, but doctor Francis slipped inside and slammed the door behind him. I was on my feet, but too late to stop him from snatching a metal IV pole and barring the door.

Emma was awake and starting to cry.

"Give her to me!" he demanded, striding toward the girl. "Where are the others?"

"What the hell do you think you're doing?" I asked.

I tried to maneuver around him to unblock the door, but he shoved me roughly back onto the bed.

"I won't let you hurt her!" I said, jumping upright once more.

"Hurt her? God damn idiot. Emma was stillborn. There's nothing that can hurt her now."

Emma was wailing now, frightened high-pitched sobs.

"She's obviously not—"

The doctor shoved a folder into my chest. Security was pounding on the door. Francis wasn't moving toward Emma anymore though, so I allowed myself the time to look inside the folder.

"Where are the others? Don't tell me you..."

"I sent them home," I said. "They were obviously happy, healthy, living..."

I was staring at a set of x-rays, but I didn't understand what I was seeing. The outline looked like a child, but there was something like an eel or a snake coiled tightly within, filling the entirety of the body.

Emma wailed louder as the door rattled harder.

"Can't you hear how scared she is?" I demanded. "You've got to stop this."

"Her mouth is closed," the doctor replied.

"What?"

The wail intensified into a shrill shriek, although it still sounded muffled. But he was right. Emma's mouth was still closed.

"She isn't crying," he said, his voice softer now but still audible because of the terrifying intensity. "Dead children can't cry. But the thing inside them can."

Emma was starting to squirm. Not just her arms and legs either—it was more like the skin was being pushed from something within.

"Do you want to call the parents, or should I?" he asked.

THE MERCY KILLING APPOINTMENT

"I live in hope I can jump before I am pushed."
-Sir Terry Pratchett on the right to die.

Is any life better than any death? Even a life of profound grief and suffering, carrying the guilt of knowing how much of a burden you've become to those you love? Should our spirits be kept locked in a feeble corpse until the last drop of blood has dragged to a stop through withered veins? Or should we alone be the judge of what burden we can bear; should our pleading be heard when we reach out in our final hour?

Assisted suicides are illegal where I live. A caring doctor should not go to prison for administering the final cure to his grateful patient. When I asked openly about the option, the hospital staff couldn't even meet my eyes. They mumbled excuses and aversions as though they were embarrassed. If anyone should be embarrassed, it was me for admitting that all life had value except this one. I was given a long list of exercises and diets and painkillers intended to add a few more months, but no-one pretended it was a cure.

"A full life deserves a full death. I don't want it to linger on the doorstep. I want it done now. Actually Monday would be better. It's supposed to rain that day, anyway."

The doctor said it was quite impossible. He left in a huff, promising to return with either a psychologist, or a policeman if I couldn't be dissuaded. He of all people should understand that the tumor wasn't in the brain. This decision wasn't an idle fancy. I wasn't some teenager declaring that life was pointless after I got dumped. I was at the end of a very long rope, ready for release.

I would have done the deed myself with a gun or a bottle of pills, but I knew my wife would never forgive me in this life or the next. Better it was clean and professional and out of my hands. I sighed and made my way to the door, but Susan, one of the nurses, stopped me. She had a bright and perky energy about her that always lit up the room, but I could tell by her hushed tone that she understood the gravity of my request.

"Monday." Just one word. It was enough.

I nodded. I slipped her my business card with my address and mouthed the word 'thank you'. She returned a tight-lipped smile, and we stood staring at each other for a moment. Then she hugged me out of nowhere. I was uncomfortable at first, but I held on anyway. Just so she wouldn't see the tears in my eyes.

At last I pulled away and cleared my throat. "Now if you'll excuse me, I'd like to spend the weekend with my wife."

Of course I didn't tell my wife about the appointment. This weekend was a celebration of life, and I didn't want it to be tainted by the unpleasantness to come. We went to the beach on Saturday and dined at a waterside cafe with our feet in the sand. On Sunday we drove up into the mountains to spend time with her family. The word 'goodbye' stuck in my throat when we hugged and parted.

The sand doesn't stick in the hourglass though, and the clouds are already gathering overhead. My wife is sleeping in the bed next to me, but I still haven't told her. Tomorrow will be Monday, and I trust Susan to meet me soon.

Won't my wife be surprised when she finds out about the appointment I made for her. With her out of the way, I can really start living again.

DON'T FOLLOW TAIL LIGHTS THROUGH A FOG

I MIGHT AS WELL HAVE BEEN SMOTHERED IN A BLANKET FOR HOW WELL I could see. Sliding, oozing, pouring through the air to swirl around me. The thick fog that rolled in from the ocean behaved more like a wave of viscous liquid than it did a cloud. The road I was driving on ran parallel to the water, and it only took a couple of minutes after the fog hit the beach before it had fully encompassed my car.

I've never seen anything like it in my life. Leaning out the window, I couldn't even see the ground a few feet below. I would have been smart to pull off the road and wait it out, but I was suffering from an acute case of love at the time and my rational voice was a ghost beside the thundering of my blood. My son was going to be born today, and I was going to be there to see it happen.

Despite my best intentions, it would have been impossible for me to continue without the taillights in front of me. I'd been following this beat up old pickup with a "Crazy8" license plate for the last few miles, and if it wasn't going to stop, then neither was I. The lights in front of me slowed to a crawl, and I kept pace going as close as I dared for fear of losing him.

The two of us were the only ones stupid enough to still be driving. We passed a half-dozen other cars all pulled off the road with their emergency lights glowing through the heavy air. The lights in front of me never stopped though, deep red beacons promising me a safe road ahead. I figured that even if he hit something, then I'd be going slow enough that I could still stop in time. I was more worried about him running off the road, but he continued to navigate the winding way flawlessly and I never even brushed up against the rumble strips that warn when you're getting too close to the edge.

It was slow going, but it gave me a chance to check in with my wife. The contractions were becoming more severe, and I told her not to wait, but she just pretended it was no big deal.

"I'm going to be telling this story for the rest of my life," she said through heavy breath. "Do you want to know how it ends?"

"With me holding the baby so you can get some God damned rest?"

She laughed. "Damn straight. You remember our deal, right?"

"Of course. It's not going to be like with your dad. I'm always going to be there for both of you."

"Well you can start any time now. I swear to God that if you don't show up I'm going home with the first doctor who smiles at me."

I think she was saying something else too, but my focus was diverted by the latest car I passed on the side of the road. A beat-up pickup—the Crazy8 plate whose tail lights were still glowing through the fog ahead of me.

"Okay honey I'm going to focus on driving, but I'll see you in just a few minutes."

I hung up and gripped the wheel with both hands. Is it possible that the car in front pulled off the road and another car had taken his place without me noticing? Absolutely not. I'd been directly behind him with my eyes glued on the lights the whole time. They hadn't changed either—it was the same red glow. I checked my mirror, but the old pickup had already disappeared into the fog behind me.

I put a bit more weight on the gas and surged closer to the car in front of me to check for the "Crazy8" license plate. The lights ahead of me sped up in perfect unison as though we were magnets repelling each other. I dared going as fast as 30 mph, but I couldn't close the distance and quickly dropped back down to 15. The lights maintained their distance exactly—just close enough for me to see the light, but not close enough to see the car.

Fast, slow. Fast, slow. I played this game for the next minute. The distance between me and the lights never changed, and the obscured landscape made me feel as though I was standing still. No one could have the reflexes to keep matching my speed like that. Or even if they could—then why? Unless of course, they wanted me to follow.

I slowed to a stop to check my GPS and make sure I hadn't accidentally missed my turnoff. Right on cue, the lights ahead stopped as well. I fiddled with my phone to bring up the maps, breathing a sigh of relief to see my next turn a few hundred feet away. Looking up, the breath caught in my throat. The lights were coming closer now, burning through the fog with a nameless menace that raised the hairs on the back of my neck.

The lights flashed once. As they drew closer, a shape began to resolve itself from the fog. The lights flashed again—no, not flashed. They didn't go on and off. Something slid over them and then slid back. It would be more accurate to say that they blinked. It took about ten seconds for my brain to process that I was staring into a set of red eyes, much larger than could fit in a human head.

My first instinct was to slam the horn for all I was worth. The eyes immediately retreated, but only a few feet. A torrent of sound replied, like a whole herd of braying animals, berserk with fear and pain as they trample one another to death in their mad dash to escape their own slaughter. Only a herd of animals wouldn't all start and stop at the same time. The whole chorus fell eerily silent together. The eyes turned away from me, the light vanishing into the mist to leave me suspended in the opaque white walls which felt closer than ever.

My suspended breath exploded out of me in a gasp. The creature was leaving, and I was safe inside the car. I started to inch forward again, now using the rumble strip to guide me toward my turn. I white-knuckled the steering wheel, trembling with the car as it eased along the invisible bend.

The turn the creature had taken a few moments before. The turn which led to the hospital where my wife was giving birth. But it couldn't be...

I had no warning before the massive impact broadsided my car. The wild braying mingled with the screech of twisted metal. The car spun almost ninety degrees from the force of the blow, leaving me even more lost and disoriented than I already was. I stomped the gas and shot straight off the road, bumping and lurching and spinning my tires to a standstill in the sandy ground.

Another impact—this time from behind, propelling me back onto the intersecting road where I'd been trying to turn. 30—40—50 mph, I accelerated blindly through the fog. The red eyes filled my mirror, easily keeping pace with me. I was pushing 70 before they started falling behind. My front right wheel kept slipping off the road, but I kept readjusting and didn't dare slow down. If there was a sudden curve, then I was dead. If there was a tree, or a sign, or an invisible barrier hidden in the fog—dead. My whole body was rigid with tension, braced every second for a collision that could happen any time.

I didn't see the eyes anymore though, and gradually I slowed once more. I started to pull up my GPS again, but the second I took my eyes off the mirror I heard the sound again. Red eyes filled the mirror, rushing toward me in a reckless charge as though planning to barrel straight through my car. I swerved to get out of the way, sliding off the road once more. The wall of sound crashed around me, then just as quickly it was gone.

The fog was lifting with it. I sat stunned for several seconds as the air miraculously cleared around me. Directly ahead was the hospital. The relief only lasted a moment. I hadn't gotten away from the creature. It had gotten away from me. I hadn't escaped its pursuit. I'd lost the race.

I was inside the hospital by the time I heard the sound again. Rabid, feral, and yet with such focused intensity that there was surely a malevolent intelligence behind its bestial roar. I sprinted to my wife's room, terrified of what I'd find yet dreading not knowing even more.

My wife sitting up in bed, holding her son—our son, in her arms. The sweat on her brow, the sweet smile on her lips, and the proud victory in her lifted face.

"He's beautiful," I whispered, hardly daring to breathe and disturb the perfect moment.

"Shh—you'll wake him."

But I was too late. He was already stretching his tiny fists and opening his little red eyes.

ALEKTOROPHOBIA: A FEAR OF CHICKENS

HER FRECKLES MAKE MY KNEES WEAK. I CAN FEEL HEAVY DROPS OF sweat squeezing through my pores. It's going to be my turn next, and I've spent the last few minutes carefully rehearsing my words and their casual inflection in my mind. Missy's left knee is almost touching my right one as we sit on the same log, and the faintest sensation of her body heat is burning a hundred times hotter than the campfire.

"Your turn, Wobbles," Jeff says. I don't bother correcting him because my real name of Webster is just as bad. "Truth or dare?"

"Dare," I say without hesitation.

My face is a carefully maintained a mask of boredom. Jeff is smirking at me because of our deal. I've been giving him my dessert for the last week, even though the camp always has the best food at the end. I've been doing his craft projects to cover for him while he sneaks behind the toolshed and drinks with a few of the older boys. I even let him beat me at ping pong while a dozen people watched, even though I could have kicked his ass, and he knows it. It's all going to be worth it though, because he's about to dare me to kiss Missy.

"You sure you're brave enough for a dare?" Jeff asks, languidly drawing out each word. He's trying to make me squirm, but I'm not taking the bait.

"I'm ready. Shoot," I say. My breathing is almost steady.

"'Cause I'm sure everybody is just dying to know more about that time you took a piss in the creak, and—"

"Come on Jeff, just dare him already," Missy says.

Every muscle in my body is a painful knot. Somehow all the moisture in my mouth has teleported into my armpits. Missy shouldn't be able to smell it over the burning logs though. I hope.

"Okay Wobbles. By the power invested in me by the sacred games of Camp Tillwaki, I dare you to..."

I was already standing. I wasn't going to over-think it. I wasn't going to give anyone else the chance to over-think it. I was just going to duck in there, and...

"... try to catch Scar Face, the one-eyed chicken!"

I'd already turned toward Missy in anticipation. She got a full view of my gaping mouth and the startled fear stamped across my face. She covered her mouth and tried not to laugh, failing in the most delightful way. I spun to face Jeff and his giant sloppy grin. He'd stepped aside to reveal a cage containing the most hideous monster I've ever seen. A few other boys had already taken up chanting "Scar Face... Scar Face...".

Jeff's hand is poised on the latch to open the cage. "Unless of course... you're scared of him."

Scar Face cocked its mangled head to the side and glared at me. It was all black except for its disgusting fleshy red crown and malicious beady eyes. The counselors said that a fox almost got Scar Face once, but it fought back and pecked out both the fox's eyes. Legend has it that it didn't stop there either, but continued to attack the blinded fox until it had pecked its way straight to the brain through the eye sockets.

"Afraid of a chicken? Don't be stupid," I said. Even with my back to Missy, she's still the only thing that I can see.

The cage flies open and Jeff scrambles backward to get out of the way. Scar Face takes his time strutting out, eyeing us all one at a time like a lord surveying his subjects. I crouch, ready to spring, but that only makes the trembling in my legs more evident.

I don't give myself a chance to over-think. Before the chicken has taken two steps, I dive on it with outstretched arms. It gets a vicious peck into my shoulder, but my adrenalin is raging through me and I barely feel it.

I'm about to stuff the creature back into its cage when my legs give out beneath me. I'd been so busy trying to keep its beak away that I hadn't noticed Jeff sneaking around the side. He'd swept my legs with a sharp kick, and Scar Face and I tumbled to the ground. By this point the creature was berserk with rage. Catching it again wasn't nearly as important as making sure it didn't catch me.

"Come on, that's cheating!" Missy wails. Her sympathy was a small condolence beside the throaty squawks.

I was still laying stunned on the ground when Scar Face began his attack. The razor beak sank into my chest again and again, and the more I tried to fight it off with my hands, the farther it worked its way up my neck and face. Jeff was howling with laughter, egging the chicken on by nudging it in the butt with his foot. I managed to drag myself to my feet, but the enraged bird launched itself into the air to continue its relentless assault.

I'd been using my hands to push myself up and wasn't shielding my face for just a moment, but that's all it took. The talons planted themselves around my shoulder and the beak dove straight into my face. I could see it growing exponentially larger by the second as it hurtled towards my eye, and the next I knew an explosion of pain cascaded through my body. The surrounding laughter turned to screams and mad panic as the blood ran freely down my face. I flailed madly until the bird dropped back to the ground. I stumbled blindly trying to get away until I tripped over a log and fell too.

I still had one good eye, but it was so filled with sweat and blood that I couldn't see a thing. I curled into a fetal position, listening to the awful squawking and screaming, just waiting for the unpredictable beak to gouge into my prone body.

I vaguely heard the gruff voice of one of the counselors, but I was loosing a lot of blood and nothing seemed quite real. I passed out shortly afterward. The last thought in my head was back to the fantasy of being dared to kiss Missy, and the softness of her lips against mine.

Camp ended one week after that. I spent most of the time in a medical building with a giant swathe of bandages compressing where one of my eyes used to be. Missy visited once, but only briefly to check in. She stayed near the back of the room and showed about as much interest in resuming my fantasy as I had in kissing Scar Face.

Yeah it was a tough week, but there was one silver lining. The counselor (who was probably just desperate not to get sued), told me that the chicken had been put down. He practically begged me to tell him if there was anything else he could do to make this right, and I told him that there was: I wanted to cook the chicken myself for the farewell banquet, and I wanted him to assign Jeff as my assistant. The counselor blurted out immediate consent, talking over himself in his hurry to promise us the whole kitchen for as long as we needed it.

Some might think this is petty revenge, but I don't. I'd need a glass eye to replace the one that was gouged out, not to mention a lifetime of alektorophobia. And when I stood at the head of the long table and watched everyone eat the final meal I'd prepared, well that felt almost as good as a kiss.

I don't know if they were just being nice because of the incident, but people raved about that meal. I tried to stay humble, but I had two plates myself and know it wasn't just empty words. Jeff really did taste better than any chicken would have.

MY STALKER WISHES ME HAPPY BIRTHDAY EVERY YEAR

"HAPPY BIRTHDAY MAHJOUBA. I HOPE SOMEONE GETS YOU THE NEW phone I saw you looking at last week."

-Love X

"Another year already. It seems like only yesterday your mom dropped you off for high school. It's been such a pleasure watching you grow up."

-Love X

"You should be more careful about closing your windows at night. You never know when someone might climb up from the balcony below. Happy birthday, stay safe."

-Love X

They might sound creepy to you, but you have to understand that I've been getting these cards every year for as long as I can remember. My mom made a big fuss about them for a while, but we never got the slightest clue where they were coming from and nothing bad ever came from it. Over the years it just became a fact of life; I even looked forward to the mysterious messages.

We all had our theories, of course. Mom thought it was some socially handicapped secret admirer with a lifelong obsession. My half-sister Amina couldn't stand the idea of anyone being in love with me. She insisted it was a psychopath who was just biding his time to strike. I even caught her slipping her own menacing anonymous letter into the pile one year just to scare me.

Personally I always thought (or at least hoped) they were coming from dad. He left my mother while she was still pregnant with me. Mom thinks that's proof that he doesn't care and wouldn't bother. I think it's proof that he knows I exist. The fact that Amina never gets a card seems to support the idea.

This never caused a problem until I was in my twenties and living on my own. I'd started dating a guy named Ranja who was almost charming to a fault. He wouldn't say that I looked beautiful. He'd tell me that the rain came from angels weeping over losing me from heaven. Or that the puddles loved me so much that they'd hold on to my reflection even after I'd left. A little over the top maybe, but I'd be lying if I didn't admit to feeling myself all mixed up at his words.

Ranja and I had been together for almost eight months before we celebrated my first birthday together. That's the first time I saw the other side of him. I guess I never realized how closely linked passion and jealousy are before he opened my mysterious card. His brows knotted together while he read, his pressed lips began to tremble, and all the color drained from his face.

"It's no big deal, really," I told him. "What's it say?"

Ranja didn't answer. He threw the card down on the table and walked to the other side of the room, breathing heavily. I picked it up and read:

"He's going to hurt you, Mahjouba. You wouldn't be the first either. Get out, or this may be the last card you ever receive."

-Love X

When I looked up, Ranja was standing on the opposite side of his living room, just glaring at me. "Well?" he asked. "Explain yourself."

"Me? What did I do?"

The space between us closed more rapidly than I was comfortable with. I took a step back, but that only brought him closer—trapping me against a wall.

"What's his name? How long have you been seeing him?" Ranja pressed.

What followed was the worst argument we've ever had. He refused to believe me when I told him it might be my father, and I got a glimpse of the person the message warned me about. I told him he could check with my family, but he seemed to think they would lie to protect me. We managed to avoid talking about it for a few days until one morning when Ranja triumphantly slammed a piece of paper on the table.

"He's dead. Twelve years he's been dead."

I don't know how Ranja did it, but I was staring at my father's death certificate. Have you ever felt a lifetime of hope shatter in a few seconds? It's like being conscious of your own death. Your body keeps moving and you can feel it go, but there's no one inside anymore.

"Stop pretending you care just to get out of trouble. I know you never met him."

And then the argument started again, but my heart wasn't in it anymore. I couldn't explain who was sending the letters. I could barely even talk, and he took my silence as an admission of guilt. He didn't understand that I wasn't hurt because I lost my father. You can't lose something you've never had. I was hurt because I lost every possible future with my father in it. I lost him dancing with me at my wedding and carrying my future kids on his back. I lost him telling me that he never stopped thinking of me, or loving me, even if it was only from afar.

And all I gained in return were threats, insults, and the unsettling realization that a stranger really had been following me my whole life long. Now Ranja was laying it on the line—I could either trust him, or the letter writer. He demanded to know why I would throw away the life I was building for some creep I'd never met. How could I possibly take care of myself without him? How could I find another man as good as him when even my own father didn't want me?

If my life was a movie, then things would have gotten better after that. I would have stood up for myself and learned to live on my own terms. But I was scared, and I was alone, and I thought that someone who said the angels wept for me would never dare blasphemy the object of their love.

I thought I deserved it when he started to lock me in my own room. What else could he do if he didn't trust me?

I thought I could be strong when he hit me or pulled my hair. At least he didn't leave. My mother would have been lucky to have found a man like Ranja.

And for the next year, I hated myself for spending my whole life waiting for a fairy tale that would never come true.

Until my birthday came again, and I finally found the will to leave. It wasn't what the card said that convinced me—just a benign, generic well-wishing straight off the shelf. It was where the card came from, because this was the first time there had ever been a return address.

In the cool and safety of the dark I stole out of Ranja's house with only what I could fit in a suitcase. It was hard going dragging my things, but I knew that if my life was going to start over, then it was going to start with the only person I've ever trusted—the one sending the letters. And when I found myself entering the cemetery, I knew I had found what I was looking for.

My father's headstone, which read: "Are you there, Mahjouba? I will always be with you."

MY DIARY THAT I DIDN'T WRITE

I'M THAT GUY WHO WILL SWERVE ACROSS THREE LANES OF TRAFFIC without hesitation because I spotted a sign for a garage sale. Doesn't matter that I don't need anything, doesn't matter if there are three other people in my car with busy lives and no interest in digging through someone else's trash. Garage sales are like magical dimensions where anything is possible and reality is only a suggestion.

Entire sofa for $50? No problem, they're just happy for someone to get rid of it.

Grandpa's medals from the war? Well, who is he trying to impress now?

The literal holy grail? Why not? It's got to be somewhere. Some dude's kids were probably eating cereal out of it.

But by far the strangest thing I've ever discovered in years of hunting was a little black notebook bound with leather straps. When I noticed there was writing inside, I snuck behind a big stack of old garden chairs to snoop mercilessly through someone's personal life. The erotic short story of a bored housewife? Maybe the daughter's scandalous journal full of young love and heartbreak? It's a garage sale, baby. It's all fair game.

I was immediately disappointed upon closer inspection. The first few entries were composed of big blocky letters like a child might write. A day at the pool, the stuff he learned in class, the new friend he met at the park... I was quickly losing interest and was about to return the notebook when I realized I recognized the person he was talking about. Devin was my best friend in third grade. We used to build pillow forts in his parent's house—And there it was. The next entry talking about the fort. About the secret passage we made in the back so his cat could still visit when the door was closed. It's been years and years since I last thought about that. But how did these people get my diary? I wasn't even in the same state that I grew up in anymore. I watched the homeowner suspiciously while he bartered over an old TV. Clean face, slightly balding, a broad smile—nothing out of the ordinary. I considered asking him about it, but decided it was too personal to explain.

I slipped the notebook into my pocket and stood to leave. It couldn't have been stealing if it belonged to me, right? As I headed for my car parked on the street, I heard him call after me:

"Couldn't find anything you liked?"

I gave my best straight face and shook my head. "Plenty I liked. Nothing I need."

"It's hard to tell what we're going to need... until we need it. Take care now."

I was gone without looking back. Too impatient to drive all the way home, I stopped in a coffee shop around the corner to continue pursuing this bizarre discovery.

Flipping through the book, I noticed the handwriting slowly refine as it progressed until it identically matched my own. This wasn't just a childhood relic: the entries spanned over the course of years. It seemed impossible that I could have kept this for so long without any memory of it. There was no denying it was mine though, complete with my fleeting obsession over a girl in one of my college classes. I was too shy to talk to her, so I'd just sit in the row behind and daydream the hour away. She dropped out a few weeks later, and I missed my chance of ever saying hello. I was so embarrassed by my ineptitude that I never breathed a word about her to anyone. And yet here she was, immortalized on paper in my own hand.

So why didn't I remember writing it?

The farther I got through the book, the more unsettling that question became. The writing became sloppier as though rushed. Entries became short and far between, just a few lines per month. I could still recognize the events of my past, but the language became darker than I was expecting.

I should just kill her. Necks break as easily as hearts, maybe easier. She didn't love me, she can't love anyone but herself. I'd spare the next sucker she decides to fuck a lot of pain if I just killed her now.

That was written about my ex fiance, only a few months ago. The breakup was stressful for both of us, but we'd parted on good terms. Sure there was some lingering resentment and disappointment, and I'd had some pretty nasty thoughts about her, but I never once considered something like that. My diary said otherwise.

She gets home late on Tuesdays and Thursdays, it read. 10:30 PM at the bus stop. She has two blocks to walk, and there won't be any people around. All I've got to do is take her purse and it will look like a mugging gone bad. No one will ever know.

The next few pages were hard to read. I kept glancing over my shoulder in paranoia as though someone in the coffee shop would read over my shoulder and call the police. I moved to a corner table which had opened up and continued reading.

It was even easier than expected. She didn't look up from her phone, even when I was right behind her. One hand under the jaw, the other on the top of her head. One quick motion—I can still hear the splintering crack, like stomping on dry wood except for the wet, sucking sound of separated vertebrae.

I stopped reading and looked away. For a second I thought I remembered what that sounded like, but it might have just been the power of suggestion. I pulled out my phone to text her and make sure she was okay, but changed my mind at the absurdity of it. I flipped ahead to the last page containing writing. It was dated yesterday.

It was supposed to be easier this way. I thought killing her would be the end, but I'm thinking about her more than ever. Every face is her reflection, every smile a sneer, every voice heavy with accusation. I think I'm going to go insane if I can't get her out of my head. I want to forget. I need to forget. And yet if I do, how much of me will disappear with her?

Need to forget. The words rang a bell in my mind. As I was leaving the garage sale, the man had said it's hard to tell what we're going to need until we need it. It had to be a coincidence. Or maybe I just needed it to be. I scanned every page until the end of the notebook, but they were all blank.

I picked up my phone and called my ex. The ringing seemed to go on for an eternity, but it was only three repetitions before it connected. I asked if she was there, my voice catching in my throat.

There was crying on the other line, then a sniffled apology. I recognized the voice as her mother.

"She's gone. Last week—please don't call this number again."

The call ended abruptly. The coffee shop suddenly felt much louder than it had a moment before. The sound of the cash register opening made me jump. People seemed to shout at one another across the room. I stumbled outside, and the traffic was a hurricane whirling around me. Then to my car, lurching onto the street with a chorus of horns shaking me to the bone. I didn't slow down until I slammed to stop at the garage sale once more.

All the other perspective buyers had gone home. It was just the homeowner sitting in an old garden chair facing the street. He wasn't reading or doing anything, just sitting there and waiting. He smiled as though expecting me when I got out of the car.

"Forget something?" he asked, his voice coy.

"I didn't kill her," I blurted out. I hadn't intended to say that. I don't know what I'd intended to say, but it wasn't that.

He only laughed. "Why not?"

"Because I'm a good person. We both are—were, whatever. It didn't go like that."

"How did it go then?" he asked, casually reaching under his chair. "Like this, maybe?"

He produced a small stack of notebooks, each a different color. He opened the red one seemingly at random and began to read: "Love survives, love endures. There was once a time when we fought a lot, but in fighting we learned more about each other than we ever did from the easy times. We showed each other our deepest insecurities and vulnerabilities—we gave the other the power to destroy us, and we loved each other for our mercy. I liked her because of her virtues, but I loved her because of her faults, because I knew she trusted me enough not to hide herself from me."

"What's that supposed to be?" I asked. I'd been moving closer while he read until I was only a few feet away.

"You were working on your wedding vows. Don't worry—it was just a first draft. Here, take it." He handed me the red notebook.

I snatched it suspiciously as though the man taking me hostage had just offered his gun. I immediately flipped to the end and saw my handwriting with yesterday's date once more.

1 dozen eggs.

Diapers—not that plastic crap.

Garden hose...

"What the hell is this?"

"Things your wife wanted you to pick up on your way home. You'll find her waiting for you if you go now. Or maybe you'd prefer the blue notebook. You never met her at all because you went back to finish your PhD. Is that what you want?"

My face must have betrayed my confusion because he laughed again. "A lot of folks think they can only affect their present because that's all they see, but every second you're alive you're only making more past. Keep that in mind next time you make a decision—is this the past I want to live with someday?"

He offered his open hand to take the red notebook back, but I clutched it to my chest. I turned away without another word, gripping the notebook so tightly that the cover cut into my fingers. I was scared to think what might happen if I spent anymore time here.

Besides, my wife was at home, and I wasn't going to keep her waiting forever.

RELIVE YOUR CHILDHOOD

THE ONLY REASON TO GO TO A HIGH SCHOOL REUNION IS TO RUB YOUR success in everyone's faces. For me, that meant letting them know I married the prettiest girl in our grade. There's nothing more satisfying than watching them glance at me, then at Kimberly holding my hand, then quickly back to me with the wide-eyed shock of realization.

I'll just smile and nod. Yep, you caught us. Me, a little fatter with rough stubble on my face. Her as beautiful as ever, the short tangle of ginger hair she wore in high school replaced with a luxurious wave flowing halfway down her back.

"I want everyone to remember that as long as you're here, it's still 2008."

That was Brandon with the microphone standing at the head of the gymnasium. He was always a weird loner that I never knew very well, but I'd gotten the Facebook invitation from him because he did all the organizing for the reunion.

I have no idea how he got permission to use our old school which had been out of operational for years. An overly ambitious remodeling project had been terminated halfway through for whatever reason, and there were still discarded building supplies and stacks of lumber everywhere.

"I'm serious," Brandon growled, hands plastering his greasy gelled hair back against his head. "Smart phones in the plastic bin. Those things didn't exist when we were in school."

Nobody wanted to make a defiant scene in front of their old classmates, so we all reluctantly dumped our gadgets into the bin as we entered.

Brandon had gone to great lengths to make the place feel like it used to. Old science fair posters were hung on the walls. Stacks of molding brochures advertised Grease with the 2008 school cast. There was even a collection of trophies that our track and field team had won that year, God knows where he got them.

"Kimberly, huh? Congratulations man." My old friend Chase clapped me on the back. "I'd always hoped you two would end up together."

"As if." I grinned. "You told me my only shot would be to wear a wig and ask out the only lesbian."

Kimberly snorted as she laughed in the most delightful way.

"Shit, is Casey here? Don't tell her I said that." Chase laughed too, but the sound cut suddenly short as he became aware of Brandon standing behind him.

"Strike one," Brandon said, his voice barely above a whisper.

"Huh?"

"They weren't married in high school. They weren't even dating," Brandon grunted. "That means they aren't together here."

"Chill out Brandon," Kimberly said. "We can be nostalgic without literally repeating high school."

"Seriously," Chase added. "I didn't have a tattoo in high school. You want me to scrape it off?"

Brandon seemed to seriously consider this for a moment. "No, that's not necessary." Chase had already half-turned away from him before Brandon grabbed his shoulder and turned him back. "You can just cover it up with some foundation."

"You're being ridiculous. Nobody cares."

"I care," Brandon said softly. "The spell doesn't work unless everything is perfect. Strike two."

"Screw you, man." Chase turned away and started walking toward the door.

"You can't leave before the bell rings!" Brandon shouted. Kimberly gave me a tight-lipped smile and rolled her eyes.

"No wonder you never had any friends," Chase shot back. "Guess some things never change after-all."

Snickers from all around. Brandon looked like he was holding his breath. His face was going bright red. Chase reached the door and heaved, but it didn't budge. Again, this time with both hands, grunting in exertion.

"You seriously locked us in here?"

"Strike three."

The gunshot shattered the air into so many ringing shards. We were all too stunned to make a sound as Chase's body slumped against the door and slid to the ground, leaving a great red smear on the door to show where the bullet exited his body on the other side.

Then the screaming started all at once. Still clutching his handgun, Brandon sprinted back to the microphone and howled at us until it was quiet enough for him to be heard.

"That's enough!" he shouted, still brandishing the hand gun in his free hand. "If you're not going to play by the rules, then you shouldn't have come. We didn't all get out of here in one piece. We didn't all get the job of our dreams, or find someone who loved us, but that doesn't matter anymore. Tonight we're back in 2008 with our whole lives ahead of us, and anything is possible."

He strutted to the stereo and turned up the music—Viva La Vida by Coldplay. The screams gave way to an electric silence as the assembly stared at Brandon in disbelief. He was getting red in the face again.

"Well?" he shouted. "What are you waiting for? Start dancing!"

The only movement was a few people cowering a little closer together. Kimberly hung onto my arm, her nails digging through my shirt.

Brandon was getting visibly more irritated the longer we waited. "You with the green dress," he shouted at a woman who was kneeling over Chase's crumpled body. "You used to date him, right?"

That was Emma. She and Chase had been together for a few months, but they split upon graduation. She held a hand over her mouth, stifling back sobs.

"Yeah, I remember seeing you together," Brandon continued, his words slurring together in their haste. "Act like it."

Emma stared in confusion, her face a mess of running tears and snot.

"Grab him by the hand. Dance with him," Brandon ordered.

"He's dead!" she shrieked. "You killed him!"

"He wasn't dead in 2008!" Brandon screamed back, limp hair whipping across the ghastly shade of purple his face as turning. He might have been intoxicated, but I'd never seen alcohol affect someone like that, the strange light almost glowing from his face. "Strike one! Don't let me get to three."

Still sniffling, Emma hoisted Chase's body up to its knees with visible effort. She kept looking back at Brandon and his leveled gun. Emma let the body's weight lean against her, his blood soaking through her dress. They began to sway to the music as she broke into fresh sobs.

Another gunshot. Emma gasped and let the body fall. It wasn't her though—it was Brody who used to play football. He'd tried to sneak into the cell phone bin while everyone was distracted. The shot hadn't hit him, but it was enough to make him freeze—standing stiff as though he were a scarecrow with a wooden pole up his ass.

"Brandon, please stop!" Kimberly shouted. She broke away from my arm. I tried to stop her, but she gave me that look that said 'trust me' and I let her go. The funny thing was that I really did trust her. More than the gun, or the dead body, or my own terror—she was more real than any of it, and she would know what to do.

"Why? Did you fuck him too?" Brandon asked, his face twisted into a cruel sneer.

"If we're all getting another chance," she said in a forced calm, walking toward Brandon with small, tense steps, "then I want to use mine to get to know you. We never talked much in high school."

I don't know what game she was playing, but I didn't like it. She was back in 2008 and wasn't my wife anymore though. She was her own person making her own choices, and anything I did to interfere would probably just get us both killed.

Brandon looked as uncertain as I felt. He shifted from one foot to the other, still loosely pointing the gun in her direction.

"No, we didn't talk much," he conceded at last. "I wanted to, but I didn't know how."

"I know," Kimberly said gently, still edging closer. "I felt the same way. Did you know I used to watch you when you weren't looking?"

Brandon opened and closed his mouth, but no sound came out.

"I used to see you eating lunch all alone and wonder what secrets that boy was hiding," Kimberly said, her voice trembling ever so slightly as she continued her approach. "But you never told me."

Brandon glanced nervously around the room. All eyes were on him. "No. I guess I never did."

Kimberly looked around as though noticing everyone for the first time. "It's not too late. You and I, we could go somewhere private. Everyone else can go, and you and I can have a chance to be alone together."

So that was her plan. To sacrifice herself so the others could escape. I had to do something, but what? I couldn't think of any way to interfere that wouldn't put everyone else in danger.

"Would you like that, Brandon?" Kimberly was close enough to his microphone that her seductive whisper was carried across the whole room. "Would you like to be alone with me?"

Brandon swallowed hard. Then nodded. He fumbled around the stereo controls until he found a button that made the bell ring. A heavy click resounded as the doors unlocked.

"Everyone out," Brandon ordered, not taking his eyes off my wife.

The doors burst open and everyone flooded through them. Everyone except me, still frozen in place.

They hadn't had a chance to get their cell phones. How long would it be before one of them was able to call for help? I had to stall.

"Strike two." The words as sharp as a slap across the face. Brandon was looking at me though—the barrel of his gun was looking too.

"I didn't do anything—" I protested.

"Strike one was pretending you were married to Kimberly when you came in," Brandon said. "Strike two was not leaving when the bell rang."

I took a hesitant step toward them, but before my foot had even touched the ground a bullet planted in the floor with a cascade of splintering wood.

"Please go." Kimberly's whisper still traveled across the room, so intimate yet so cold. Her eyes were pleading. "Brandon and I want to talk in private."

"I'll find you," I promised.

What else could I do? I turned and ran. I'd get to the closest store that was still open and call the police from there. Or knock on houses if I had to—one of them would see the desperation on my face and let me in.

It took less than five minutes of sprinting before I found a gas station, but it felt like hours. Every step was taking me farther away from my wife, and every second was bringing her closer to disaster.

The police didn't find them at the school. They didn't find them in their sweep of the neighborhood, and even more peculiar, didn't even find a trace of the bullets that had been fired.

They did find Brandon eventually though. He was sleeping in bed in his home a little over ten miles away. Kimberly was there too, confused as to what all the fuss was about. She'd spent a quiet evening with her husband, a high school sweetheart whom she'd gotten to know after an unlikely intimate conversation the two had shared 10 years ago.

Chase was at his home too. He'd never heard about a reunion, but he was happy to hear from me and didn't understand why I was so upset. No one understood why I was still so hung up over a girl from high school. Or why it hurt so much when she smiled her secret smile at someone other than me.

HEART EATER

I'd already found the engagement ring my boyfriend Niles hid in his sock drawer. Now he was taking me on a romantic weekend getaway with a private dinner at the base of a waterfall. It was supposed to be the best day of my life, but now he's dead and it's all my fault.

I was ready to say yes. It's all I could think about on the drive through the state park. My family never thought it would last, but I was going to prove them wrong. Dad called Niles a "pretty boy", and every time he saw a Disney Princess he'd point and ask "Hey, isn't that your boyfriend?"

I'd just smile and roll my eyes. They thought that just because Niles was handsome that I was superficial for being with him, but he was so much more than that. He was kind, and smart, and funny, and even more important, he made me feel like that's exactly what I deserved.

Everything was perfect that night except me. 'Something' by the Beatles was playing on a handheld stereo, and a dozen candles were scattered on the surrounding ground. There was chilled champagne in the ice chest, and stars in the sky, and the love of my life getting out of his chair to drop to one knee.

"Umm," probably wasn't the answer he was expecting. It wasn't what I was expecting to say either, but it was the best I could do.

"Umm?" Niles asked in disbelief. "I didn't drive all the way out here for an 'umm.'"

I was frozen. I'd rehearsed this moment a thousand times in my head, but my rehearsals hadn't prepared me for the breathless terror of the actual moment. All I could think about was my dad's words, wondering if it really was just his looks that I was attracted to.

In ten years, when he's started to bald and put on weight, am I still going to think his jokes are funny? When we settle down and have kids and romantic moments like this are replaced by daily chores and routines, will I still look at him the same way? Or even more likely, what if he's the one who gets bored of me?

"Umm," I said again.

"Unbelievable," Niles said. "Un-fucking believable."

"What? I didn't say no!"

"You didn't have to." Niles wasn't kneeling anymore. He wasn't even facing me—just staring off into the emptiness of night.

"It's a serious question!" I could have said yes then, but I felt obliged to defend myself. "There's nothing wrong with taking a moment to think."

"Take all the time you need. I'm going for a walk."

Again I had a chance. I could rush up to him and hug him and say of course I want to spend my life with you. But it only took him a few steps to exit the meagre light of the candles, and Niles was gone before I could gather my wits.

The song finished playing, and I was able to distinguish a strange plopping sound separate from the crash of the waterfall. My rapid breathing became louder, but it didn't drown out the mumbling whisper from the dark water.

"Niles? Are you still there?"

The whispering grew louder—a low rasping voice that sounded nothing like Niles, coming just beyond the ring of light. I couldn't make out every word, but a few were unmistakable.

"... your doubt... your fear... delicious."

That last word sounded with particular clarity, drawn out and savored as though each syllable was tasted.

Niles was playing a trick to get back at me. That meant he couldn't have taken my hesitation too seriously. I breathed a deep sigh of relief, but didn't even have a chance to fully exhale before I heard the crack of twigs. Then a muffled swear—all the way up the hill we'd hiked in on.

"Niles, was that you?" I called, my own voice so feeble and insignificant in the looming wilds. "Come back! Let's talk."

"Alright. I'm coming." That was from the hill again. So he hadn't been the one whispering.

"I can tell you," hissed the whisper. A stir of movement behind me. I spun just in time to catch something like a long slug disappearing beyond the light. "How he feels," the whisper came from the same place. "What he's really after, and whether you can give it to him."

I heard Niles stumble—still a fair distance away.

"Okay yeah," I said. "I need to know."

If a sound could curl like a smile, then that's exactly what the hiss did. Then it was gone, its barely perceptible shadow slipping into the deeper darkness beyond.

"Hold on, I'm almost there," Niles shouted from the same direction.

"Niles watch out!" It had only just occurred to me what I'd done. "There's something out there—"

His scream overwhelmed the splashing water and filled the sky from horizon to horizon. Tortuous, guttural, and long enough that he had to pause to draw breath to begin screaming again.

I was rushing toward him as fast as I could, but I made slow progress as soon as I pitched into the blackness. I kept stumbling over hidden rocks or blindly charging through thick underbrush, led by nothing but his screams which seemed to go on forever.

But forever is a dream from which all are forced to wake, and he was silent by the time I found him. The slug I'd glimpsed rested on his chest, pulsing as it burrowed its way into his flayed chest cavity. It was as wide as a tree trunk, maybe four feet long, perhaps more depending how deeply it sank within Niles' body.

"Do you still want to know?" The whisper came from the free end of the slug. "Everything he knew, everything he felt, his heart is not hidden from me."

Would it be wrong to listen to this monster which feasted upon him? Or would it be disrespectful to turn away and forever lose his final thoughts? For the second time that night, I was frozen and said nothing.

"I can taste his admiration," mused the creature. "From the first time he saw you, sitting alone reading a book. The intelligent focus on your face—the way the light played through your hair—he watched you for almost an hour before he worked up the courage to say hello."

"He never told me he was watching…"

"I can taste his love," it hissed. "Fresh from his heart, it fills me up. Enough to endure a hundred years of adversity. Until the night at the end of all days when age has stolen everything but the grace of your spirit, he would have loved you."

I had to hear this. Even though I was crying, I wouldn't leave. This was my solace and my punishment in one. The monster was silent for a long moment before it said:

"I love you too."

It was enough of a shock to suspend my heaving sobs.

"With everything he was, I am," it hissed. "I love you with all his heart."

The creature pulsed. Then again, the ripple cascading up and down its fleshy mass as it wriggled free. Niles heart was in full view, raw and wet and still beating where it was clutched in the creature's mouth. Then swallowing, the heart vanished still beating all the way down.

"I'm back," the second mouth said, speaking with Nile's voice as clear as the mountain air. "Let's just start over, okay? Don't overthink. Don't make assumptions. Don't be afraid. Will you marry me?"

I started to cry again. "Yes Niles. It was always yes."

I wasn't about to lose true love twice in one night. Besides, maybe now dad will finally shut up about me only loving him for his looks.

XENOPHOBIA

Patient Name: Jordan Malone
Age: 42
Sex: Male
Diagnosis: Xenophobia
Time of death: To be determined

THIS REPORT DOCUMENTS THE PERFORMANCE OF MJ220717 IN THE Skinner Prison Experiments. Due to the overcrowding of [REDACTED] State Penitentiary, we have been provided with an operational license to transfer qualified subjects to our rehabilitation facility.

MJ220717 was selected based on the following interview that our agent recorded in his blue notebook.

Agent: Please state the reason for your incarceration.

MJ220717: A beaner was threatening me, so I set his house on fire. You guys going to get me out, or what?

Agent: The police statement says that you were armed and accompanied by three accomplices. The victim was unarmed and living with his wife and five children. How was he threatening you?

MJ220717: Five children? Damn.

Agent: You were unaware?

MJ220717: I knew there were too many of them, but I didn't know they bred like roaches. They're threatening our way of life and will flood the country if somebody don't burn 'em out.

Agent: Do you plan to 'burn out' all 11 million illegal immigrants estimated living within the country?

MJ220717: We killed 6 million Jews last time. Yeah, I reckon we can do 11 if we work together.

Agent: So you and your hate group—

MJ220717: Hate group? Shit, we don't hate anybody. My momma don't raise me like that. Let me ask you something though—you go to church?

Agent: That's not relevant—

MJ220717: 'Cause I do. Me and [REDACTED] were doing God's work. Doing the Law's work that the police are too chicken-shit to do. Now I'm in jail while those fuckers walk around free in my country. So yeah, maybe I do hate that. That's injustice, pure and simple.

Agent: I understand. Thank you, Mr. Malone. I think we can help each other here.

MJ220717 was transferred to our facility two days later. He was happy to be released and provided no resistance as he was introduced to his new living quarters. He was provided with a standard suite, approximately 500 square feet with a private bathroom and mini kitchen.

There were no altercations when he was briefed on the details of his rehabilitation.

Agent: Our team has diagnosed you with xenophobia. Are you familiar with the term?

MJ220717: I'm not sick with nothing.

Agent: It means a fear of the unknown, based on your fear reaction with unfamiliar races and cultures—

MJ220717: I'm not afraid of them! I'm standing up to them. If a snake got in my house and I strangled it before it bit somebody, that's bravery right there. I'm protecting my country.

Agent: ...are we finished?

MJ220717: You said we could help each other.

Agent: I got you out of prison, didn't I? Now it's your turn to help me with my study. Unless you'd prefer to go back, of course.

MJ220717: Let's get this over with. What do I have to do? Talk to a counselor?

Agent: Something like that. We're pursuing a form of exposure therapy. It's only going to take two hours a day. The rest of the time will be yours, with access to television and recreational facilities.

MJ220717: I've heard of the exposure thing. So what, you're going to lock me in with a spic? We gonna play checkers or some shit?

Agent: This isn't about your relationship with foreigners. We're more interested in the deeper underlying issue—your fear of the unknown.

MJ220717 did not protest as he was locked inside his living quarters. Security footage continued to monitor him as he paced the room in agitation. This continued for several minutes before he returns to his bed and points the remote at the TV.

The screen remains black. He points again, mashing the buttons in visible frustration. He gets off the bed and approaches the TV, reaching to turn it on manually.

He isn't expecting the hand which reaches out of the screen to intertwine its fingers with his own. He stumbles backward and falls onto his bed. The hand is gone by the time he returns to the screen to smash it with his fist.

MJ220717 hyperventilates as he removes the shards of glass from his knuckles, but he otherwise seems unaware of the [REDACTED] entity now sharing his living space. All agents have vacated the area to give it space to work.

MJ220717 goes to the bathroom, presumably to look for medical supplies. He isn't expecting the swarm of spiders that flood from the medicine cabinet. The capacity is only a few cubic feet, but the contents are sufficient to cover the entire surface area of the bathroom within seconds.

MJ220717 flees the bathroom and closes the door behind him. He presses his back against it for several seconds, his hyperventilation exasperated. When he notices the spiders crawling under the door, he retreats to the bed and pulls the sheets to seal the gap.

He's hammering on the apartment door, calling for help. There is still an hour and forty minutes left of his session, and the door remains locked.

The [REDACTED] entity doesn't remain idle during this time. The hand has reappeared out of the garbage disposal, feeling its way around the kitchen sink.

MJ220717 notices it now. He approaches and stares at the thing, apparently realizing that it is growing into the room rather than reaching. Similar to the development of a time-lapsed plant or mushroom, the hand and arm are swelling. The joints grow more gnarled and misshapen, and additional fingers begin to bud.

MJ220717 tries to turn on the garbage disposal, but the hand intercepts him and interlocks its fingers once more. They struggle briefly before the subject is able to maneuver his free hand to reach the switch. He turns it on, but the intertwined hands drag him into the blades.

He manages to turn off the garbage disposal before his hand enters. He flees once more to the front door, pounding and screaming.

The bathroom door opens. The spiders have been growing in the same manner as the hand, and each are now the size of a rat. They're now large enough for him to realize that they are scuttling on tiny fingers instead of legs.

MJ220717 spends the remainder of his two-hour session pressed against the door while the growing [REDACTED] entities crawl over him. He's still crying when the agent retrieves him and permits him to move to a fresh living space.

Agent: Ever see anything like that before?

MJ220717 is quietly crying.

Agent: We're not so different, you and me. Or you and those people whose house you tried to burn down. Or you and your ancestors ten thousand years ago. We're all pretty much the same, compared with something like that. Don't you think?

MJ220717: I want to go back to jail. Please.

Agent: You have 22 hours before your next session. Feel free to take comfort with your fellow humans in the recreational area until then. You have more in common than you think.

A GLOBAL RELIGION

IT BEGAN WITH ALCOHOL, AS MORE THAN ONE RELIGION MUST HAVE done before. I wanted to be drunk by the time I got home. It's a habit I picked up after my divorce when I realized how cold an empty house can be without a little fire in the blood.

There's a pub around the block that lets me park my car overnight. I'd stop after work and walk home when I couldn't feel my face anymore. The chill morning air on my walk back helped wake me up enough to drive to work, and then I'd do it all again.

I'd thought about going to Alcoholics Anonymous, but I figured I could do the same stuff they did on my own. All I had to do is surrender myself to God, right? To admit that I'm helpless and he's all powerful, and to accept that he doesn't want anyone to have any fun.

It's getting to be winter here though, and one night it was so damn cold that I felt like my skin was peeling off just standing outside. I'd drive home—just this once. No one else was on the road, and I thought I could inch along without any trouble.

I don't know how I turned down an unfamiliar road this close to my home, but whether it was a trick of the darkness or the alcohol, I presently found myself before a row of strange houses. Piles of trash, boarded windows, and even the gutted skeletons of burned houses loomed above me on either side. I was about to turn back when something dark dashed in front of my car.

I slammed my foot down, but somehow the shock crossed my wires and I hit the gas instead. The car lurched forward, and I heard a loud, wet noise, like someone belly flopping into a pool from ten stories up. I heard the second bump as my back tires rolled over it before I could stop.

I threw open my door and stumbled out. There was a long glistening streak behind my tires. A crumpled shape in the road, and one naked white bone jutting out to reflect my taillights.

I threw up. It was a long one where I kept heaving and spitting up bile and drool long after my stomach was empty. I could hear this pitiful moaning the whole time, but I was helpless to my trembling contractions and couldn't help him.

I thought I was too late by the time I walked back to the mess on the road. There wasn't an inch of unmarked skin or a limb that wasn't folded back on itself. The broken form looked more like it had gone through a blender than been hit by a car.

"Please..." the voice said, gurgling and spluttering as it did. "Please forgive me."

"Forgive you? Shit, I was the one—hold on, I'm going to call for help."

"I'm sorry. I'm sorry. I know I deserve this, but have mercy."

It took supreme concentration to force my clumsy fingers to dial 911, but I froze before I hit call. The broken form was rising, and dozens of fingers were intertwining in front of it in a gesture of prayer.

Dozens. I kept blinking, sure that the alcohol was playing tricks on me. As it continued to stand, it became undeniable though: whatever I was looking at wasn't human.

I couldn't understand how my car could have done that much damage, but now I saw that it hadn't. The creature's body was covered in boils and welts, many of which were long since ruptured to weep rivers of dried blood and pus. Its third leg was shriveled as though devoid of muscle or bone, dragging limp on the ground behind it.

Veins across its body stood out like knotted rope beneath the skin, except in the many places where they exited the skin entirely to tangle with one another before sinking back into the flesh.

I felt the nausea swelling up within me again, but I was too empty to vomit again. We stared at one another for a long moment before it said:

"You're not one of us."

I shook my head.

Something like a snarl crossed its face, destroying its last visage of humanity and replacing it with a mask of bestial terror.

"You don't know how long we've waited for you," it hissed.

I turned and began walking toward my car, swaying but remaining upright.

"Please don't leave us!" The terrible wail behind me only made me hasten my pace. "The others are coming."

I dropped heavily back into the driver seat and slammed the door. I spent a few moments fumbling with the buttons before I heard the doors lock. I re-locked them a dozen times just to be sure. When I looked up, I could see the face of the creature filling my rearview mirror.

It bore traces of being human, but only so much as butchered meat hints at the finally prepared meal which might be made from it. The car's side panels on either side shook, and there were more of the creatures peering through the windows. Then a loud thump on the roof, and the pitter-patter of those dozens of fingers probing along the surface, feeling each ridge for a way in.

Though mired in the dead of night, the surrounding street had come alive. The light of flames flickered into existence in the surrounding houses, and where there was no flame a sea of eyes reflected the light from the shadows. Long fingers pried away the boards on the windows, and much of what I'd mistaken for trash now shifted with the teeming beings which had huddled underneath.

"Don't leave us, my pure-skin, my love." A living echo which multiplied with every utterance. "Love, love—never leave."

I maneuvered the car forward, trying my best not to hit anyone.

My hesitation only made it more difficult as the creatures continued pressing in around the car. I had no choice but to floor the pedal and press through them, hoping they'd get out of the way.

They didn't. If anything, they made an active effort to hurl themselves before the car as though their bodies could slow my departure. The wails rose in pitch around me, the agony of the fallen growing more frenzied and desperate by the second.

Each that was crushed or wounded by the relentless passage of my car would be swiftly seized by their massing brethren. Such victims could not defend themselves and were swiftly torn to shreds, devoured alive before my eyes. The empty space was filled at once with more creatures who hurled themselves before me only to be met with a similarly gruesome fate.

Crawling headfirst down from windows, or digging up from the ground, or manifesting from the darkness, this swarming legion flooded toward me from all directions. I increased my speed and gave no regard to the constant buckling of the car as it rolled over the incessant mob.

But I could not block out the wailing grief, nor the chanting which arose from every corner of this blasphemous street. Dark hymns whistled and shrieked with feverish pitch, and again the echoes which spread through the chaos like an infectious disease.

"We need you—we love you—our pure-skin God. Take us with you —don't leave us—our pure-skin God."

Until I'd finally gained enough acceleration to tear through the last of them and break free onto the open street. Many tried to race alongside me for as long as they could, their deformed bodies moving with desperate urgency until they collapsed in exhaustion and were beset by those behind.

I didn't dare slow until I'd left that madness far behind and found myself on a solitary hill. I paused to look at the view and get my bearings, but I recognized nothing that I saw.

Unfamiliar towers gouged the sky, mountains lit by firelight. The neighborhood I passed was no anomaly, for as far as I could see the ruined buildings were writhing to life with the swarming creatures. I couldn't stay long though, for already bright eyes were reflecting from the darkness around.

I drove again until I found a larger road, and then taking that I kept going until I found a highway. The echo had spread far past the street of its origin, and I heard the phrase "pure-skin" follow me where I went like rolling thunder across the land.

I was the only car on the highway and remained so for many miles while fleeing that awful den. My head ached, and I was exhausted, but I forced my eyes to remained locked on the road ahead of me and didn't deviate from my path.

It wasn't until the early hours of the morning when I heard a siren and suddenly realized I was no longer alone on the road. The daily traffic had gradually resumed around me, each car occupied by a human driver—bored, sleepy, and ignorant to the denizens of that dreadful night.

"Do you know why I pulled you over?" the policeman asked when he got out of his car.

"Because I'm wretched and I deserved it," I managed to reply.

"I'm more concerned about the blood on your car," he said.

Good thing it wasn't human blood, or I could have been in real trouble.

I don't know how I stumbled into that world, but I think I accidentally started some sort of religion there. So must all things seem glorious to the wretched. If only they understood how small and powerless their pure-skinned God really was.

FIRST RULE OF FRIGHT CLUB

The first rule of fright club is that you can't join if you have a heart condition or high blood pressure. That's just common sense though, right?

The second rule is that you can't leave the room until the bell rings. Whatever you see or feel in there—whatever sees or feels you—that's your reality until the round is over.

The third rule is that you cannot take anything with you or let anything follow you out. The poster said that breaking any of these rules makes the participant ineligible to win the $10,000 grand prize, which comes with a unique internship opportunity.

The cartoon pumpkin and witch stickers didn't make it sound very threatening. Besides, the poster had my University logo on it, and everyone knows that school-sponsored events are lame and politically correct by necessity.

"You can't not do it," my friend Jesse told me. "It's free money." This coming from the guy whose retirement plan is buying a lottery ticket every month.

"There has to be a catch," I told him. "They charged me to print out my resume so I could apply to their own job offers. You aren't going to get it."

"Let's make it more interesting then," Jesse said. "Bet you $100 bucks that I last longer than you, whatever it is."

$10,000 is $10,000, but showing up my friend and taking his money? Now that's priceless. I agreed to check it out, and we both went to the specified room in the psychology building after our classes finished for the day.

The stickers made it easy to find the right place. Big black cauldrons with frothing brew, zombies and skeletons, ghosts with their billowing sheets and demons with pitchforks. The scrawny teenager in the long black cloak who checked us in was even less intimidating.

"You know the three rules?" the guy in the cloak asked when we said we'd like to join.

"Yeah. But what's up with something following you out?" I asked.

The teenager shrugged. "Donno. I figure they just don't want to make a mess in the rest of the building."

"Has anyone won yet?" Jesse asked.

"Maybe?" The teenager scratched the back of his head with the intensity of a dog chasing fleas. "Man, just let me read from the script, okay?" He coughed and held up a clipboard, beginning again in what he must have thought was a dark and spooky voice. It sounded more like Dracula's gay lover to me.

"Once upon a time in a far away land, an aging King had to decide which of his three sons would next sit upon the throne. Believing bravery to be most important, the King devised Fright Club to test which of his sons were worthy."

"Seriously? What self-respecting King would call his test Fright Club?" Jesse asked.

The teenager gave us a long suffering look, like a waiter when you ask him to taste your gluten-free food to see if he thought could still taste the gluten.

"Ever since, Fright Club has been passed down through the generations," the cloaked guy continued. "Dare ye enter to see if you too are brave enough to be King?"

"Is that what we're interning for? Being King?" Jesse quipped.

"Just sign the damn form," the teenager snapped. "I don't know anything more than you do."

I picked at one of the pumpkin stickers on the wall while Jesse was signing. It peeled cleanly back to reveal a little hole in the wall. It was time for me to sign though, so I pressed the sticker back into place and pretended I didn't see anything. I thought that I might be able to get an advantage from this insight later.

The teenager meanwhile produced a large uncarved pumpkin from beneath a table and left it in the middle of the room. He set a timer on the table for ten minutes and said he'd check back after the first round was over. Then he was gone, and it was just me, Jesse, and the pumpkin.

"I don't get it," Jesse said, pacing the perimeter of the room. "What are we supposed to—"

The lights went out, suspending the room in nearly complete darkness. The only glimmer came from the stickers which apparently glowed.

"Oooh I'm a four-year-old. I need a nightlight because I'm scared of the dark," Jesse whined.

"Shut up. Do you hear something?" I asked.

"Yeah, I think so. It sounds a bit like the easiest $100 I ever made."

I didn't reply. I was intent on the scraping, scratching sound. Like a knife peeling a potato, or—

"Something is carving the pumpkin. Listen."

I felt my way toward the center of the room and the sound grew stronger. It was a wet, juicy sound, and I could clearly smell the freshly cut pumpkin.

"My phone isn't turning on," Jesse grumbled. "Can you see what's happening?"

I fumbled in my pocket. My phone was dead too, although it had been at half battery the last time I checked. I gingerly probed the darkness with my foot until I found the pumpkin. I reached down to feel it with my fingers, but immediately recoiled at the soft, warm touch.

"It doesn't feel like a pumpkin..." I said.

Jesse traced my voice and quickly located it as well. I felt him kneeling beside me.

"That's a head, dude. Check it, I've got the nose right here."

I felt along his arm until I reached his hand. Then back to the invisible 'pumpkin'. It was undeniable. The shape, the flexible cartilage, even the lips and teeth below it. There was a human head where the pumpkin had been.

"This is kid stuff, dude," Jesse said with the slightest tremor in his throat. "I wonder how much time we've got left."

"So what's the sound coming from if it's not a pumpkin?" I asked. My hand was still tracing the face when I felt the jaw suddenly open. The scraping sound grew louder. Something brushed against my fingers, evidently exiting the mouth.

I stumbled back a few paces. "Jesse? Did you feel that? Where are you?"

"Over here man. I'm getting some glow stickers to try to see what's going on."

I spotted him against the wall, his hands vaguely illuminated by the small stack of stickers he'd already peeled off. The scraping sound was coming from the walls now too. Something was coming through the holes behind the stickers.

"Stop it. Put them back," I said.

"Chill, dude. You're just jealous you didn't think of it first."

"Hurry then. Come on, that's enough."

His pale illuminated hands were carrying about a dozen glowing stickers. I watched him grab two more before carrying the pile toward the middle of the room. Then his hands hesitated, and he changed direction.

"Hold on a second. I'm just going to check the timer."

The scraping was getting louder by the second. Like sandpaper along a rough surface, or hundreds of tiny legs skittering—

"Three minutes left. No big deal."

Something flying brushed my face. Then another one. The whirr of unseen wings beat against the blackness all around me.

"I want out of here," I said.

"Come on, we're almost there. I bet it's just like stuff on strings swinging around." His glowing hands were moving toward the center of the room.

"Are you encouraging me to stay now? Don't you care about winning anymore?"

"Whatever, I can win next round instead. I just don't want to be alone in here."

"Aha! I knew it! You are afraid!" The triumph of that realization gave me courage. It was easy to forget that we were still at school with the dark buzzing all around us.

"Do you remember when we were freshman and those three guys started following us one night?"

Jesse was standing directly over where the head was, but the light didn't reach far enough down.

"Yeah, so what?" I asked.

"You remember how we kept taking random routes to lose them, but they kept making all the same turns?" He still wasn't moving.

"What are you waiting for?" I asked. "Light that sucker up."

"Then how we started running, and they ran too? But they were just playing a prank on us to scare us."

More flying things were brushing against me. They kept landing on my face or the back of my neck. My hands were nonstop windshield wipers now, but it still wasn't enough to keep them off.

"What does that have to do with anything?" I asked. "Is this a pep talk or something?"

"No," Jesse said. "I just wanted you to remember." He finally knelt down with the glowing stickers. If that was a fake head on the ground, then it was the realest fake head I'd ever seen. From the congealed blood at the base of the severed neck to the flies and maggots swarming out of its mouth, everything looked exactly how I'd imagine it should.

"I just want you to know how well I tricked you. I know everything Jesse knew, because I already got him the second the lights turned off."

The glowing handful of stickers illuminated Jesse's head on the ground. But it couldn't really be him because I've been hearing his voice the whole time. Hadn't I?

I studied the hands that were holding the glowing stickers. For the first time I noticed how large and rough the fingers were. How much hair was on the knuckles. The light wasn't strong enough to see the rest of him, but in that moment I was 100% certain that those were not Jesse's hands.

"Run," Jesse's voice said from the darkness.

"I'm not leaving before you do, Jesse," I said, addressing the head on the ground. "$100, that's the deal. But I'm not leaving without you either."

"That's good," said Jesse's voice. The pitch of the voice grew deeper with each word. "I'll see you again in round 2 then."

The hands cupped to cover the glowing stickers and disappeared along with the head. There was no sound but the mad buzzing of insects, although this too grew fainter and more distant by the moment.

I crossed my arms and stood stubbornly still until the bell rang. The lights came on an instant later, just in time for me to see the last few insects crawling back into the holes in the wall. They looked like wasps, but were at least three inches long with monstrous spiral stingers. They reminded me of those army knives that were supposed to leave wounds that couldn't be closed.

"Round 1 clear!" the teenager said with forced enthusiasm. "Congratulations."

I blinked rapidly to readjust to the light. There was a pumpkin in the middle of the floor again. Jesse's head and the other figure were nowhere to be seen.

"What about Jesse?" I asked. "Did he leave early?"

"Who?"

"Jesse. The other guy who took the test with me."

The teenager scratched his head vigorously. Hard enough for there to be blood under his fingernails when he withdrew his hand.

"I don't know what you're talking about. Only one person at a time is allowed to take the tests. You came in here alone."

Jesse hasn't answered my calls since I got out. No one has seen him anywhere. I can only hope there will be more answers in the second round.

SECOND RULE OF FRIGHT CLUB

THE SECOND RULE IS THAT YOU CAN'T LEAVE THE ROOM UNTIL THE BELL rings. Whatever you see or feel in there—whatever sees or feels you—that's your reality until the round is over.

I guess I shouldn't have been surprised to find Jesse waiting for me inside the Fright Club room. The severed head had been pretty convincing though, and I was cautious not to close the door completely behind me. We were the only ones in the room, and it was empty except for a table covered by a white sheet.

"Nice robe," I told Jesse. "What happened to the other guy?"

Jesse was scratching his right forearm. Hard. It sounded like the nails were splintering. I studied his face hard, trying to discern whether it was really him or only the thing pretending.

"Huh? Hey man, haven't seen you in..." his voice trailed off. He turned his attention back toward scratching his red arm.

"So you work here now?" I asked, trying to keep my voice casual.

"Yeah since..." Scratch. Scratch. Scratch. Then he stole a glance at me, shying away from meeting my eyes. "Your hair is different," Jesse said. "Longer. A lot longer—is that a wig?"

The shock of finding him occupied my initial attention. Now that he mentioned it though, he looked different too. He was paler and skinnier than he was yesterday, with rough stubble that couldn't have grown overnight.

"No. Just combed weird," I replied cautiously. I could only hope that this was the real Jesse, but I couldn't let my guard down.

"You know how it is, man," Jesse said. "It's not like the King asks whether someone wants the job or not. Someone's got to do it though, right?"

"Sure," I lead him on. "Otherwise how would the King know who was going to rule after him?"

"You know what's up," Jesse bobbed and nodded. He moved towards me, but I got out of the way to give him space.

My mistake—Jesse was headed for the door, not for me. Now I'd let that thing get between me and my only exit. He roughly closed the door and turned to face me.

"Are we ready to begin?" Jesse asked.

A muffled ticking began before I could answer. I couldn't make out where it was coming from though.

"How long have we had a King?" I asked.

He grinned like he was in on the joke. I didn't follow up with anything though, and gradually the smile cracked at the edges to draw the lips tight and thin.

"Always. But you've just got ten minutes." I felt an anxious rush as though it was my time running out instead of the game's.

"I saw you dead," I said accusingly, unable to maintain my forced nonchalance any longer.

"Yeah..." Jesse replied hoarsely. "I felt it too. Like lightning through my throat, and then everything went numb, and I saw my body tumbling away..." He turned away, his hands on the back of his neck. Scratching. Blood between the nails. "That was only my other, though. I guess your other is still alive?"

I hadn't considered that. I didn't want to consider what he meant.

"The King said we'll know when our double dies, even if he's in the parallel universe," the other Jesse continued. "I thought it would be more like a notification though. I didn't expect to actually feel him die."

"I don't understand this round," I interrupted. I was getting impatient and frustrated. "What's supposed to be scary about this?"

"This one isn't supposed to be scary," the other Jesse said. He went to the table and began rolling back the sheet. "There's more to bravery than not being scared. Like enduring pain, for example."

A thin naked body was revealed beneath the sheet. I winced as it turned toward me, recognizing my own face staring back.

"Yeah, that's the short hair I remember," Jesse said, staring at the thin body. Then to me: "I guess that makes you the other."

The ticking was louder now. It was coming from the body on the table. Jesse continued rolling back the sheet until he reached the stomach, revealing the alarm clock embedded deep within the flesh. It looked like an old wound because the skin had grown around it to hold it in place with hardened scar tissue.

"What's it like? The other side?" Jesse turned away from the body. I wish I could too, but my eyes were fixed. "What's the King like?"

The ticking stopped. My other groaned and shifted on the table.

"We don't have a King," I told the other Jesse.

"No King..." the other Jesse sighed. "I wish I could go back with you."

I may have been slow to realize it, but that's when it really hit me. This room—maybe the whole building, but definitely this room—wasn't in my reality. I was already on the other side.

"What's going on?" I asked. "Why did the clock stop?"

"You've got to take it out to resume it," Jesse said. "Otherwise the round will never end."

The face of the clock barely protruded from my other's skin. I didn't know how far back it extended, but removing the clock would leave a gaping hole that would doubtlessly be a mortal wound.

My other whimpered and closed his eyes. My eyes—his eyes—it didn't matter. I shook my head and went for the door.

"I'm not going to kill him," I said. Jesse didn't move to stop me, so I accelerated until I reached the exit. "I only came back because I thought I could save you. You can come with me—"

"Third rule," Jesse replied.

"Fine, suit yourself. I'm going."

Only I wasn't. Opening the door, there was no school hallway or decorated walls. There was a long corridor of rough stone with red flickering electric lights. And a rising echo—a distant scream reverberating through the stone. I swiftly closed the door again.

"The second rule—"

"Shut up. Shut the hell up," I said, angrily pacing back. "I'm not going to do it."

Jesse shrugged and resumed scratching.

"What the hell is wrong with you, anyway?" I asked.

He shrugged again, focusing on his task.

I was getting really agitated, but I couldn't control it. I paced restlessly, trying not to look at my other's frail body. The only other place to look was the other Jesse and his incessant scratching.

Scratch scratch scratch—he was beginning to draw blood again. It beaded out of his forearm to dribble down toward his wrist. I stared as he picked at the tattered skin, peeling it back like a child playing with dried glue.

There was something moving underneath. Small black fingers, quick as anything, darted out of the wound to draw the skin back together. I only saw it for a moment, but it was enough.

I worked up the courage to stand over my other on the table. He wasn't me, no matter how much he looked like it. He wasn't human, although that thought was an even harder sell because his face held so much suffering and resignation.

"Okay. Okay okay." Deep breath. "I'm sorry," I said to the thing wearing my face. It didn't hear, or didn't react if it did.

I grabbed the clock with my fingertips and began to pull. My other started to scream, and I reflexively released, feeling the building pressure in my own stomach release as well. Then gritting my teeth I grabbed again, dragging it out one excruciating centimeter at a time.

Blood was swelling from beneath the clock, soaking my fingers and making it slippery and hard to hold. At the same time I could feel the gouging pressure in my own stomach explode into a white-hot knot of pain.

My other began to thrash on the table, but I pulled even harder. This wasn't happening. He's not human. I'm not really killing him. I'm not really dying. The words made no impact on the agony of the moment. It doesn't matter whether this was reality or not. It was real to me.

The small black fingers emerged from my other's open wound and danced around the clock, dragging it back inside. I wrestled with them, but they were incessant and I was growing weak from pain. I needed something sharp—something to cut it out with, but I had nothing but my own hands.

I managed to get the clock completely out of the skin, but I couldn't break the grip of the dark fingers. My only choice was to hold the clock with one hand while using the other to reach inside the wound, feeling around the back of the clock to try to turn it back on. This blind maneuver was subtle, and it as almost impossible to concentrate because I could feel a hand rummaging around in my own stomach the whole while.

Click—then ticking—at last the clock was going again. I released the clock and dragged my hand out of my other's stomach cavity. The pressure immediately vanished in my own stomach, but the shock was enough to leave me panting and heaving on all fours.

I heard my own scream, but I couldn't be sure whether it was coming from me or my other. I stayed there on my hands and knees, waiting for the pain to slowly subside until it was nothing more than a dull ache.

The bell finally rang.

"If I finish all three trials, do I become King?" I asked at last.

"That's how it's usually done," Jesse said.

"And I could do whatever I want then, right? I could break my own rules and let people out, or stop playing games with them, or anything I wanted?"

"I don't see who would stop you."

"So when does the final round start?"

THIRD RULE OF FRIGHT CLUB

THE THIRD AND FINAL RULE IS THAT YOU CANNOT TAKE ANYTHING WITH you, or let anything follow you out. It's the only rule I broke during my trials.

I wanted to bring my double with me when I left the second round. The black fingers did wonders to mend his wound from the inside, and though broken in spirit, there was still breath dragging from his lungs when I left.

But for an accident of birth, I could have been that tormented pawn in this unholy game. Or maybe I was no less of a pawn than him —maybe I was him, and there was no difference at all—it's still very confusing for me. Ultimately, I decided that I would do no good for anyone unless I could pass the third round though, and I left him so as not to jeopardize my chances.

The King was waiting in the open door of the Fright Club room for the third round. On his head rested a thin crown of twisted black wire, but I didn't need that to recognize him. The thick hair on his hands—the deep voice when he welcomed me—he was the man who had killed the real Jesse in the first round. More than that though, it was the familiarity in his ancient face that made me so certain.

"Is that really what I'm going to look like when I get old?" I asked him. From the set of his jaw to the sharp angles of his nose and high arching brows, I knew I was looking at another version of myself despite the toll of years.

"If you get old," the King replied somberly.

He smiled and stepped aside graciously, gesturing for me to enter. The room didn't have the facade of a classroom anymore—cold stone and red electric lights trailed off into a sea of shadows in the massive space.

The air was musty and cold when I stepped inside, and sound echoed and lingered beneath the massive dome overhead. It reminded me of a gothic cathedral, except that in place of religious iconography there were only statues and carved designs of strange and monstrous creatures that had never been seen on Earth.

"Stand with your others," the King said in a voice accustomed to being obeyed. "We'll begin when the last contestants have arrived."

I shivered as I moved toward the dozen other shapes. They were sitting on a row of benches which were arranged around the perimeter of the round room. I can't say I was surprised to see each wearing my face as they tracked my progress toward them.

That's not to say that there weren't still variations between us though. One was young—looking just as I had ten years ago, wearing the bright red sweatshirt that I remember wearing to school every day. Another was hardly recognizable because of his dozens of piercings, and a third was even female, sharing my features in the way twins might. Their clothes ranged from coarse hand-sewn linens to sleek suits and everything in-between, including two wearing a seamless metallic substance which fit them as close as a second skin.

"Um, hi," I said to the assembly of my others. "My name is—"

They knew my name because it chorused back to me at once.

"That's what we're all called," the youngest one chimed in.

"Sure, okay," I said. "That's going to get confusing though, don't you think?"

The female version of myself said: "It shouldn't be a problem. Only one of us will leave this place."

"Did the King tell you that?" I asked.

They all glanced back and forth, reading each other's faces with unspoken acknowledgement. No, they didn't have to be told. Deep down they just knew—and so did I.

"How are we the only ones to make it to the end?" I asked. Again I knew the answer before I'd even finished asking, but the cold silence of this place begged to be filled.

"The rest of us didn't survive the first two rounds," the woman said. "We're the only ones he wants."

"But why?"

The King's deep voice echoed indistinctly. All froze and turned their attention toward two more of us—me twenty years from now, with a large belly and receding hair, and another me whose gaunt and haunted expression looked like the mugshot of a heroin addict.

"It would be best if I answered that," the King said, following the two latest arrivals toward us. "It all begins with a King and his three sons. Stop me if you've heard this one."

"None of the three sons passed," my other in a suit said. "They all died in this round."

The King beamed. I half-expected him to take a treat from his pocket and throw it at my other. Instead, he said: "Correct. And it is a blessing that they did, for it would be a greater tragedy by far to have a weak King sit upon the throne. Imagine now that poor old King whose sand ran swift through the hourglass. He had watched all three of his dear sons die, and now his Kingdom would be lost without a strong hand upon the reigns. Follow."

The King continued walking toward the center of the great chamber as he drew level with us. We stood and followed him across the uneven stone.

"None were worthy to sit upon the throne," the King continued, "save for the King himself. If he could conjure a magic draught to live forever, doubtless he would be ruling still. Instead he did the next best thing—he found a way to create his other and crown a younger self, and so he began his rule again."

The King stopped at the center of the room where a large pit was carved into the floor. Inside the three-foot drop, the pit was filled with fine-powdered sand. Embedded in the sand were swords, spears, axes, and other strange bladed devices that I could not recognize. In the very center of the sand was a large-faced clock.

"Each King has refined this subtle art and passed on his knowledge, until now we are no longer limited to a single other. We create all the variations of ourselves and spread them so each may have different experiences and lives. Each comes from different epochs with different talents. Only this King among Kings is fit to rule hereafter, and only one of you is worthy to replace me."

I closed my eyes but could not block the image of what must surely come next. He would have us fight and kill one another here until only one was left. And worse still, each wound and death that we inflict upon one another must also be felt upon ourselves, such was the agony of the clock in the second round.

"And if we don't?" I was first to break the heavy silence. "If we all refuse to rule and you are left to wait for age to take you?"

"You aren't the first to ask that." The King sneered. "It only takes one of you to want it though, and knowing myself, at least one of us is ready to kill."

My others sensed it too, as they must thinking with my mind. We looked to one another for comfort, but saw only the eyes of our victims or our murderer looking back at us. The same ambition which drove me to return for the final round must also burn in their hearts. I could trust none of them any more than I could trust myself, and in such desperate circumstances I did not value my nobility high.

"I won't kill you," whispered the girl out of the corner of her mouth.

"Thanks," I whispered back. "That's the nicest thing anyone has said to me all day."

She coughed discreetly. The King glanced at us, then turned away.

"And?" she prompted urgently. "You're supposed to say you won't kill me either."

"Oh right, yeah. Definitely not. I mean, there isn't really another option, but hopefully not."

The King was starting to pull the weapons from the sand. He was still talking—something about the glory of victory and the honor of besting yourself. I wasn't really listening anymore.

"We could run." She barely mouthed the words, but our minds were already running down the same road.

"We'd have to break the third rule," I said. "The King—"

"The King is our other too," she interrupted. "When one of us is killed—he'll feel it too. That will be our chance. I don't want to go alone."

The King was looking at us again. I didn't reply, but I gave the slightest nod. That would be enough for her to understand. It was enough for the King too.

"You, boy. From the University. You're first." The King hurled a sword at me, handle first. I snatched it and almost dropped it immediately, surprised by its weight. "Suit—you too. Let's make this quick."

I felt several hands on my back pushing me toward the pit. I glanced back at the girl—the subtlest nod. But before we could break for it, someone had to die. And if I was in the first round, that meant that I had to kill.

The suit was fumbling a set of javelins when I dropped onto the sand. If I were him, I wouldn't hesitate. That's why I rolled the instant I hit the ground—just in time before the first spear quivered in the sand beside me.

The ticking of the clock began, but I wasn't playing anymore.

There wasn't anywhere left to hide. He'd expect me to charge straight at him, trying to close the distance to use my sword. I took a sharp right instead, feeling the air of a second javelin digging into the ground. He'd be ready for that trick next time, but I wouldn't give him the chance.

I dashed across the sand directly toward him. My feet were sinking with every step though, and it was taking longer to reach him than I expected. I tried to dodge again as he raised his arm, but he held the javelin this time and waited until the last possible moment. I tried to switch directions again, but I lost my footing in the loose sand and tumbled to the ground. A few feet away from him and helplessly mired, he wouldn't miss again.

The pain came with an explosion of light and heat. In one side and out the other, straight through the heart. I was dead, and the only mystery left was wondering how I knew I was dead.

"Run! Everyone now is your chance!" the girl screamed.

I was back on my feet before I realized what happened. My combatant fell to his knees, the tip of a knife protruding from his chest. The girl was standing behind. He never threw the last javelin—it was his death that I'd felt.

I scrambled out of the pit and helped her out behind me. The old King was clutching his chest and gasping for breath—everyone was in an equal state of shock and pain, but the older ones were slower to recover.

Some of us broke away and started running for the door—the youngest boy, the girl, and the middle aged man.

"Kill them!" the King roared. "Shoot them in the back. It'll save you trouble in the arena."

Swords bouncing off the stone, the whir of projectiles in the air, neither as terrifying as seeing my faces contorted in rage and bloodlust as they charged after me.

"He recovered too fast," I yelled. "He won't let us escape."

"Keep going, trust me," the girl said. I wanted to explain that I couldn't trust her because I couldn't trust myself, but I decided not to waste the air.

We leapt over the benches. Behind me I heard one of them turn over as someone stumbled and fell. It was the youngest boy, sprawled out on the stone on the other side of an upturned bench. The boy was on his knees again in a second, but not fast enough—

The whir of a crossbow and the fatal pain returned. Like a drill bursting through the back of my skull. I kept running—there's no way someone could have survived a blow like that.

It bought us enough time to get to the door. I flung it open and stood staring at the empty stone corridor beyond. I slammed the door shut again and re-opened it to the same sight.

"No one is going anywhere," the King's booming voice reverberated through the chamber. "Not until they finish my game."

The girl arrived beside me a second later. She ripped open the door a third time to see the same hall.

"His game, his rules," she sighed in exasperation. The others would be on us in a matter of seconds. "On my signal, you open it again."

"It's no good. We're still stuck in—"

"You have to trust me," she said.

"What signal?"

But the signal was impossible to miss. A blade in my heart, staggering me to my knees. I forced myself upright and opened the door at once, seeing my school corridor with the Halloween stickers beyond.

I leapt through and turned to see the girl still on her knees, hands pressing the knife into her own heart. The King was bellowing somewhere beyond—the shock must have been enough to break the spell separating the two dimensions for just a moment.

With the last of her strength, the girl lunged forward and slammed the door in my face. I instinctively tried to open it once more, but the pain which overtook me was unbearable.

I died a dozen times in the next few moments. My head was caved in, or lopped off entirely. The piercing of blades sliding between each rib, and other wounds which were harder to classify. There was a slaughter in progress on the other side of the door, and I was helpless to stop it.

By the time the worst of it passed I stood and flung the door open, ready to rush back and save who could be saved. I nearly tripped over myself entering the empty classroom. Lights off, desks pushed against the wall, there was no sign of the other world which I'd been cut off from.

I don't know who survived in the end, if anyone. I can only hope that whatever black magic preserved us with the mending fingers saved her somehow. I hope that there is a Queen who sits next upon the throne, and that she will break the tradition and go in peace.

I tell myself that I'm the lucky one, but I don't know. How can I go back to living my life when so many parts of me will never leave the Fright Club room?

ANTENNAS ON EVERY HOUSE

THE ANTENNAS WEREN'T INSTALLED DURING THE DAY. SOMEONE WOULD have noticed the electrician's van in the street. I don't see how they could have been put in at night either though. I can clearly hear when squirrels chase each other on my roof—there's no way I wouldn't notice someone walking around up there.

Mrs. Jackson on my left noticed first. She had already called the power department, our internet and cable provider, and the home-owner's association—none of which had a clue.

She insisted that I step outside and look at them, despite my face clearly expressing zero interest. Her voice was getting more shrill with every word though, so I eventually allowed her to drag me outside to avoid waking my six-year-old daughter Emma.

Bleary-eyed and still in my bathrobe, I followed Mrs. Jackson to the street to get a proper view of the thing. The antennas had three metal prongs a bit like a pitchfork, pure black unlike the typical metallic ones. I spent several minutes nodding seriously as she rambled, wondering how long I was expected to stand there before I could politely resume my apathy.

"You can probably climb there from your balcony," Mrs. Jackson told me. "All you'd have to do is jump up and grab—"

"Wouldn't it be just as easy from your balcony?" I asked.

Mrs. Jackson gave me a critical look as though trying to decide whether to be offended. It was only a subtle change from her usual expression.

"My husband won't be home until tonight," she said, as though that was my fault somehow. "It'll only take a minute."

It was just cold enough for politeness to suddenly become optional.

"Oh, wait, I remember what that is," I said, turning back. I drawled out my words so I could make it all the way to my door before I finished. "That's just the government secret surveillance program. Don't blow up anything and you should be fine."

I swiftly shut the door before she could reply and congratulated myself on a successful escape. I let my wife answer the door next time and heard her apologizing on my behalf. My wife managed to get me out of climbing on the roof, but somehow we lost Emma to our neighbor's daughter's sleepover during the negotiation.

I didn't think anything more of the antennas until I left for work and they caught my eye. There were two dead squirrels on my roof beside them, lying in a small pool of blood which dribbled into the gutter.

When I got home that night I found Mr. Jackson kneeling on his roof beside his antenna. He was motionless and intent upon the thing, staring with such ferocity that I expected him to lunge and snap it off at any moment.

"Hiding from the Misses, huh?" I called up to him. "Good spot."

He started to move his head toward me but stopped part way, his eyes never leaving the antenna. Slowly his head returned to its fixed position. I thought he might not have heard me and was about to try again when he said quite softly, "Can you hear it? Like static in your brain."

"Hear what? Hey look, while you're up there would you mind tossing those two dead—those four dead squirrels from my roof?"

Four now. I shuddered, trying not to look at them. There must be a hawk or something that lived up there.

Mr. Jackson slowly turned his head toward me again, his eyes finally breaking away from the antenna at the last moment. His mouth seemed to be moving, but I couldn't hear anything.

I stepped closer until I could hear a faint buzzing sound. He was blowing air through his lips like Emma did when she was trying to make a fart noise. The vibrating of his lips sounded more like static though. We locked eyes for about ten seconds, him softly blubbering the whole while. Without another word I turned and went inside my house, glad to be rid of him.

I didn't feel comfortable about Emma sleeping there that night, but I couldn't think of a good reason not to let her go either. I packed her school bag with her dolls, a board game, and a whistle—just in case. I told her all she needed to do was blow the whistle if anything was wrong, and I'd hear and come get her.

After ten minutes of continuous whistle blowing—including once when she tried to make it sound different by sneezing into it—I'd changed my mind and was happy when Mrs. Jackson knocked to pick her up.

"Did you ever figure out what the antennas are for?" I asked her.

She gave me the stink eye. "Government surveillance, no doubt."

"Oh that's nice. You hear that Emma? You've got to be good or the government will take you away."

"Sounds good!" Emma said cheerfully.

"What a horrible thing to say to your child," Mrs. Jackson sniffed.

"How do you get your daughter to behave?" I asked.

"Shirley doesn't need to be threatened. She knows good girls go to heaven and bad girls go to hell, and that's all there is to it," Mrs. Jackson huffed without the slightest sense of irony.

We were interrupted by the blast of a whistle.

"I want to go!" Emma demanded. "What are we still doing here?"

I felt slightly sick watching Mrs. Jackson take Emma by the hand and walk away. I watched them all the way until they got to their house. Mr. Jackson was still on the roof, but he turned away from the antenna to watch them go inside. It was hard to tell from here, but it seemed like his lips were still moving.

I closed the door and took a deep breath. My wife and I had the house to ourselves though, and that was enough reason to celebrate.

It was freezing outside, but I left the window open that night so I could hear the whistle. My wife thought I was being paranoid, but apparently paranoia is cute when it comes to our daughter, so she let me keep it open. That should have made me feel better, but it didn't. In fact I felt even worse because every moment that I didn't hear the whistle made me wonder whether something had already happened to her.

I'd bothered my wife enough already though, and I kept my fears to myself. I lay awake listening for the static in my brain—for the whistle—for something on the roof—for anything. But the night was dark and still, and little by little I allowed myself to lower my defenses and drift off to sleep.

That night I dreamt of falling from a dizzying height as though I was dropped from space. I kept going faster and faster, the wind whipping around me. But no matter how fast I went or how far I fell, I never seemed to get any closer to the ground.

I could still hear the wind when I woke up the next morning. It sounded a lot like a whistle. The next I remember, I was in my kitchen with three police officers standing around the table.

They believe that Mr. Jackson had killed his wife during the night. The hushed tones and ashen faces of the police told me not to ask exactly how. Most of their daughter Shirely was found in the living room beside her mother, although they're having trouble finding the rest. Mr. Jackson was nowhere to be found.

Thank God that Emma escaped in time. The police found her hiding on the roof, clinging to the antenna all night long to keep from sliding off. She must be suffering from shock and cold, they said, because when they found her she barely responded. She couldn't tear her eyes away from the antenna, or reply with anything besides the soft static nosies she made with her mouth.

I LOST MY INNOCENCE AT SERENITY FALLS

My father was a diplomat who shook hands with the most powerful people in the world. A business man with foreign affairs, managing an empire so vast that the sun never sets upon it. He was an army veteran in Afghanistan and a doctor in Ethiopia. In fact, he was so important that he went everywhere and did everything—except for coming home, that is.

When I was little, I used to love hearing stories about him. I liked to imagine that I'd get to meet him someday, and the two of us would go everywhere I heard about in mom's stories. It wasn't until I was eight years old when I realized how strained her voice was when she talked about him, or how selfish I was for always bringing him up. I didn't ask for any more stories after that, and mom never brought him up on her own.

She must have loved him terribly for it to still hurt after all these years. My mother once said the longer you wait for something you want, the better it is to have, like interest building up in the bank. So every day he didn't come home wasn't a punishment; it would only make their reunion that much happier when it finally did happen.

It would have been so much easier if he did come back though. I wouldn't have to walk home from school because mom would be there to pick me up. And I wouldn't have to make my own dinner, because mom wouldn't need a second job in the evening. Some nights I'd try to stay up until she got back, but I'd usually fall asleep on the couch watching TV and wouldn't see her until the morning when she woke me in my bed.

The older I got, the more mother's stories didn't make sense. Even if only one of them was true, my father must have had an opportunity to visit by now. Army contracts are only 4 years, and if he was as rich and important as she said, then he must have been able to send a little money so mom wouldn't have to work so hard.

The only explanations I could think of was that he was either dead or lost. If he was dead, I intended to find out where he was buried so mom wouldn't have to keep waiting. If he was lost, I'd help him find his way home again. A friend suggested that my parents might have gotten divorced and just didn't love each other anymore, but I didn't think that was true. Mom wouldn't still be hurt if she didn't love him, and I didn't think it was possible for anyone not to love my mom.

So I started my search. I asked my grandparents on my mother's side, but they were tight-lipped and quick to change the subject. I spent my lunches looking for him online on the school computers, but there were hundreds of people with the same name, and I only had a single grainy photo to compare with. He might have gained weight, or grown a mustache, or even lost an arm in battle for all I knew.

The one thing I was sure about was that he never changed his name, because if he was lost then he'd want to be found again. So I started going down the list of the hundreds of people with the right name and sending each a message asking if they were my dad.

Most didn't reply. Some seemed concerned, others creepy, but I didn't let that bother me. I started out with my city, Serenity Falls, but quickly expanded my search to the whole state of Wisconsin. We'd moved around quite a bit when I was younger, but we'd never left the state so I thought that's where he must be looking for us.

Then one day I messaged someone and asked if they were my father, and he replied with my mother's name and I knew I'd found him. He was older than I expected and most of his hair was gone, but he still looked a lot like the photograph. A lot like me. And no one using the other school computers could understand why I started to cry.

He asked a lot of questions about my mother. He asked for pictures of her and wanted me to tell him everything. I told him what city we lived in, and he promised to drive there right away even though it was over a hundred miles. He didn't seem to mind that mom would still be at work, because he was excited to meet me too.

For the first time in my life my dad was going to pick me up from school. I couldn't focus or sit still through any of my remaining classes. When the final bell rang I exploded out of my chair so fast I knocked my whole desk over, but I didn't stay to pick it up. I was the first out of the building and was waiting on the sidewalk within a minute. He was already waiting for me.

My dad had even less hair than his picture, but I didn't mind because he drove a red sports car. I asked if he really was an international businessman, and he laughed and said he did that in his spare time.

He didn't want to meet mom at home or at work because that wasn't romantic. Instead he wanted to take me to the real Serenity Falls the town is named after. That's where they had their first date, and mom could meet us there. I texted mom and let her know a surprise was waiting for her there, and she promised to get off work early.

It was only about a twenty minute drive, but I feel like we really bonded in that time. Dad didn't like talking about himself and asked me a thousand questions instead. What games did I like to play? How was I doing in my classes? Who were my friends, and on and on. His eyes would light up with even the most boring answer as though it was a miraculous revelation from on high.

I teased him for that, but then he got all serious and said, "You don't understand. I didn't even know you existed until today. You aren't just telling me about yourself—you're being created from nothing right here in front of my eyes. It really is a bit like a miracle."

Serenity Falls was quiet around the Christmas season. We were the only ones in the parking lot, so we got to drive all the way to the head of the trail which led to the viewpoint. The water was all frozen in snow and ice, and it wouldn't be a waterfall again until the thaw of the spring. It was still beautiful because of the long icicles lancing off the jagged rock. The light seemed trapped within the crystals which shimmered as the light faded.

We stood together in silence overlooking the falls for several minutes. I started to shiver, but he put his arm around me and drew me close, and I almost started to cry again without knowing why.

"When is your mom going to be here?" he asked at last.

"Not for at least an hour."

"Do you want to wait in the car where it's warm?" he asked.

"Why did you really leave?" I blurted out.

He withdrew his arm from around my shoulders and we stood together in silence again.

"I lied earlier," he said, still staring at the hanging ice. "I did know you existed before today."

"Then why did you—" I cut myself short.

"I wasn't ready. I loved your mother, but I didn't want to have a family yet. I'm sorry."

I shrugged as if it had nothing to do with me, but I couldn't look at him.

"Were you really in the army?"

"I was."

"And a diplomat? And a doctor?"

He laughed in response. It was a warm sound, and I wasn't shivering anymore.

"But you really did love my mom?" I asked.

"I still do. More than anything," he said. "That's why I'm here. But I'm still not ready to have a kid. I don't think I'll ever be."

It hadn't gotten any colder, but I started shivering anyway. He put his arm around me again, but it didn't feel as comforting as it had before. His fingers were gripping my shoulder a little too tight.

"It's only going to be cold for a minute," he said. "After that you won't even feel it. It'll just be like drifting off to sleep."

"I want to go back to the car." I tried to pull away, but he wouldn't let go.

"Everybody wants something," he said, "but not everybody is willing to do what it takes to get it."

He slid behind me, and suddenly both his arms were around me. I struggled and kicked, landing a solid one into his thigh before he got me off the ground. He grunted but didn't let go as he lifted me over the railing. I braced my feet against it and tried to push back, but he lifted me even higher until I couldn't reach it anymore.

My dad flung me over the ledge to tumble down the twenty foot drop to the frozen water. I smashed straight through the ice and plunged into the numbing depths. I spun over once or twice trying to orient myself, and by the time I was able to surge upward again I couldn't find the hole I'd broken through.

All I could feel was the underside of the ice. It was thicker than it seemed when I fell through. My numb fists moved sluggishly through the water, pounding feebly. I went back to searching for the hole instead, but the freezing water stung my eyes so badly I could barely see.

I saw the vague outline of his shape through the ice though. He was standing directly over me, looking down. He watched me flail against the underside. The weight of my wet clothes was beginning to drag me down, and my chest felt like it was about to explode. Each time I surged upward it became a little harder to reach the ice, until the time I couldn't reach it at all and began drifting down.

I watched him turn and begin climbing up the slope, and everything went black. I came to a moment later when I heard the sports car rev to life and pull away. I lurched upward again, and by blind chance one hand slipped through the hole in the ice. I couldn't feel my fingers as they latched onto the edge. Somehow the air was even colder than the water, but inch by excruciating inch I dragged myself upward until I'd pulled myself from the water.

I was barely alive when my mom found me. I didn't want to tell her what happened, but even lies meant to protect someone can do more harm than good. I told her everything, and she promised never to let that man back into our life again.

If my future children ever ask me about my father, I'm going to tell them the truth. That he tried to kill me, that he was never caught, and that no family is incomplete that has love.

BURY THE PAIN

MY GRANDFATHER JERRY HAS A MEAN TEMPER, BUT YOU'D NEVER GUESS it from looking at him. He's got these little spectacles which slide all the way to the end of his nose that do nothing to hide his twinkling eyes. The poof of white hair around his head looks almost like a halo, and the lines of his face are so deep that he seems to be smiling even when he's not.

I've never seen him yell, or swear, or break anything, but I'd hear him whenever I spent the weekend. The first time was one night after I'd already gone to bed and the lights had been off for a little while.

I was laying real still, getting ready to fall asleep, when the porch-light starts sneaking past my curtains. I peaked out to see Jerry softly closing the backdoor behind him and creeping down into Grand-mother's vegetable garden. He went about twenty feet from the house at the very edge of light and began to dig, even though the ground was hard and frozen and the wind must have been bitter cold.

He dug for a few minutes before dropping to his knees to bring his face against the hole. Then he started to scream.

For a good few seconds there weren't any words to it—just a rush of anguish I didn't know one man could bear. I thought he was having a heart attack or something, so I rushed out of bed and opened the backdoor.

"Whiny, ungrateful little bitch. Somebody ought to bleed him dry and make him drink it back up."

The earth muffled a lot of it, but I heard enough to stop me from running to his aid. He couldn't see me while his face was pressed to the ground like that, so I just stood and watched from the porch.

"The girl's no better," he shouted. "Should have raped her when I had the chance. She would have liked that. Deserved it even if she didn't."

The words morphed into another wordless, guttural scream. I turned around and raced back inside, heart pounding 100 for every breath I took. I jumped back in bed and pulled the blankets over my head, just laying there shaking and listening until he fell silent.

The porch-light went off, and I heard the backdoor close real soft again. Then not another sound for the rest of the night, which I know because I didn't fall asleep until morning.

I got a few hours sleep before I woke to a knocking on my bedroom door. It was Grandmother promising fresh pancakes in the kitchen. Grandfather Jerry was there too, all smiles and cheerful jokes about the newspaper he was reading. And life went on like it was supposed to.

Until the next night when the porch-light flicked on again. I didn't get out of bed that time. I just lay there and listened to the distant muffled screaming. I caught the phrase, "Nail him to a cross if he wants to act so damn holy." I wouldn't have gotten out of bed again for anything.

Jerry continued to be as pleasant as always, graciously thanking anyone for the smallest service and going out of his way to help whoever needed it. But every time I stayed the night I'd watch for that porch-light, and every time I was falling asleep I'd hear him going on.

When I got old enough to stay home alone, I stopped sleeping at my grandparents. I moved to another city when I went to college and never told anyone. I didn't even like to think about it. Then my parents moved for my dad's new job, and I didn't see my grandparents so much after that.

Fast forward to a week ago when we got the news that Grandmother died. My parents had long since sold the house I grew up in, so we were all going to stay at my grandparent's house for the funeral. As chance would have it my parent's flight was delayed though, so the first night I arrived it would be just me and Grandfather Jerry in the house.

I could have handled it if Jerry had been in mourning. It would have been tough to see him like that, but at least it would have been natural. Instead he was just as cheerful as he'd always been. He whistled to himself while he cooked me dinner, making a show of juggling cans of green beans with a great wide grin on his face.

By the evening I'd half-convinced myself the whole thing was in my head. I still felt like a little boy when I got into bed in that old room though, and I still dreaded seeing the porch-light through the window as I waited for sleep.

And there it was. Half-past 11 when I'd just plugged in my phone and was starting to undress. The soft click from the backdoor sent a shiver down my spine. It was absurd for a grown man to be afraid of that decrepit tottering fool. I reasoned that I couldn't be afraid of him, that it was only the memory of being afraid as a child that I was holding onto.

To prove the point, I forced myself to go to the backdoor and open it. It took a moment for my eyes to adjust to the dark before I spotted him. He was kneeling down into the earth again, but he wasn't screaming this time. I watched his old shoulders tremble as he wept into the hole for a long time before I quietly closed the door and went back to my room.

Soon after I saw the light go off. I waited until I was sure he was in his own room before stealing out of the house. It wasn't hard to find the place where he'd been digging because the garden had been neglected for a long time, and there was only a single spot where the ground had been disturbed.

So I began to dig. I didn't know how deep I was supposed to go, but it only took him a few minutes so I was careful not to push the blade too far. I didn't know what I was looking for, but I knew I I'd found it when I saw the earth start to move on its own.

Slow, even pulses, like breathing which raised and lowered the last layer of dirt. I produced the flashlight on my phone and turned it on, staring at the beating heart embedded within the earth. With every beat the heart pushed a small gush of blood out of its aorta to dribble down the sides and soak into the ground, despite there being no obvious source for the blood.

The house was dark and quiet except for the porch-light. I briefly considered screaming at it like Jerry did, but I didn't see the point and didn't want to risk waking him.

I wanted to get a better look though, so I reached down with my hands to clear more of the dirt away. One of my fingers accidentally brushed against the thing's side while doing so, and that's all it took. A flood of feelings swept over me all tumbling over one another, senseless and maddening in their conflicting natures. I'd never had a panic attack before, but that's the closest parallel I can draw.

Grandfather took two bullets in the Vietnam war. I'd forgotten, but I remembered it now because I suddenly felt them in my left shoulder and thigh. He'd once been swindled by a building contractor —his name was Jeffery Wallace, and I'd never hated anyone so much in my life. He'd been cheated on by a girl he loved, fired from a job he put his soul into, and once falsely accused of rape.

All the rage and injustice and misery he'd felt in his life was all coming to me at once. Voices in my head were shouting over one another to be heard, and more voices were joining by the second. I couldn't tell one from the other, or even understand where the hurt was coming from, just that it was all there at once in one great red wave of anger and remorse. It flooded through my veins, poured through my body, then up through my throat and out my mouth in one long wordless scream.

The one wound that rose above the rest was the absence of my Grandmother. She wasn't the old lady who let me watch cartoons and made pancakes though—in that moment she was the center of my life that everything else revolved around. But she was gone, and everything else had stopped revolving, and I didn't see how anything in this world was going to make it start again.

I don't know how long that lasted, but it didn't stop until I felt a hand on my shoulder. The scream cut short, and I collapsed on my hands and knees, gasping for breath.

My grandfather didn't say anything. He just stood behind me and squeezed my shoulder. Once I'd steadied myself I turned to look at him, standing there in the cold with just his pajama bottoms on. My eyes fixed on the long scar on his chest, right over where his heart should have been.

"I can take yours out too, if you want," he said. "If it gets too much."

I didn't realize how much I wanted that until he said it. How much easier it would be to leave all this behind.

"Please," I begged.

"But I'll tell you something I wish my father told me before he showed me how," he said. "You can bury it and keep walking, but it never goes away. And you'll have to come back to it every time you bury a new hurt, and it'll be worse than ever because all that stuff you tried to bury will be right there waiting for you."

"I don't want to feel like this," I told him.

He squeezed my shoulder again. "You're going to feel it," he said, uncompromising but not without sympathy. "Either when it happens, or years down the road. And it's a lot easier to feel one thing fully at a time than bury it for when you're ready. Even if you live to be as old as I am, you're never going to be readier than you are now."

My parents arrived the next morning, and we all attended the funeral together. I don't think there was a dry eye in the house except for Grandfather. I overheard a few whispers looking down on the man for his lingering smile, but I knew better. She had a special place in his heart that none of them would understand, and she'll still be there long after he's gone.

THE SCARIEST STORY IN THE WORLD

THOUGH THE WIND BELLOWS FIERCE ACROSS MY FACE LIKE THE HOWL OF a nameless beast, though the moon twists shadows into abyssal creatures and the gates of Hell within my companion's eyes, I am not afraid. I will be, he promises, but not yet.

You see this is not the scariest story in the world. This is just a tribute.

My brother Jake read the fabled story on an ancient scroll, or so the old man swore to me. I believe the psychiatrist preferred the explanation of "sudden onset psychosis".

All I know for sure is that last week I met Jake for a drink after work and listened to him complain about his wife for an hour. The way she bossed him around, the way she never considered his feelings, then on to ramble about his job and a camping trip he and his coworkers had planned to get away from it all.

Three days later, I received a phone call from the police station. Did I know Jake? Of course, he's my brother. Did I know why his naked body was covered in blue paint, or why he was running down main street screaming at pigeons?

No, officer. I'm not sure why he was doing that.

Speaking to Jake in the hospital was the most difficult thing I've ever had to do. His eyes were milky pools which bulged so disgustingly from their sockets that I was afraid they'd fall out. His breathing came in short bursts of ragged gasps as though he was constantly forgetting and then being reminded that he was being chased. Even his skin seemed to have aged, fresh wrinkles threatening to melt off his face entirely.

"I never knew a nobody. Nobody never knew me." He repeated that line frequently, sometimes looking in my direction though never quite seeing me.

It was punctuated with other nonsense, such as:

"You see 'em born, but you never see 'em unborn."

Or

"I felt it drinking me. Like I was a bottle and it couldn't be quenched."

I couldn't make heads or tails of it. Neither could our parents, or our relatives, or any of the long line of doctors who paraded through the room. By the third visit I was seriously considering leaving and never returning. What was the point? Whatever had happened to him, my brother wasn't in there anymore.

I wrestled with that thought all day, making excuses to delay until finally near midnight the guilt overpowered my hesitation. I decided to drop by for just a moment to see if his condition changed.

It hadn't. But something had. There was an old man sitting beside his bed, endlessly wringing his hands and muttering to himself. His stained trench-coat and wild matted hair suggested a homeless person, and I wouldn't have been surprised if he had his own room in the psyche ward.

"Do you know Jake?" I asked cautiously.

"Does anyone, anymore?" the old man replied with the articulate, measured words of a stage actor.

"Do you know what happened to him?" I asked, still standing by the door.

"Mr. Sandman," Jake's voice gurgled like wet mud. "Mr. Sandman, dream me a dream..."

"I do," the old man answered. It was almost surreal to hear such an even, intelligent voice from such a disorderly man. "He read something he oughtn't to, and it's driven him quite mad."

Convinced by my companion's certainty, I sat in the chair beside him and searched his face for answers. The eyes which met my gaze, as I have already mentioned, were akin to the gates of Hell. I suppose such a fanciful description requires elaboration. It's not that his eyes were abnormal, just as an arch of stone may seem quite natural almost anywhere. I simply had the feeling that the world on the other side of those eyes had very little in common with our own.

"What did you read?" I asked my brother, needing an excuse to look away.

Jake's breath was coming fast again. His fingers gripped his bedsheets on either side of him as though he was hanging from a precipice and clinging for his life.

"The scariest story in the world, that's all," the old man said. "Would you like to read it too?"

Jake was practically convulsing at the words. I was about to call a nurse, but the old man ran his long fingers down my brother's face and his breathing immediately eased.

"You can't get through to him if you don't know where his mind has been," the old man's voice had grown as melodic as a lullaby. "Read the story, and if you keep your wits about you, then you will find the words to call your brother home."

"Okay. Sure, yeah," I said. Part concern for my brother, part sibling rivalry in wanting to test myself, but mostly it was just morbid curiosity. "Is there a chance I'll end up like that?"

The old man smiled and stood. Saying nothing, he turned to exit the room.

"You can't expect me to follow you if you don't answer," I called after him.

"I absolutely can," he replied, and he was gone. And of course he was right. How could I not follow that begging question mark?

And so the wind howled as I walked into the night with my companion. I asked his name, and his voice betrayed nothing when he answered "Mr. Sandman." I assume it was in jest, but I can't be certain. While we walked, he told me the tale of the demon scroll.

"The story was written over the course of four generations, beginning in the 6th century. After the man had fathered a son, he would take up the story and pour all he knew of fear into the manuscript. Once he had contributed what he was able, the man would collapse into insanity, passing the manuscript onto his heir when he came of age."

"If they knew the thing was evil, why wouldn't they just destroy it?"

"Will you destroy it?"

"Not until I've read it..."

"Ah," Mr. Sandman said, tapping the side of his nose. "And so it passes. Each son thought they could save their father through their own sacrifice, yet each fell as their fathers had into madness."

The old man had taken a turn on a street I didn't recognize, but I was too absorbed in his tale to pay it much mind.

"Well maybe I will destroy it then. If everyone who has ever read it—"

"Not everyone," my companion interrupted. "Four generations passed the scroll, until one son endured the trial. He maintained his sanity, helped his father to recover, and even prospered for his greater sight into the heart of terror. Such was his love for the fear he found that he kept the scroll hidden and safe. Until your brother discovered it by accident, of course."

"What happened to the boy? And how do you know this?"

The old man smiled over his shoulder, saying nothing.

"Well what made him different that allowed him to prevail?" I pressed.

"The boy wasn't brave like the others." Mr. Sandman had left the road entirely and was now walking along a dirt path through a dark copse of trees. I was helpless but to follow. "When you are brave, you fight against fear as though to conquer it. Only the cowardly know how to make fear their friend as that boy once did. Here we are though, just where your brother left it."

Mr. Sandman reached inside a rotted stump to produce a scroll. It was a stretch of animal hide, about three feet tall, its surface yellowed and edges burned or tattered by age. He offered it to me freely, and I accepted.

"Can't you give me any idea what to expect?" I asked. The thing was clenched in my hand, still rolled.

"I already have." Mr. Sandman's eyes didn't waver, fixed on my own. The wind held its breath as I held mine. I nodded, my mind made at last. Still meeting Mr. Sandman's eyes, I took a lighter from my pocket and set the flame to the scroll.

If his eyes were the gates of Hell, then now they were opened. An animal snarl escaped his throat as he launched himself at me. Decrepit fingers clawed at my face, feeling like shards of bone digging into my skin. I tried to fend him off, prompting him to sink his yellowed teeth into my defensive forearm.

There was no chance to reason with him. I couldn't flee with him latched onto me. All I could do was pummel his scruffy head with my free hand, over and over, each blow harder than the last as his teeth plunged deeper into my skin. By the time he let go his mouth was a fountain of blood which spurted between his rotten teeth.

"You've read it, haven't you??" I demanded, looming over the crumpled body. "Tell me what's inside!"

The wet laughter was nauseating. Then it stopped, and that was even worse. The wind started to whistle again, finally daring to breathe.

The thick animal hide was slow to light, but I got it going with a little kindling. The stump, the scroll, and Mr. Sandman's body all joined in the pillar of flame. Fear is an evil thing. That's what I told myself in the heat of the moment, my bloody arm in agony. That it was a cursed knowledge the world would do better without.

But each night as I lie awake my thoughts are bound to what was inside that scroll. And when my brother took his own life in the hospital, I had to wonder how things would have been different if I had striven to understand fear rather than flee from it.

Maybe fear is an evil thing, but the fear of fear is even worse.

GRAB YOUR FREE BOOK!

Read more from Tobias Wade
download a **FREE BOOK!**
TobiasWade.Com

READ THE FULL COLLECTION

Click the image or get it on
TobiasWade.Com

PUBLISHER'S NOTE

Please remember to
honestly rate the book!

It's the best way to support me as an author and help new readers discover my work.

Read more horror at
TobiasWade.Com

Printed in Great Britain
by Amazon

36940521R00165